A BLACK HEARTS STILL BEAT STORY

RUIN

l. a. cotton

USA TODAY AND WALL STREET JOURNAL BESTSELLING AUTHOR

I0718876

RUIN

A Black Hearts Still Beat Story

L A COTTON

Published by Delesty Books

RUIN
Copyright © L A Cotton 2020
All rights reserved.

This book is a work of fiction. Names, characters, places, and events are the product of the author's imagination or used in a fictitious manner. Any resemblance to actual persons or events is purely coincidental.

No part of this book may be reproduced or used in any manner without the written permission of the publisher, except by a reviewer who may quote brief passages for review purposes only.

Edited by Andie M Long Editing Services
Cover by Opulent Designs

PROLOGUE

HER BANSHEE-LIKE SCREAMS filled the house. I crouched down against the wall, pressing my hands to my ears, trying to block it out.

It never worked though.

Once my mom got into one of her fits, she wouldn't stop until she was passed out from drinking a bottle of vodka. Sometimes, I thought about lacing her tea with the damn stuff. At least then she'd pass out quicker and I wouldn't have to listen to...

"Where the fuck are you, you disgusting little—"

"Levi, I'm scared." My baby brother Rafe crawled into the gap between the closet and the wall and snuggled into my side.

"S'okay, Rafe, she's just in one of her moods again."

"Why does she hate you so much?" He stared up at me with his big gray eyes, and my insides twisted up.

Mom did hate me.

Made sure to tell me every day of my life.

I was almost nine, so there had been *a lot* of days.

A loud crash followed by the sound of glass shattering echoed through the house, and Rafe whimpered, pressing further into my side. Slipping my arm around his shoulders, I hugged him tighter. "Try and block it out," I whispered. "Try and think happy thoughts."

"Sing to me," he croaked.

"Rafe, buddy, come on..."

"LEVIATHAN!" she shrieked, making us both flinch.

"Please, Levi." He tugged the hem of my t-shirt. "I like it when you sing."

He might have, but our mom sure didn't. She'd washed my mouth out with soap twice last month when she caught me humming a tune in the shower. I'd puked for three hours straight.

"You know I can't," I sighed, dropping my head back against the wall, the words cutting me up inside.

"Please..."

"Okay, buddy, but I have to keep it quiet." I couldn't tell him no. No kid should have to witness the things he did, to hear the vile and twisted things she said. It was different for me, I'd always been the subject of her hatred. But not Rafe. He was her favorite. Her sweet and gentle Raphael.

"Sing the one about the rainbows," he whispered, "I love that one."

I inhaled a sharp breath, letting it fill my lungs. If she heard me, it wouldn't end well for me, it never did. But I couldn't deny my little brother. And singing...

Well singing made all the bad things disappear.

CHAPTER ONE

LEVI

BLACK HEARTS STILL BEAT POSTPONE TOUR AMID SEX TAPE SCANDAL.

TEN DAYS AFTER THE TAPE WAS LEAKED, THERE HAS BEEN ONLY ONE STATEMENT FROM THE BAND'S LABEL, RAZORSHARP RECORDS.

BUT THE REAL QUESTION ON EVERYONE'S LIPS IS: WHERE IS LEVI HUNTER?

I THREW my phone down on the coffee table and ran a hand over my head, feeling anger ripple up my spine.

Ten days.

Ten fucking days since my life blew up in front of my eyes, and the press were still chomping at the bit. They were like sharks circling, waiting for the first scent of blood.

I'd fucked up.

The grainy video of me snorting a line of coke off Riley's stomach was evidence enough.

Conniving fucking bitch.

The band's ex-assistant—she had been fired when it came out that she was leaking private information about us to the press. What nobody realized at the time though was she had an ace card up her sleeve.

An ace card I'd forgotten all about because I'd been off my face on a lethal concoction of liquor and drugs. She'd set me up and like the reckless fucking idiot I was, I'd fallen for it hook, line, and sinker.

"Motherfucker," I yelled, kicking the table. My boot collided with the wood, sending the thing toppling over. Pain ricocheted through my big toe and shot up my foot, but I barely flinched. The anger in my veins doused some of the other shit running through my head, but it wasn't enough. My blood craved something else.

Something stronger.

Hunger pulsed through me, my skin itching for a hit. Coke. Crack. Molly. I didn't discriminate. Right now, given half a chance, I'd snort, smoke, or swallow anything I could get my hands on...

Except, the label had me on house arrest like I was a fucking toddler in timeout.

Johnson, my bodyguard stood guard at the door,

watching me like a hawk, with another two guys out in the hall.

Alistair, the band's manager, said it was for my own good. I called it some kind of mental torture. I'd been cooped up here, in an apartment on the edge of the city, for almost ten days.

After the story broke, everyone expected me to explode. To plummet headfirst over the thin ledge of control I walked every day of my existence. They expected me to reach for the bottle or slip our security detail and go hunt down a dealer to score whatever drugs I could get my hands on.

I'd surprised them—and myself—when I'd done neither of those things. Instead, I'd punched the wall, split my knuckles wide open in the process, and then shut down. But as the pain subsided, the urges stirred to life. So I was shipped here, and told to stay put until the label could figure out what to do about Riley.

My patience was wearing thin though. If they didn't let me out soon, I'd be forced to take matters into my own hands. Because I needed to do *something*.

For a guy like me, carrying the kinds of demons that haunted me, sitting around was like a fucking death sentence. Being on alone with my thoughts wasn't therapy, it was my own personal version of hell.

Too much time to think.

Too much time to reflect and dwell.

Too much fucking time to remember.

My mind was a dark place to be at the best of times, but after almost two weeks of being locked down in this apartment, my thoughts were borderline morbid.

The blare of my cell phone cut through the unrelenting silence. I snatched it up and barked, "About fucking time."

"How are you?" My brother's voice filled the line.

"How do you think? I've been locked away here—"

"It's just until Ali and the label deal with Riley."

I sneered. "Because I'm a liability, you mean."

"Levi," Rafe sighed. "The whole world saw you snort coke off her body. The video went viral—"

"Don't fucking remind me." I sank back against the couch and let out a frustrated breath.

"I didn't know she would do that."

"Yeah, well it's done now." His voice was thin. And I hated it. Hated that yet again, I'd disappointed my little brother. But it was the story of my life. Rafe was the good one, the righteous one. And I was the thorn in his side. The devil on his shoulder.

"We need to look forward."

Forward... yeah, right.

This was just another black mark against my name. I was already on shaky grounds with the label. But what did they expect signing on someone like me?

Someone with a heart as black as the night and a soul full of torment and nightmares.

I was the label's poster boy for a reason. And it wasn't for my squeaky-clean reputation and charity work.

But where they needed me and the band to make them their millions, I needed them to allow me to keep performing. It gave me an outlet, a way to channel all my anger, the pain festering inside me. It was cathartic; for those few minutes while the beat thrummed through me and I lost myself in the lyrics, I was free.

It made sense. I was an addict, after all. I craved the high, the rush of endorphins and adrenaline. And there was no better feeling than performing to a sold-out arena of tens of thousands of screaming fans.

Now I had nothing.

No music.

No liquor or drugs.

I was in withdrawal from everything good in my life, and it fucking sucked.

"Forward?" I snapped, feeling irritation roll up my spine. "What I need is to get out of this fucking cell."

"Levi, it's the penthouse suite in The Louisville Regency. It's hardly a prison."

"Do you know what, brother? Go fuck yourself."

He let out a sharp hiss but didn't respond, choosing to change the subject. "Eva wants to come out and see you."

"No."

I didn't want her here.

I didn't want her anywhere near me.

Eva Walker, my brother's girlfriend, was a sweet little thing. She'd been signed on to tour with us as our opening act, and somehow managed to worm her way under my skin. But she was Rafe's.

"I told her as much," Rafe sighed, "but you know Eva."

Yeah, I did. Which is exactly why I didn't want her anywhere near me right now. I couldn't be trusted. Not while I was itching for something—*anything*—to take my mind off of the shitshow that was my life.

A knock sounded at the door and I glanced back at Johnson. He frowned and turned to answer it. "Levi," he shouted. "You have a visitor."

Realization slammed into me and anger exploded in my veins. "What the fuck did you do, Rafe?"

"I told her not to come." He didn't sound pleased. "But she insisted…"

"You're her fucking man. You should have—"

"What? I should have what?"

"Whatever. I'll tell Johnson to send her away. Next time she wants to stick her nose where it doesn't belong, try fucking harder, *brother*." I hung up, bolting from the couch and storming over to the door.

"Levi, thank God." Eva smiled, relief glittering in her gaze.

"You should go," I said, the words rough against my throat.

"G- go? But I came to—"

"Yeah, well, I don't need another fucking babysitter, not when I already have Johnson."

He didn't flinch. Staunch motherfucker.

"Levi, please…" Eva's expression softened as she stared at me with her big blue eyes. "I just want to talk."

Talk.

Because talking solved everything.

"Go away, Eva. You can't fix this." *You can't fix me.*

Once upon a time, when she'd first joined the tour, I'd thought that maybe she could. That maybe she could fill some of the darkness in my heart with her light. But I'd quickly realized that she wasn't meant for me.

She was too good, too pure for the likes of Leviathan Hunter.

Eva was the sun, and I was a giant black hole, sucking everything good into oblivion.

I turned my back on her and stalked into the bathroom, stripping out of what little clothes I had on. I couldn't drown myself in liquor or numb the pain with a synthetic high, but I could stand under the hot shower jets and try and burn away my sins.

———

WHEN THE WATER began to run cold, I finally dragged myself out. My skin was shriveled, red and sore, but I welcomed the burn.

Wrapping a big fluffy towel around my waist, I padded out of the bathroom, stopping dead in my tracks at the sight of Eva sitting in one of the chairs.

Her head whipped up. "You're okay."

My brow arched.

"I knocked, twice... but you didn't..."

"I was taking a shower."

"I figured." Pity glittered in her eyes.

"I told you to go."

"Levi, please..."

"What, Angel?" I drawled her nickname. "Come to save my soul? You might as well save your breath."

"We need to talk about this." She shot up, glaring at me defiantly.

"No, we really don't."

"Riley set you up, she betrayed you, all of you. And now... Phoebe."

"Don't." It came out harsh as my eyes shuttered at the mention of *her* name.

Phoebe Halstead.

Riley's replacement.

The second girl to get under my skin.

For a second, I'd thought she was the one. The girl who could handle my demons and keep them at bay.

I was wrong.

The second the story broke, I saw the look in her eyes.

Disappointment...

Regret...

Disgust.

I hadn't spoken to her since.

It had been foolish to think that someone could ever look past the darkness surrounding me. I was unhinged. Reckless and volatile. I was a sinking ship slowly drowning in angry seas.

I didn't blame her for wanting to get as far away from me as possible.

I blamed myself.

But no one knew what it was like to walk in my shoes, to be so worshipped and adored and feel nothing but gaping emptiness. The fans, the shows, the tour, the number one hits, it was everything... and yet, it was nothing.

Talk about fucked up.

I had it all. Money, fame, and power. A string of fangirls all looking to ride the Levi Hunter happy train. I wanted for nothing.

Except the one thing that nobody could give me.

"How have you been?" Eva changed the subject.

"That's a loaded fucking question, Angel, and you know it."

She didn't want to hear how I'd sweated in bed every night, curling my fists into the sheets, fighting the urge to escape my prison and go score off some back-alley dealer.

"I know it isn't ideal—"

"Ideal?" I balked. "I think rehab was better than... than this." And rehab had been a fucking nightmare.

"The label just wants to get a handle on everything. Figure out a way forward."

"You mean they want to make sure I don't spiral and end up back in rehab."

She let out a small sigh. "We're all worried." Her eyes drilled holes into the top of my head as I looked down at the floor. She meant well; Eva always did. But I wasn't in the mood to be coddled. Least of all, by my brother's girl.

"Rafe is—"

"Save it," I groaned. "He doesn't get it. No one does."

The self-hatred.

The loathing.

Riley might have set me up, but I'd played right into her hands. I'd wanted to forget. I'd wanted to get off my fucking face and forget everything.

Me.

But I couldn't stop.

Even now, after everything, I knew if Eva offered me a bump of coke, or a little white pill, or a syringe full of crack,

I'd take it. Because feeling something, even for a second, was better than constantly feeling nothing.

"This will all be over soon, and then we can get back to the tour."

"And then what? We go on as one big happy family?" I sneered. "Pretending I didn't screw up again?"

"I'm not saying it'll be easy, but the guys understand—"

"Understand what? That I snorted coke off Riley's body and then fucked her until I passed out?"

Eva blanched but I was too worked up to care. This wasn't some game, it was my life.

My fucking disaster of a life.

"Yeah, I didn't think so," I added when she didn't reply. "We can all pretend, go back to normal again, but we all know, everyone will just be waiting for me to screw up again."

"You're wrong." Eva gave me a sad smile. "So wrong," she said.

"Nah, Angel. It's you who's got it all wrong. I'm not some project to be fixed, some charity case to be saved. Everything I touch turns to ash. You're better off without me."

"Levi, that's not—"

I flopped back on the couch, feeling myself begin to crash. Here, away from the fast-paced life of touring, it was harder to stave off the exhausting lows.

"Just go, Eva," I said through gritted teeth, refusing to meet her sympathetic gaze. "Just go and don't come back."

The air shifted as she got up. "You think you're unredeemable, that you don't deserve to be happy or loved, but you're wrong, Levi. And I hope that one day, you realize that."

A few weeks ago, her words would have touched something inside me. But not anymore. The video of me and Riley wasn't just a betrayal, it was a reminder.

Just as my mother used to tell me, I was and always would be, a worthless fuck-up.

CHAPTER TWO

PHOEBE

WHEN MY DAD got me the job working at Razorsharp Records, I'd expected to be making coffees for music execs and filing paperwork in some back room office. I hadn't expected to find myself interning with Letty Panem, PA to one of the hottest rock bands of the moment—Black Hearts Still Beat.

But where Black Hearts went, scandal and chaos usually followed.

Thrown into a world of sex, drugs, and rock and roll when they were just teenagers, Levi and Rafe Hunter, Hudson Ryker, and Damon Donnelley had whipped up their fair share of media frenzies. Crazed crowds of teenage girls, out of control parties, and rumors of a revolving door of women were but a few of the band's escapades.

But no member attracted media interest more than Levi Hunter.

He was the band's enigma. The brooding and arrogant bad boy with the voice of a rock god. Levi gave zero fucks and the fans lapped it up.

Before joining the label, I'd heard their music, seen the odd performance on the television, but nothing could have prepared me for experiencing it firsthand. Levi didn't just perform their songs, he bled them out on the stage. His lyrics were ammunition, his voice the weapon, and the crowd his battleground ... and he slayed it every damn time.

But the Black Hearts front man was damaged. Tortured in the way that most rock stars were. A string of drug induced misdemeanors had landed him in rehab last year. By the time I joined the band, he'd been doing better...

Until the story hit.

It had been ten days of madness while the label tried to get the fallout under control. Letty and Alistair, the band's manager, were working around the clock to get the video pulled from social media, but it was no easy task once something had gone viral the way it had.

"Phoebe," she called. "We're ready."

I followed her into the conference room of the hotel we were staying at. Alistair joined us and after pressing a couple of buttons, the PR team at Razorsharp Records appeared on the screen.

"Ali," Dusty Higston said, "tell me something good."

"She won't budge." Alistair grimaced. "She wants one mil to disappear."

"The label will never agree to it. Legal will nail her ass to the wall."

"But it'll be too late by then. If she gives the exclusive, the story will be out."

"Fucking traitorous little…" he stopped himself, yanking his collar from his thick neck. "Options people, give me options."

"We negotiate—" someone around his table started.

"Not an option."

"We offer her five-hundred grand," Alistair piped up, "and hope she takes it. The band will take the hit."

"Too fucking right, they will. We wouldn't be in this mess if Levi had managed to keep his nose clean and dick out of the staff."

"Dusty," Alistair warned.

"Ali's right," Letty added. "Riley is just looking for her meal ticket. Offer her the money and I'll arrange an exclusive with The Rock Report to spin this in a better light."

"There's a better angle here?"

"There's always a better angle, Dusty, you should know that. Levi had some bad news and fell off the wagon, and his manipulative assistant saw an opportunity to make a quick buck. The Die Hearts are already backing Levi and the band."

"Yeah, but the ratings with the younger demographic are falling through the floor."

"You need to use Eva. She's the key." Letty sat back, completely calm and composed. "You wanted to get her into the studio, now's your chance. But I think it should be a collaboration with the band."

Silence filled the room as Dusty steepled his fingers. "A collab, you say?"

She nodded. "The fans love it when Levi brings Eva out on stage. Their hashtag #HunterWalkerMagic trended for two weeks straight. We can harness that."

"Alistair?"

"It's the best option we have right now. Levi has a history of bad behavior, it's nothing new. But the video forces people to acknowledge it. If we can bury Riley..." He hesitated, running a hand down his face. I'd heard rumors he and Riley had history, so I couldn't imagine how he must be feeling. "And flood the channels with a collab and The Rock Report exclusive, we might be able to turn it around."

Dusty considered Alistair's words for a minute, conferring quietly with his team. "Make it happen. I want them in the studio pronto. But you'd better tell your boy he's walking a fine line, Portman. He needs to get his shit locked down or the band could lose the Masterpiece endorsement and they might as well kiss the international leg of the tour goodbye."

Letty sucked in a sharp breath, as if Dusty's threat was worse than she expected. I didn't know what to expect because I'd never been an assistant to a band before, let alone sat in a meeting such as this one.

But I didn't doubt that if they knew how well I knew Levi, there was every chance I wouldn't be sitting here right now.

I forced down *those* thoughts. Levi was a mistake. One I didn't intend on making again. The second I saw the video, I knew I couldn't do it again. I couldn't be second string to a substance addiction. I'd walked that road before, and it had gotten me nothing but a broken heart and scars so deep I wasn't sure they would ever fade.

From now on, my relationship with Levi and the band would remain strictly professional.

Because that's all we could ever be.

He was an addict, and I was an addict's ex-girlfriend. We were like fire and ice—a disastrous combination.

"Phoebe?" Letty's voice made me blink.

"Sorry, what?"

"Alistair wants us to go and see Levi, prep him on everything." She gave me a tight smile. It was then I realized Alistair had already left and the screen was off.

We were alone.

"I can do it if—"

"No, it's fine." I nodded, unsure who I was trying to convince more.

"Okay, then. I'll call ahead and let Johnson know we're on our way." She gathered up her things.

"What will happen with Riley?" I asked as we exited the room and headed for the elevator.

"Legal will handle it. She'll get paid off to keep quiet, and they'll lock her into an airtight contract."

"Didn't she have the contract before though, and that didn't stop her manipulating the band." The words soured on my tongue. I didn't know Riley from Adam, but I hated her for what she'd done to the band. To Levi.

"This industry is all one big game." We entered their

elevator and Letty hit the button for the ground floor. "She made her play, now it's our turn to make ours."

"And Levi?" Just saying his name made my heart clench. He reminded me so much of my ex, Zephyr. Lost, angry... afraid. Levi had issues; everyone could see that. But music was his salvation, his therapy. It wasn't a cure though. That could only come from inside.

Letty gave me a weak smile. "Let's go see what he has to say."

I TOOK a deep breath as I followed Letty inside the suite where the label had banished Levi. It was everything I'd come to expect from my short time with the band: big, modern, with no expense spared where the furniture and décor was concerned.

"Levi," she called.

"Fuck off," he grumbled from somewhere inside the room.

I leaned over her shoulder and pointed at the bare foot just visible over the top of the huge sectional.

"Come on, Hunter, we need to talk."

"I said fuck off."

She let out an exasperated breath.

"Let me," I mouthed at her and she nodded, giving me space to move around her.

"Levi," I said. "We really need to talk."

"Phoebe?" He sat up, rubbing his eyes. "What are you—"

He glanced down at his tight black boxers and muttered under his breath.

"Maybe go get dressed?" I suggested, heat rushing through me. "And then we'll talk."

"Uh, yeah." He clambered to his feet, and I tried to look anywhere but at his ripped, inked body.

God, he was magnificent.

"I'll just..." He ducked into one of the other rooms.

"Okay," Letty said, "that was just weird. I don't think I've ever seen the infamous Levi Hunter act... embarrassed."

"I fucking heard that, Panem," he yelled.

Less than thirty seconds later, he reappeared dressed in jeans and a *Blood Runs Thicker* tour t-shirt. He ran a hand through his hair. It had grown longer in the last couple of weeks.

"You should try opening a window in here," Letty teased. "The place smells worse than a men's locker room."

"Are you here to bust my balls or because you have actual news?" His eyes flicked to mine, softening.

"We had a conference call with Dusty and his team. Riley is asking for one mil."

"I hope they told her to go fuck herself. Traitorous bitch."

I flinched at the venom in his tone. But I knew Levi well enough to know he didn't appreciate disloyalty.

"Levi, you know that's not how this works."

"She broke the NDA," he hissed, "legal should nail her ass to the fucking wall."

"But it wouldn't stop her leaking the full story. The video has already caused enough damage. If she gives the exclusive who knows what bullshit she'll say. That wouldn't be good for you or the band."

"Fuck." Levi clenched his hand into a tight fist. His jaw was set, his dark eyes narrowed to thin slits. He was furious, anger rolling off him like a volcano on the verge of erupting.

"I'm not giving that manipulative bitch a cent."

"Good thing you don't get to make that call then. Dusty agreed on five-hundred grand. They'll call her bluff with court action if she doesn't take it. But she will."

He scrubbed his jaw, studying Letty. "How can you be so sure?"

"Because I worked with her for the last two years. I know how she thinks, and she only wants the money."

"What do you think?" Levi fixed his eyes right on me and I felt myself grow hot all over again. He didn't just look at me, his eyes seared me to the very bone.

There was intense, and then there was Levi Hunter.

"M- Me?" I choked out.

"Yeah, Intern, you."

Intern.

My fingers curled around the edge of the couch. It's what he'd called me when I'd first joined the tour. I suspected it was Levi's way of distancing himself from people, of reducing them to something less than their given name.

But now... now he said the word with such intimacy, I couldn't help but wonder if he was toying with me.

Steeling my spine, I replied, "Well, I don't think you have much choice. This is bigger than just you, Levi. You have to think about the band."

Something flickered in his dark gaze, and a shiver ran through me.

"Levi," Letty hissed, drawing his attention. Released from his scrutiny, I let out a shaky breath. "We didn't come to debate the plan. This *is* the plan. Legal will handle Riley. It's my job to handle the band's image."

He groaned, sinking back against the huge cushions littering the sectional. "And what, pray tell, do you have in mind this time?"

A faint smile traced Letty's mouth. "You're in the studio first thing tomorrow."

"The studio?" That piqued his interest.

"Everyone agreed we need a distraction, something to draw people's eye off your latest indiscretion."

He scoffed at that. I pressed my lips together, trying to focus. The last thing I wanted to think about was Levi snorting cocaine off that traitor's body.

"You talked to the guys about this?"

"Not yet. We wanted to talk to you first."

Confusion clouded his eyes. "What's the catch?"

"It's a collaboration."

"Eva..." Her name was a whispered sigh on his lips.

"The label has been wanting to get her into the studio, and what better way to improve your image than have the band release a record with the sweetheart of Country?"

"Shit, Letty..."

"It's the right move, Levi."

"I don't like the idea of using her like that."

"It's not like that and you know it. Masterpiece wanted Black Hearts *and* Eva because Dowager saw what everyone else sees, the two of you together, it's effortless. It shouldn't work, but it does. We have to play on that, now more than ever."

"Do you have a song in mind?" There was a cautious edge to his voice.

Letty glanced between us and smiled. "Actually, I do."

CHAPTER THREE

Levi

"It's good to see you, man," Damon pulled me in for a guy-hug, slapping me on the back.

"Yeah," I clipped out, feeling irritation trickling up my spine.

"How was lockdown?" Hudson asked from across the room.

"Fuck you, Ryker."

"Glad to see you didn't lose your sense of humor." He smirked.

I flipped him off and moved deeper into the studio, dropping down on a leather couch. The recording booth was beyond the huge glass partition. But I didn't feel the usual tingle I felt whenever we were about to record something new.

There was a commotion over by the door, and my brother and Eva entered the studio, laughing and joking. They might as well have been in their own little world.

I rubbed my jaw, stuffing down the urge to run. I was contracted to be here. That's what happened when you sold your soul to the devil.

Razorsharp Records owned my ass, whether I liked it or not. I could refuse to be here, take off on one of my benders and leave it to Rafe and the guys to pick up the pieces... and believe me, part of me wanted to. Part of me didn't want to be here, watching my brother and his girl, feeling their love infect everything around them. But the other part, the tiny sliver of humanity I managed to cling onto, knew I couldn't walk out on them. Not this time.

This was my mess.

I did this.

So come hell or high water, no matter how much it sucked for me, I had to try to fix it.

But a collaboration with Eva?

Fuck.

I would have gladly taken anything but that.

It wasn't that I didn't want to sing with Eva, she was amazing. Talent bled from her pores like sweat. We sang all the time together on stage for the tour—but this was different. This was us creating something together. Inviting her into my head like that, it scared the fuck out of me.

"Levi." Her voice was like an explosion in my brain.

"Y- yeah?" I blinked up at Eva, and her smile softened.

"I asked how you were?" Concerned glittered in her eyes.

Once upon a time, I would have mistaken it for a play. But I knew she was Rafe's. She'd chosen him. My brother. The better half of my fucking soul.

"I'm here, aren't I?"

"Levi." The warning in Rafe's voice made my jaw tic.

"Yeah, yeah, okay. *Fine.* I got the memo, *brother.*"

Just then, Letty and Alistair entered their studio. "How are we this morning?" he asked, letting his narrowed gaze settle on me.

"Peachy with a side of keen," I drawled.

"Good to hear it. This is Letty's idea so she's running the show."

"Where's Pheebs?" Hudson chimed, throwing me a knowing look.

Fucker.

"She's... taken a personal day. Don't worry, she'll be back tomorrow."

My brows furrowed.

A personal day?

Something inside me twisted. Was she avoiding me?

I couldn't blame her if she was.

After Alistair announced the label wanted to take the tour international—with the band and Eva—we'd celebrated. Nothing crazy, just the band, Eva's parents, and her best friend from back home, and some people from our inner circle. I'd ended up spending the night with Phoebe.

She'd blown my fucking mind, and I couldn't get enough of her. But then, morning had rolled around and with it, news that a video was going viral of me and Riley. Phoebe had barely looked twice at me since.

Fuck.

My fist clenched against the arm of the couch. Just when

things were starting to look up. The band was in a good place, the tour was going better than any of us expected, and I felt more stable than I had in a while. Then everything came crashing down around me, reminding me that my life would never be my own. That every mistake, every moment of madness, every time I slipped off the wagon... a hungry pack of wolves would be right there waiting to capture it on camera and share it with the world.

Newsflash: Levi Hunter fucked up... *again*.

But this time was different because Riley had betrayed us. She'd manipulated me and used me to her own ends, and now, all I could think about was destroying her. The need for revenge was like poison in my veins. She came after me, came after the band. And now I wanted her to pay.

But the self-loathing I felt was almost as bad.

"Okay," Letty pulled off her skull and bones scarf and draped it over a chair. "So this is what I was thinking. What about if we take the song Levi played at Damon's party, *Drown*, and develop it into a power ballad?"

"No."

No fucking way.

Drown was *my* song. It was personal. Sure, I'd sung it at Damon's birthday party a couple of weeks back, but there had been a good reason for that.

"Do you have a better suggestion?" Letty scowled at me.

"We write something new. I'm sure Eva has plenty of ideas."

"We don't have time to write something new," Letty interjected. "We have the studios for the next three days. We need to nail this. *You* need to nail this." She let out an exasperated breath, flicking a concerned brow toward Alistair. His cell began ringing and he held up a finger, checking the screen.

"I need to take this. You need to figure this out and fast. If we don't get the tour back on track ASAP, I don't need to tell you there will be no more studio time."

A tremor rippled through the room. Hudson looked at Damon, who looked at Rafe, who looked at me.

"What?" I shrugged.

"You're a real fucking asshole sometimes," Hudson sneered. "It's just a song."

But it wasn't just any song.

"This is the plan." Letty rolled her shoulders back and I knew she meant business. She'd been with us since the beginning. Our rise to fame and fortune didn't intimidate her. To her we were nothing more than her responsibility... her job. Sometimes, we were also her friends.

But right now, she was our boss, and we were going to fall in line whether we liked it or not.

"How much of the song is written?"

"Knowing Levi, it's a whole goddamn album." Hudson snorted and I flipped him off.

"Everyone just take a breath." Damon stepped forward. "Maybe we should hear Levi out. If the song is personal to him—"

"It can't be that personal, he sang it for you in front of half of the crew."

"Hud," Rafe warned, glancing at me with concerned eyes.

"You really don't want to use it?" Letty asked. "Because we all heard you that night. It was something special, Levi. I think we can really make something of it, especially with Eva on the track."

"I don't want to upset anyone," Eva said. "Maybe this isn't the best—"

"We'll use it," I said with a defeated breath.

"Yeah?" Relief washed over Letty. "I wouldn't have suggested it if I didn't think—"

"Yeah, yeah, Panem, save the dramatics." I got up and headed for the door.

"Levi, where are you going?" she asked.

"What?" I glanced back. "I can't take a piss now without everyone needing to know?"

No one else said a word as I slipped out of the room. Truth was, I didn't need a piss, I needed a second.

Drown was my song. Something I'd been working on the last few weeks. Yeah, I'd sang a couple of verses at Damon's party, but I never wrote it for public consumption. They owned enough of me already. Now Letty wanted to have the guys and Eva come in on it.

I hated the fucking idea.

Storming into the bathroom, I went straight to the basins and braced my hands on the counter. Beads of sweat rolled down my back as I tried to regulate my breathing and focus on anything but the constant scratch under my skin. The scratch that no matter how hard I tried, I couldn't quite itch.

My skin was sallow, my cheekbones hollow. I looked like

shit, felt like it too. But I knew I was on a shaky ledge. One wrong step, and I would be back in rehab. And I couldn't go back there.

Not again.

For someone like myself, who fought his demons day in day out, rehab was the worst kind of hell. Even if it had saved my life on more than one occasion.

Turning on the faucet, I splashed some water on my face before rubbing my hands to the back of my neck. The blast of cold helped me focus.

Six months ago, I would have told Letty to go fuck herself. I was Levi fucking Hunter. I did what I wanted, when I wanted, with little regard to the consequences. But things were different now. Eva was on the tour, she was one of us, and we had the endorsement from Masterpiece. I couldn't just walk out on them, no matter how much I wanted to.

This time, I had to suck it up and go along with the plan.

This time, I had to fall in line.

This time, I had to try to be better.

EVA SANG THE LYRICS AGAIN, her soft, sultry voice filling the recording booth. I could just make out Letty standing over the sound engineer, a guy called Brad. We'd been at it for hours. First, Eva had to learn the lyrics and then we had to figure out the arrangement. Once we had that nailed, we'd bring in the guys.

"It's good," Letty came over the speaker. "But something is missing."

She wasn't wrong.

There was no doubt our voices blended together effortlessly, but it lacked energy and emotion, and I was pretty sure I knew why.

"She's right." Eva tore off her headphones and took a deep breath, hitting the microphone button so that no one else could hear us. "Maybe it would help if you told me the meaning behind the lyrics."

My brow quirked up. "Nice try, Angel. But never gonna happen."

"Levi, come on. You can trust me. It's such an amazing song but it's *your* song."

"You cover songs all the time." They were a staple of her set on the tour.

"Yeah, but that's different. I'm trying to sing your words, and I know you well enough to know everything you write means something."

Eva was special. Kind and gentle and so damn intuitive. It wasn't any wonder her light had burrowed its way into the darkest part of my soul. For a second, I'd wanted her to be mine. I'd wanted to revel in her purity and let it wash away my sins.

But I always knew she was Rafe's.

Just as I always knew a girl like Eva was too good for a guy like me. I tainted everything I touched, and left to my own devices, I would have tainted her. I would have sucked dry her overflowing well of goodness and turned her soul into nothing more than a black abyss.

Because that's who I was.

Levi Hunter: stealer of hearts, reaper of souls.

Therapists liked to tell me that I couldn't expect anyone to love me until I learned to love myself.

So I was shit out of luck... because loving myself?

Yeah, never going to happen.

PHOEBE

"You're late," my father rose from his chair, a scowl of disapproval etched in the harsh lines of his face.

"Sorry, the traffic was a nightmare."

"Yes, well, you should have left early enough to account for that."

My teeth ground together.

Peter Halstead was a hard man to please. Shrewd and cold with little time for pleasantries. Great for the movie industry; not so great for me, his only daughter.

After an awkward kiss, we both sat down.

"This is great, Dad," I said, pretending to take in the restaurant. The truth was, I hated these places. Rich. Ostentatious. Full of fake conversation and even faker clientele.

He signaled a server and ordered our usual, a bottle of Perrier for me with ice and lemon, and a glass of Jameson eighteen-year-old reserve. "How is at the label?"

"It's... uh, good." I swallowed. My dad had gotten me the internship through a friend of a friend.

"I think this could be a good thing for you, Phoebe. After Zephyr, you need to keep busy."

"Got it, Dad." My lips pursed.

"You haven't spoken to him?"

"I promised I wouldn't."

"Good." He gave me a stiff nod. "That man needs help, sweetheart. Professional help."

"Hmm-mm," I murmured, too choked to reply.

Thankfully, the server chose that moment to bring our drinks over. I grabbed my bottle of water and added it to the glass, wishing it was something stronger.

"If he does try to contact you, I want you to inform me immediately."

Zephyr wouldn't try to contact me. That ship had long sailed. No, it had run aground in after a tumultuous storm.

Ignoring his comment, I mumbled, "And here I thought this was supposed to be lunch with my father because he wanted to actually see me."

"Oh, save me the dramatics, Phoebe." He sipped his whisky. "All I'm trying to say is, you can't save everyone. You need to move on from—"

"Already moved on, Dad. Zephyr who?" My lips twisted into a saccharine smile.

He rolled his eyes. "I see you haven't lost your sense of sarcasm. You know, it's the lowest form of wit. It isn't very becoming of a young woman such as yourself, with so much untapped potential."

I wanted to disappear. I wanted the floor to open up and swallow me whole, if it meant avoiding this conversation.

When I'd gotten the call from my father's assistant that he was on business in Memphis and wanted to have lunch, I'd contemplated making an excuse. But Peter Halstead was not the kind of man you turned down. Besides, if I wanted to keep him off my back, I needed to play nice.

He picked up the menu and began scanning it. "So, tell me about Razorsharp. I hope they've got you doing something a little more useful than making coffee and filing paperwork?"

"I'm the intern, Dad, that's kind of par for the course." The lies rolled off my tongue with ease. I'd spent the better part of the last five years lying to him.

I hadn't grown up living with my father. He and my mom had separated not long after I turned four. He travelled a lot for work, and she didn't like being second best to his job. It wasn't until she died when I was fifteen, that he finally stepped up to the plate. He took me in, and for those first few months, I'd been the center of his world. Mom's death had hit me hard, and I spiraled into depression. Dad took some time out of work to help me through it all. But the second I was better, he returned to his job, and I was left to fend for myself.

I was at a new school with no friends and a whole heap of grief. It was hardly any surprise when I fell in with the wrong crowd. I was desperate for attention, craving intimacy and comfort. I was a teenager in pain, and it wasn't long before I found my cure.

Zephyr Marek.

Tortured bad boy with a penchant for broken girls.

Our love story was a whirlwind. Reckless and chaotic, we fell hard and fast. He was a couple years older than me, but it didn't matter. I was infatuated, swept away with stolen kisses and secret touches.

Until it was too late.

Until I was hooked on him and he was hooked on anything that gave him a high.

I gently shook the thoughts out of my head, watching my father as he ordered his meal.

"Phoebe?" he said.

"I'll have the seared chicken breast with greens please." I folded the leather-bound menu and handed it to the server.

"I'm proud of you, sweetheart. I know I don't say it often, but I am. It took a while for you to come to your senses where Zephyr was concerned, but you got there in the end, and that's all that matters. You're still young. You have your whole life ahead of you." He sipped his whisky again. "You could always give college another try—"

"I think I'm done with that, Dad." I forced the bitter memories down.

"Never say never, Phoebe. You're only twenty-one."

Sometimes I felt about thirty. Like I'd lived too much life for a young woman of my age.

"I'm in a good place at the label, Dad," I said, hoping he wouldn't read too much into it.

I knew he'd find out about the band eventually. He'd call his friend at the label and it would come out, but I wasn't about to give him the ammunition he needed to ruin things for me.

If he got wind that I was working with Black Hearts, he'd pitch a fit. Everyone knew the hype surrounding the band.

Around Levi.

Just thinking about him made my heart flutter. He was everything I needed to avoid, and yet, like the foolish girl I was, I'd allowed myself to get close.

My father got a lot of things wrong—he was aloof and hardly present—but he wasn't wrong about not being able to save everyone.

Love didn't fix people. It only masked some of the cracks. I knew that better than anyone.

Our food came and the conversation turned from me to my father. He talked about the latest A-list celebrities he'd been rubbing shoulders with, and the most recent secrets and scandals. He told me all about Jan, the agent he was dating. He talked and talked and talked until his voice became white noise and my smiles and nods of agreement became robotic.

Then, after we were done, he dabbed his mouth before requesting the check. "This was nice," he said. "We should do it again soon."

And like that, I was dismissed. My father had fulfilled his parental duties enough for the month until the next time his assistant reminded him we were due to do lunch.

It was that he didn't care, I knew that.

He just didn't care enough.

———

WHEN I GOT BACK the hotel, I was exhausted. It had been six-hour round trip to Memphis, but of course, my father hadn't thought twice about expecting me to make the journey to see him.

I slipped into the suite, expecting to find it empty, but Letty and Eva were curled up on the sectional sipping hot chocolate.

"Hey," I said, making my way over to them.

"How was it?" Letty asked.

"Oh, you know. He berated me for my poor life choices, we ate lunch, and then I listened to him drone on for an hour about his work. The usual."

Eva frowned, and I let out a weary sigh. "Sorry, my dad." I sank into one of the armchairs. "That's where I was today."

"He sounds... charming."

"Peter Halstead, charming?" I snorted. "Now there's a joke if ever I heard one. How'd it go at the studio?"

I was bummed to miss their first session, but I figured it might make things easier all round. From the looks on both their faces, I realized I might have assumed wrong.

"That bad, huh?"

"It wasn't bad, but it wasn't quite right either. Eva tried to get Levi to open up about the song, but you know what he's like."

"If anyone can get him to talk, it's you," I said, hating how the words made my stomach sink.

"Phoebe, that isn't—"

"Can we not do this." I sighed. "What happened between me and Levi was... a mistake."

Eva blanched. "This thing with Riley, she set him up."

"Maybe, maybe not. But she didn't force him to snort that coke. And we all know it didn't end there." I hadn't watched the rest of the video circulating the internet. I didn't want to see him with another woman.

I couldn't.

"I hate her for this," She snarled. My eyes widened, surprised at the venom in her voice. She was usually so meek and quiet.

"Yeah, Riley is a real class act," Letty sneered. "But legal will shut her up soon enough. Then we can try and focus on the tour."

"Is there any talk of when the label wants the band back on the road?" They had already postponed five shows.

"If everything goes to plan, we'll head for New Orleans on Thursday. It gives us enough time to produce the track and get it out there."

"If we ever finish the song." Eva tipped her head to the ceiling, letting out a heavy sigh. "I'm worried about him, he was in a better place." Her eyes slowly lowered to mine. "And now he's lost again."

"He's survived worse," I said, trying to ignore the plea in her gaze.

I couldn't fix this. Not without sacrificing part of myself, and I'd promised myself I wouldn't do that again.

"We still have time," Letty said. "He might be a mess, but Levi has always managed to pull it out of the bag when it counts."

"I really thought he'd lose it," Eva added. "Something this huge, I thought he'd spiral out of control."

"Just because he seems okay doesn't mean he isn't one second away from relapsing." The words were out of my mouth before I could stop them.

Letty and Eva both looked at me. Sympathy shone in my mentor's eyes. She knew my story... well, some of it.

"I had an ex," I said for Eva's benefit. "He was an addict. It ended badly." I inhaled a shuddering breath.

"I'm sorry."

"Don't be. I should have walked away long before I did." But love was a funny thing. Once it had its claws in you, it dragged you under deeper and deeper.

"It makes sense now."

"What does?" I asked her.

"How you are with him."

My cheeks heated. I didn't want to think about Levi, about the innate need I felt to protect and shield him from not only himself but the world who would so happily chew him up and spit him out.

"I overstepped and I shouldn't have." I stood, too overwhelmed by the conversation. "I'm going to get an early night. See you both tomorrow."

"Phoebe, you don't have—"

Eva's voice melted away as I shut my bedroom door. I kicked off my pumps and lay on the bed, scrolling my social media apps. Part of my day-to-day responsibilities was to help manage the band's website and official fan pages. Since the video leaked, the Die Hearts—the die-hard Black Hearts fans—had positioned themselves as one-hundred percent supportive of Levi. They provided a wealth of commentary on articles and social media about their favorite tortured bad boy of rock. But the younger fans, the ones whose parents cared a little more about what music their kids were listening to, didn't want to see their favorite rock star snorting coke off a woman's stomach.

Before I knew it, I'd been sucked into a black hole of social media uproar over Levi Hunter and his sinful ungodly ways. I didn't realize what I was looking at until it was too late. The label's PR team had done an excellent job of removing the video from all viable sources. But screenshots were forever.

And there, staring me in the face, was Levi and his betrayer in the throes of passion.

Phoebe was back.

I'd spent most of the morning watching her as she and Letty did whatever it was they did when they were together.

"Levi, earth to Levi." Eva chuckled, and I finally dragged my eyes away from Phoebe.

"Yeah?"

"You know this would go a lot quicker if you concentrated."

"I'm concentrating." I smirked. "It's called inspiration."

Fuck.

I couldn't believe I'd admitted that out loud.

Eva gave me a knowing smile. "You like her."

"It doesn't matter." I'd fucked it up before it ever got started.

My head dropped back against the wall as my eyes flicked over to where Phoebe and Letty were huddled over a binder. She was so fucking beautiful. She didn't try too hard, not like Riley who had always been dressed to the nines in designer dresses and ugly fucking pant suits.

Phoebe possessed natural beauty. Her look was effortless. Her dark hair was braided off one side of her face and hung over her shoulder in thick waves I wanted to run my fingers through. It drew your eye to the tattoo sleeve down her arm. She was inked and pierced and preferred to dress down than up.

She was everything I never knew I wanted.

And I'd already lost her.

Because Leviathan wasn't just my namesake. It was in my soul, imprinted on my fucking DNA.

My mother always said I was her little monster, sent to torment her. I guess there was some truth in her words.

I was tainted, impure. Cut me open and I was pretty sure I would bleed black sticky tar.

"I've got it," Eva said with a trace of excitement. "What if we add the female perspective?"

My brows knitted as I met her gaze. "We only hear the male point of view, but what if we write the female responding to his pain?"

My spine tingled with anticipation. She was onto something. I could already see the lyrics dancing across my mind.

"So right here," Eva held up her notes, "after your first verse, I could respond. It'll be like a conversation."

"I like it." I liked it a lot.

Even if they would be Eva's words, her thoughts and feelings in response to my lyrics...

And not the girl's they were meant for.

"Yes, yes!" Letty's shriek of approval came over the intercom. "That was... shivers, guys. I have honest-to-God shivers."

A shy smile tugged at Eva's mouth. I smirked at her. "It was all Eva," I said, knowing that everyone beyond the booth could hear us.

"Rafe is already working up a riff."

"We want to run your sections again, Levi, okay?"

"Not Eva's sections?" I scoffed.

"Sorry, champ." Letty teased. "She nailed it."

Heat exploded in Eva's cheek. I should have felt a twinge of jealousy, but I knew Letty was right—Eva *had* nailed her sections.

"Get out of here," I said.

"You're sure?"

I nodded. "You did good today, Angel, real fucking good."

There had been moments, when I'd closed my eyes, I could imagine a different voice singing the lyrics to me. But that was a fantasy, and I knew life was nothing more than a living nightmare.

"Don't work too hard." Eva gave me a warm smile. "I think the guys mentioned pizza later."

"I'm not sure—"

"Come," she said softly. "You should come."

Giving her a stiff nod, I waited for her to leave, before slipping my earphones back on and getting ready at the microphone. Brad gave me a thumbs up and I inhaled a deep breath.

Eyes so deep I fall and fall
Can't crawl out, and I can't breathe
These feelings crash over me
Until there's nothing left of who I used to be

Eye so deep I fall and fall

Can't escape, and I can't feel
These feelings crash over me
Until I'm numb inside and cut free

But I'm broken now, I'm dead inside
She can't save me no matter how hard she tries
But I'm broken now, I'm dead inside
She can't save me no matter how hard she tries

Down we go... like sinking ships
I'm drowning now... drowning now... drowning yeah...

WHEN I WAS DONE, I felt emotionally wrecked. I'd written some heavy stuff in my time. Songs about my mom, about growing up and being unwanted, unloved. I'd written about my addiction and the demons that lived inside me. I'd written about love and heartache and loss.

But I'd never written about a girl.

Until *Drown*.

I suspected Eva knew the truth, maybe Letty too. But they wouldn't push me about it. There was a good chance even Phoebe knew the truth, but it didn't matter now.

I gave myself a second, inhaling a ragged breath.

"That's great, Levi," Brad's voice came over the mic. "We got what we need for today."

Slipping out of the booth, I expected to find Eva and my bandmates all waiting for me, but I was only met with Brad and Letty.

"Where'd everyone go?" I said.

"Oh, they left already. Something about pizza."

My stomach sank. They'd left... without me. It shouldn't have mattered. Hudson was still pissed at me. Rafe too if the lingering looks he kept giving me were anything to go by. Damon was Damon. Peacekeeper. Father figure. Loyal friend. But even he'd been quiet the last couple of days.

"I think they were heading to their suite if you want to catch up with them?" Letty gave me a reassuring smile that did absolutely nothing for the pit in my stomach.

"Yeah, maybe," I lied. Because no fucking way was I about to invite myself to their cozy little tea party—the one they clearly didn't want me at.

Johnson was waiting for me in the hall. He didn't blink as I stormed past him toward the back exit of the studios. He would drive me back to the hotel, and I would retreat to my room and drown my sorrows in the mini bar. If Letty hadn't been in and cleared it out that was.

But when we got back to the hotel, Phoebe was just heading into her room. The one two doors down from mine. Our eyes collided, sucking all the air from the hall.

"Levi," she said right as I said, "Phoebe."

We laughed, hers wrapping around me like silk. Fuck. She was so beautiful.

"You go," I said.

"You're not heading up to the suite?"

"Looks like I'm still in the doghouse."

"You're not..." She gave me a weak smile. "I mean, I know things are strained. But they just wanted to give you space."

"Whatever." I shrugged, aware that we weren't alone. But

Johnson was security. A ghost. He didn't care about our conversation so long as it didn't pose a threat to my life.

You had to get used to sharing every part of your life with security pretty quickly, when you went from nobody to somebody overnight.

Silence lingered between us. She wasn't close enough to touch, too far to ghost my fingers over the ink on her shoulder.

"Well, I should probably go—"

"Wait." The word echoed through my mind. "Do you want to hang out?"

Her breath caught. "I'm not sure that's a good idea," she whispered, the words like jagged knives to my skin.

"I'll behave, I promise." I held up my hands. "I just..." I couldn't tell her.

I couldn't confess how lonely I was.

Not me.

Levi Hunter: rock god and sex symbol.

Phoebe inhaled a sharp breath, her eyes fluttering closed. When they opened again, I expected her to tell me no. But the word, "Okay," fell from her lips. "Just for a little while."

She tucked her key card in her purse and moved closer. Sweet relief flowed through me. This was a good sign. Maybe if we hung out, if we were together, she would remember how good it could be between us.

I opened the door and stood aside, letting her passed. It wasn't the penthouse suite, but it was still one of the best rooms in the hotel. It could have been a hovel for all I cared though. Because Phoebe was here.

"Drink?" I asked her, going to the mini bar.

"I'm not sure that's a good idea." Her brow went up.

"Soda then? Juice?"

"I'll take a soda."

I grabbed two sodas and went over to where she was hovering. "Here." Our fingers brushed as she took it from me, electricity sparking up my arm. My eyes lifted to hers. "Phoebe, I—"

"So today went well?" She darted to one of the chairs and sat down.

"Yeah, it was okay. Now we've figured out the arrangement, it's flowing." I ran a hand over my head, choosing the couch. It put me dead opposite her.

"Letty's right, I think this will work."

"You really want to talk about this?" I'd kinda hoped we would talk about us, about what happened with us.

"I think it's for the best if we keep things professional, don't you?"

"Actually," I said dragging my snake bit piercings between my teeth and letting them pop. "I don't think that's going to work for me."

"Levi, please..." She darted out of the chair. "I should go, this was a mistake."

"Don't do that." I got up and stalked toward her. "Don't call me a mistake."

It's all I'd heard growing up. I could be that to my mom, to the father who didn't want me. But I didn't ever want to be that to this girl.

Phoebe inched back, but I snagged her waist, pulling her closer. "We need to talk."

"There's nothing to say." She dropped her gaze to the floor.

Irritation licked my spine. She was being stubborn, and part of me understood. She felt betrayed. But Riley was a mistake, one that happened before Phoebe arrived on the scene.

"Hey, look at me." I gripped her chin and lifted her face to mine. "What happened with Riley was before you and I—"

"Stop, Levi. There is no you and me. It was one night."

"That's bullshit and you know it."

"I can't do this again. I can't be with someone who will never put me first. I'm sorry, I am... but this, us, I was a fool to think there could ever be some—"

I cupped her face, slamming my lips to hers. Phoebe went rigid in my arms, but the second my tongue plunged into her mouth, her body softened against me. The kiss became a storm, sweeping us away with every stroke and every press of our lips. My hands dropped to her ass and I picked her up, pushing her up against the nearest wall.

"Fuck, Phoebe, you taste so fucking good." I caged her body with mine, freeing up one of my hands to glide up her throat. "Tell me you feel it, tell me you're here with me..." I stared into her heavy-lidded eyes.

"I..."

Say it.

I really needed her to say it.

"You need to stop. We need to stop." She pushed around my chest, trying to wrangle out of my hold. I jerked away as if she'd slapped me and Phoebe slid down the wall, skin flushed and eyes apologetic.

"I see."

"It's for the best, Levi. You need to focus on the band and getting things back on track, and I need to—"

"Got it. You know where the door is. Don't let it hit you on the way out." I marched over to the minibar and grabbed the first thing I could find. The liquor barely registered as I chugged it down.

"That won't help," Phoebe said softly.

"I thought you were leaving?" I ground out.

She stood there for another second, before letting out a quiet breath and leaving. The door clicked shut but it may as well have been a gunshot to my heart.

What a fucking idiot.

The bottle flew out of my hand before I could stop myself, shattering into tiny pieces against the wall.

"Call someone to clean that up," I barked at Johnson. I didn't look at him, I couldn't.

Instead, I grabbed another two bottles from the mini bar and headed for my bedroom.

At least there, I would have privacy.

I'D MESSED UP.

When I'd agreed to go with Levi, I thought we'd talk. I thought it would be a good opportunity to clear the air.

I didn't think he would kiss me.

Although *kiss* didn't do justice to the way his mouth had laid siege to my emotions. I'd felt his desire for me, the hard outline of his dick pressed up against me. Levi wanted me. But he had the power the destroy me.

It had taken everything to push him away, to do the right thing. Because while nothing about kissing Levi felt wrong, it was a mistake.

One that would only lead me down a path of heartache and misery.

"We have a problem." Letty greeted me. I was barely awake, and she looked ready to take on the world.

"A problem?" I rubbed the sleep from my eyes.

"Levi, he's a mess."

Guilt shot through me.

"What happened?" Letty gave me a serious look as she barged into the room.

"I... I messed up."

"Talk."

"I went to Levi's room last night. I thought he wanted to talk..."

"He didn't?" Her brow arched but I found no judgment there.

"Not exactly. He kissed me."

"And let me guess, you rejected him?"

"How did you—"

"Because Johnson found him passed out over a collection of mini bar drinks."

"We should have emptied it." We'd discussed it but Letty decided that after two weeks of exile, treating Levi like a child wouldn't get us anywhere fast.

"He's okay," she said. "But his mood is..."

"Dark."

Her lips pressed into a thin line and she nodded.

"I'm sorry," I whispered, feeling the guilt take hold.

"Don't. This isn't your fault. It's all on that traitorous bitch."

"Is she taking the deal?"

"Of course she is. Practically foamed at the mouth when legal called her."

"At least the tour can resume now."

"Yeah. But this thing between you and Levi... a little word of advice... you need to decide what you want. Levi won't give up. Once he set his sights on something..."

A shiver ran down my spine. "I understand."

"Good, because I need him on this."

"I'll talk to him."

My stomach twisted. It was the last thing I wanted but Letty was right. This entire thing relied on Levi. The band needed him, the tour needed him, Razorsharp Records needed him. Without him, the shaky kingdom they'd built crumbled.

"They shouldn't have left without him yesterday."

"I know." Letty grimaced. "But they're not just a band, Phoebe, they're friends. Family. And he broke their trust sleeping with…" She hesitated.

"It's okay, I'm very aware of what happened between him and Riley." I'd seen enough screenshots to last me a lifetime.

"This is life with the band. It's messy and fraught and the lows can outweigh the highs… but man, those highs can make it all worth it." Her expression softened. "This will pass, you'll see."

For them, maybe.

But for me and Levi, I wasn't so sure.

———

LEVI RODE to the studio alone while I rode with Eva and the guys.

"How is he?" she asked me, keeping her voice low while Rafe and Damon chatted about the music for *Drown*.

"I don't know, I haven't seen him."

"We shouldn't have done that yesterday." Her mouth downturned at the corners. "I told Rafe it was a bad idea, but you know what boys can be like."

It amused me to hear her calling them boys. Because despite their age, Black Hearts weren't boys. They were young men thrust into the spotlight too early. That kind of exposure aged you. Forced you to grow before your time. The parties and women, drugs and liquor… it was a deadly combination for a bunch of hormonal guys on the cusp of adulthood.

"They need to figure it out," I whispered, but Hudson's head whipped over in my direction.

"Figure out what, New Girl?" He rubbed his jaw, eyeing me intently.

"Hud," Damon warned.

"Nah, man. If she's got something to say about the way we handle band business, I'm all ears. So, spit it out, *Pheebs*, what exactly do you think we need to figure out?"

The air in the SUV cooled, making my blood run cold. Tension crackled around us, thick and charged.

"You need to forgive him," I said. "Levi blames himself enough without the three of you making it worse."

"*We* need to forgive *him*?" Hudson sneered. "Do you have any idea how many times we've had to—"

"Hudson, enough." Rafe leveled him with a hard look. "No disrespect, Phoebe, but you've been here two seconds, we've been dealing with Levi for years."

"Rafe." Disbelief coated Eva's voice. "She's just trying to help."

"Yeah, well if she wants to help, she should let Levi work off his tensions on her." Hudson glowered at me and everything began to close in around me.

"I'll pretend you didn't just say that." I sat taller, my body vibrating with embarrassment.

"Everyone just take a breath." Damon made a sweeping motion with his hands. "Hudson, apologize to Phoebe."

He glared harder until Damon elbowed him in the ribs. "Sorry," he grumbled.

"Emotions are running high," Damon added. "We're all feeling the pressure. But she's right, we shouldn't shut Levi out. Not now. Not after what Riley did. An attack against one of us, is an attack against all of us. He needs to know we've got his back."

"Until the next time he—"

"*Hudson!*" Damon let out an exasperated breath. "Whatever personal shit you've got going on you need to rein it in. We're a band, a family, and right now, Levi thinks he's on his own. That's on all of us."

"Fine," Hudson grunted.

"Damon's right." Rafe looked out of the tinted windows, torment etched into the lines of his face.

I didn't know the Hunter brothers' full story, but I knew enough. He was the angel on Levi's shoulder. His protector. I knew what a burden it was to carry someone addicted to the high. What a burden it was to always come second to that devastating little thing called addiction.

Rafe had Eva now though. He had someone to lean on when the burden got too heavy. I'd never had that. I'd loved Zephyr in solitude. I was his person, his crutch, and when things got rough, I was his punching bag. Never physically, but sometimes words cut just as deep.

The rest of the ride to the studios was silent, everyone lost to their own thoughts. Eva offered me the odd smile of reassurance, but it did little to settle my soul. I was the outsider here, the enemy. But what they didn't realize was, keeping my relationship with Levi strictly professional was the only way for us to both survive the connection we shared. I couldn't be Levi's lifeline and he couldn't be the stable secure guy I needed.

We were doomed long before Riley's betrayal came to light.

Levi would get over it. Over me.

And I would file him away as another moment of weakness.

***

THE SECOND LEVI entered the studio the mood changed. He was late, and the guys were pissed. But Damon insisted they cut him some slack.

"Hey, man," he said, stepping up to Levi. "We wanted to apologize for yesterday. It was a bum move."

"It's all good." Levi wore an easy expression, but it was too easy.

"Well, we just wanted you to know we're sorry. We're in this together."

"Together, yeah."

I watched him out the corner of my eye. He was a man on the edge, walking a fine line between control and chaos.

"You guys figure out the backing track yet?" he looked to Rafe and then Hudson.

"We've got a few ideas yeah."

"Good, let's get to it then."

"Sounds good." Some of the tension eased out of Damon's shoulders. "Letty, we good to go?"

"It's all yours." She motioned to the booth. The band's instruments were all in place, waiting for the guys.

Levi grabbed a bottle of water from be mini bar and

chugged it down. His eyes flicked to me and went right past me.

Ouch.

His silent treatment hurt, but it was no less than I expected. Or deserved.

Something told me Levi Hunter was choosy about who he invited into his inner sanctum. I'd been granted access but now the doors had been slammed shut in my face.

It's for the best. He'll get over it. You'll get over it.

He dropped down beside Eva and she leaned in close, asking him something. His eyes snapped to mine again but what I saw there made me glance away. When I noticed Letty make her way over to them, I couldn't help but peek though. She perched on the table, handing him her phone.

Levi scanned the screen. "That's bullshit," he growled.

"It's for the best," Letty replied, keeping her voice calm. "We don't have to worry about her now, and you can focus on the band and the last leg of the tour."

"Yeah, whatever." His teeth ground together. "Problem, Intern?" He narrowed his eyes at me.

Heat exploded in my cheeks as I shook my head.

"Do you mind then?" Disdain dripped from his voice.

"Levi," Letty warned.

"Actually, I have some emails and calls to follow up with. I'll be in the meeting room if anyone needs me." I hurried out of there, dragging in a shaky breath the second the door closed behind me.

Levi was hurting, and when he hurt, he lashed out.

Pressing my head against the wall, I gave myself a second. But it didn't help. All I could think was…

What had I gotten myself into?

———

"WE'RE GOING OUT," Letty announced the second her head appeared around the door. It had been a long day in the studio. After retreating to the meeting room, I'd immersed myself in work; everything from social media management, to interview bookings, and replying to fan mail.

"Out?" I paled, closing my laptop. "Is that a good idea?"

"It's just dinner and drinks. Damon suggested it, a peace offering if you will, and Levi agreed."

"And we have to go?"

"Where the band goes, we lowly folk must follow." She smirked. "You good with this?"

"Yeah, fine." I wasn't, but I couldn't exactly tell her that. She was technically my boss.

"I've already made the arrangements with the club. They've promised complete discretion."

"And you believe them?"

"I already emailed the NDA's over. They have a VIP section, we'll have privacy."

"Okay." I started packing up my things. "Did they leave already?"

"Yeah, the coast is clear." She gave me a knowing look.

"How did it go?"

"Okay. Good. He seemed present, but with Levi everything can appear fine and then come crashing down."

Like most addicts.

"I think a night out will do everyone good," Letty went on. "He knows the deal. There's too much on the line."

"Yeah." I didn't want to argue, to tell her that the line didn't matter to an addict unless it came littered with white or brown powder.

He was the label's star, their leading guy. They didn't care about whether or not he was suffering, so long as he was fulfilling the terms of their contract. It was the dark side of the industry. Throwing young artists into a world of sex, drugs, and debauchery, and not caring much if they sank or swam, so long as the money kept rolling in.

"Come on, I have a car waiting."

We made our way out front and climbed into the familiar black SUV.

"I never thought I'd say this, but I miss the tour bus." Letty sank back against the leather seats.

"Really?"

"Yeah, it kind of becomes home after a while. I like life on the road, waking up in a different city every morning. The beds suck, but I'm usually so tired I don't really notice."

"I don't know, my hotel bed is pretty awesome." I smiled.

"Yeah, you're not wrong there. I guess this life is either in your blood or it's not."

"What about relationships? Friends? It can't be easy maintaining those when you're away from home so much."

Sadness washed over her. "Home hasn't been home in a long time."

"I know that feeling."

"Look at us, working with the hottest rock band of the moment and we both look like our favorite puppy just died."

Letty chuckled but it came out strained, and her expression sobered. "I'm glad you're here, it's nice to have another girl along for the ride. Although if you and Levi—"

"Letty," I said feeling my chest constrict. "There is no me and Levi."

A knowing glint sparkled in her eye and she said two little words that I felt all the way down to my soul.

"We'll see."

I DON'T KNOW why I'd fucking agreed to this. Everyone was crowded into a long booth, tucking into their food, while I sat there, trying to look anywhere but at Phoebe. She looked stunning in a simple black dress with ankle boots. She'd styled her hair into another complex braid, leaving the creamy expanse of her neck on display. I could imagine kissing her there, sucking the spot right over her pulse and making her moan.

Her eyes caught mine, but she instantly looked away, only making my mood darker.

I didn't want to be here, but Damon was trying to do a good thing, and I needed the guys to believe I wasn't two steps from falling into the deep end.

Uncapping my water, I took a long pull, letting the cold liquid douse some of the anger swelling inside me. But water wasn't going to cut it, not if I wanted to relax.

Lifting my hand in the air, I signaled one of the servers. She sauntered my way. "What can I get you?"

"I'm going to need something a little stronger than this." I motioned to the bottle of water.

"What's your poison of choice?" She batted her eyes, swishing her long platinum blonde hair over one shoulder. The Cube was a high-end bar and restaurant overlooking the city, with a nightclub below. The VIP section was a secluded mezzanine above the dance floor. It was quiet now, but later it would be filled with people all looking for a good time.

"We stock an excellent range of vodka—"

"No vodka," I snapped, feeling the icy fingers of the past wrap around my throat. "Whisky on the rocks."

"You got it. Anything else I can help you with, Mr. Hunter?" Heat blazed in her eyes, rolling off her tight little body in heady waves.

She knew who I was... and like most women on the planet, she wanted a taste.

"That's all... for now." I smirked, letting my eyes run over her chest, lingering on her ample rack spilling out the top of her crisp white blouse. Blondie looked like she'd be down for a good time. She'd probably let me lead her to the bathroom and fuck her up against the wall. There was just one problem...

She wasn't Phoebe.

I felt her heavy gaze as I flirted with Blondie, but when I slid my eyes her way, Phoebe ducked her head. My fist clenched against my thigh. She was shutting me out. Just like that, she'd decided we were done.

Well, fuck that.

I was Levi fucking Hunter.

And no one told me no.

No one.

———

THE MORE I DRANK, the better I felt. I knew Rafe and Letty were worried. They'd told me as much when they'd suggested I switch to water earlier. But I didn't listen. It wasn't like I was shitfaced and about to puke up my deepest darkest secrets. The liquor helped; it ran through my blood stream making everything numb.

Blondie kept the drinks coming. She also went out of her way to let me know she was available for more than just drinks service. The way she licked her lips, let her hand brush mine, the sheer lust swirling in her eyes... yeah, she was game for a good time.

I watched her across the room as she chatted to the bartender of the VIP section. We had exclusive use but somewhere over the last hour, a handful of other people had joined us. There were associates of another band we'd performed with a few times, and our quiet dinner became an intimate party.

"Is that a good idea?" Damon dropped down beside me, eyeing the glass in my hand.

"If you're only here to give me the speech, you're wasting your breath."

"I'm just worried."

"Well, don't be," I hissed. "I've got a handle on it. It helps take the edge off."

"You'll tell me if it becomes an issue?"

I nodded, even though we both knew I wouldn't.

"Listen, about yesterday..."

"Forget it. I already have." Another lie.

"It was the wrong call." Damon sighed. "But tensions were high, and we wanted to give you your space."

"I got that memo when I got handed my own room key."

"Shit, Levi, you could have stayed in the suite. We just thought—"

"That I wanted space? Yeah, I got it."

He let out a strained breath, rubbing a hand down his face. "The truth is, we've all been waiting for you to blow up over this shit with Riley. But you didn't. You didn't, man, and that's huge." Damon gripped my shoulder, squeezing.

"I know what's at stake," I mumbled.

"Know what I think?" His brow lifted. "I think you found someone you want to do better for." He flicked his head over to where Phoebe was talking to a couple of guys at the bar.

Red hot jealousy coursed through me, and a low growl rumbled in my chest. "She's made her choice," I gritted out.

"She's just trying to protect herself. That shit with Riley panicked her."

"Nah," I said through clenched teeth. "We're done."

"Really? You believe that?"

"I don't need her." And she definitely didn't need a guy like me storming into her life and ruining everything.

"Guys like us aren't built for relationships."

"Speak for yourself." Damon chuckled but there was something so fucking sad about the sound. "Besides, Rafe seems to be enjoying life on the dark side."

That was because Eva was special.

She wasn't like most other girls.

I watched Phoebe with the two guys. They were just talking, but it didn't stop me from wanting to go over there and claim her as mine.

Mine.

Fuck. I really needed to get over myself. She'd made her feelings on us perfectly clear. For all I knew, she was interested in one of them. They both looked like the

Alistairs of the world. Dressed in immaculate suits with their hair slicked back and polished shoes. They probably had luxurious apartments in the city and a ten-year plan.

I didn't know what I was doing from month to month. It's why we had Alistair and Letty to keep us on the straight and narrow.

Phoebe laughed at something one of them said, her eyes twinkling with delight. It drifted over to me, cutting my skin like tiny blades.

"Relax, they're just talking."

"Yeah." My teeth ground together again, and I was almost certain I would break enamel. "I need to take a piss." I got up and headed for the small archway leading to the restrooms. Johnson followed me, waiting by the entrance.

I slipped inside and braced the counter, forcing myself to take a couple of deep breaths. The liquor burned inside my veins, giving me a slight buzz. But it wasn't enough.

After I was done, I washed my hands and left the room, running straight into one of the guys.

"Hey, man." He gave me a friendly smile. "I'm Dougie. I'm with Cantor Records."

My eyes narrowed. "Good for you."

His smile fell as he ran a hand through his hair. "Phoebe was just telling us you're back on the road soon. She's a real sweetheart that one."

Anger exploded inside me and it took everything I had not to ram my fist into his face. "She's as good as family."

Dougie's eyes widened, the warning in my voice was clear. "What? Oh, no... no, it isn't like that. I have a wife. She's pregnant. I just—"

"Save it for someone who cares." I barged past him and stormed back into the bar.

"Problem?" Johnson asked me.

"Nothing I can't handle." My eyes instantly spotted her across the room. She was staring at me, confusion clouding her eyes. But then Blondie arrived with another drink for me, and our connection was severed.

"Here you go. Can I get you anything else?" She licked her lips suggestively.

Dougie slipped past us and made a beeline for his friend and Phoebe. They all glanced my way and she flushed.

Motherfucker. I hadn't expected he would run back and tattle to her.

Phoebe laid her hand on his arm and smiled up at him. My thin rope of control snapped. Two could play at that game, and I never lost.

Leaning in a little closer, I let my hand snake around Blondie's waist to the small of her back. "Why don't you come sit with me and my friends?"

"Yeah?" Her eyes lit up.

"Yeah, bring a friend or two."

"Okay." She tried to sound confident, but I heard the slight hitch to her words.

"I'll be right over there." I pointed toward where Damon and Hudson were sitting. Hudson had barely spoken two words to me all day, but if there was something we could always bond over, it was our love of hot women.

I sauntered over to their table and dropped down on the leather bench.

"You look mightily pleased with yourself," Hudson said.

"I come bearing gifts." I winked at him.

His brows furrowed. "What do you—oh, now we're talking." Hunger flared in his eyes as he watched Blondie and her two friends approach with a tray of drinks.

"Hey," she stopped just short of the booth. "This is Cherry and Jasmine. I'm Darcie." Her eyes held mine.

"Cute name. Now get over here." I slung my arm over the back of the booth, waiting for her to slide in. Hudson wasted no time lifting Jasmine over his lap so she could squeeze in between him and Damon. Damon looked less than impressed at our little party for six, but the guy needed to learn to relax.

I handed everyone a shooter and grinned. "To new friends."

"Hear fucking hear." Hudson pulled his girl close, nuzzling her neck. Her giggles filled the booth.

Rafe caught my eye across the room and frowned. I ignored him. Letty too, when she gave me one of her 'what the fuck are you doing?' glares. The only person I cared about was the one person not paying me an iota of attention.

Phoebe was deep in conversation with Dougie and his friend. The three of them were laughing and joking. Her body had even begun to sway gently to the music pumping out of hidden speakers.

"Levi?" Blondie let her fingers slide against my jaw, demanding my attention. "It's our turn."

"Oh yeah, and what are we playing?"

She leaned over and grabbed another shooter, bringing it to her lips. Taking a sip, she held the liquid in her mouth for a second before swallowing. "You have to guess the flavor."

"Oh yeah?" I drawled. "And just how am I going to do that?"

She leaned in, letting her mouth slide against mine. When I didn't push her away, she licked the seam of my lips, plunging her tongue deep inside. Sour cherries exploded in my mouth, but Blondie didn't let up. She practically climbed onto my lap, kissing me like a porn star. I heard Hudson's cheers of encouragement, alongside Damon's groans of frustration, but I didn't stop.

I couldn't.

She was too eager, too hot and soft. Her lips were pliant and skilled. Her tight little body felt too good rocking against mine. I drowned in sensation, letting my hands run over her slim curves.

Eventually, she pulled away, cheeks flushed and eyes alight with lust. "That was... wow." She dabbed the corner of her lips before dropping back into the space beside me. "I guess we got carried away, huh?"

"Something like that."

I didn't know what to think. Her body felt good pressed up on me, too fucking good. But she wasn't Phoebe.

Not even close.

"We could take this somewhere a little quieter?" She purred in my ear, letting her hand drift down to my crotch.

I glanced over at Phoebe, watching her until she finally looked my way. Her expression fell, her lips parted on a shaky breath. She cared.

She fucking cared, so why was she doing this? Why was she denying us both what we wanted?

Pick me, I wanted to scream. Choose me.

But she didn't. She gave me a sad smile and then looked away.

Pushing me right into the arms of a woman who would never be her.

I watched Levi leave with Hudson and their harem of women. They all worked at the club, but apparently, the chance to sleep with a rock star negated work responsibility. Or maybe Levi had handled their boss.

I didn't like to think about that.

"Everything okay?" Dougie asked me. He was a junior manager at Cantor Records. He and his colleague, Paul, had spent most of the night entertaining me with stories from their intern days. It was nice, normal.

At least, it had been until he returned from the restrooms a little while ago. Levi had gone out of his way to be rude to Dougie, and I couldn't help but wonder if it was because of me.

Guess it didn't matter now. He'd left with the blonde. If that wasn't a giant 'fuck you', I didn't know what was.

I suppose it had to happen eventually. If it wasn't tonight, it would be one night. Levi was a young, hot-blooded male. He had needs, and according to his reputation, he liked to get those needs serviced at regular intervals.

The pit in my stomach carved a little deeper.

"Hey, are you sure you're okay?" Dougie touched my arm making me startle.

"S- sorry." I forced a smile. "I'm just tired. It's been a long day."

"Yeah, we should probably call it a night," Paul said, shooting Dougie a strange look.

"Yes, *Dad*," he chuckled. "It's been nice chatting, Phoebe. If you're ever in town again and want to get together, here's my card." He slid his wallet out of his pocket and handed me the foil embossed business card.

"Strictly professional?" I eyed his wedding band.

"Of course." His smile suggested otherwise, and disappointment washed over me. I'd spotted his ring immediately, but our conversation had been nothing but innocent industry talk. We were all professionals in the same field.

I'd obviously misread the situation. Stuffing the card in my purse, knowing I had no intentions of ever looking him up, I smiled. "Excuse me, I need to check in with Letty."

His eyes burned into me as I walked away.

"What's wrong?" Letty asked when I reached her, Eva, and Rafe.

"Guy in the gray suit. He's married."

"And let me guess, he wasn't just talking for talking's sake."

"He gave me his card for if I'm ever in town again."

"That's so disappointing," Eva said, cuddling into Rafe's side.

"Men are dogs," Letty added.

"Hey, guy standing right here."

"You're an exception to the rule." Eva beamed up at him. "At least, you'd better be. Because if I ever find out you're giving your number to random girls across the country, I'll —" She tugged him down to her and whispered something in his ear.

Rafe chuckled. "Okay, I think it's time to get you back to the hotel, Starshine."

"Can we do that thing again? The one with—"

"Okay." He clapped his hand over her mouth. "I'm going to have Travis bring the car around. Are you two riding with us?"

"Might as well." Letty shrugged. "Since the others already left." Her eyes flicked to mine, but I ignored her.

I didn't want to think about Levi back at the hotel with Blondie.

"He's hurting." Letty squeezed my hand as we made our way out of the club. "When he hurts, he lashes out."

I mumbled some inaudible reply. Because for as much as I told myself it didn't matter, that this was the best thing for us both, it didn't change the fact that my heart—my stupid, foolish, fickle heart—didn't believe me.

———

THE NEXT MORNING, I was up early. I couldn't sleep, imagining Levi and that girl together. I knew Letty would be up and at it early too, so I decided to go in search of coffee for us both.

As I left my room, I didn't expect to come face to face with Blondie. "Oh, hi," She rubbed her bleary eyes. "You're with the band, right? I need to go. Do you think someone can give me a ride?"

Just then, Johnson appeared around the hall. "Miss Halstead," he greeted me.

"Levi's friend," the words were like ash on my tongue,

"needs to get home. Can you make the necessary arrangements?"

"Of course. Please Miss..."

"Miss Bass. Darcie Bass."

"Very well, Miss Bass. This way please."

"Oh, before I go," she dug around in her purse and pulled out a notepad and pen, scribbling her number on it, "can you give Levi this and tell him I'd love to finish what we started sometime." She thrust the note at me and skipped off down the hall as if she hadn't just decimated my heart.

I stared at the digits, anger swelling inside of me. These girls, they only wanted the rock star. Their five minutes of life in the spotlight. They didn't care about the guy underneath.

My fingers began closing around the note, crumpling it into nothing, when Levi's door opened again. He ground to a halt, his eyes red and bloodshot. "Intern?"

"Your little friend just left. She asked me to give you this." I threw the note at him and stormed off down the hall.

Levi Hunter wasn't just hazardous for my heart; he was a plague on my sanity. And I needed to do a better job of reining in my emotions around him.

Letty intercepted me at the elevators. "Problem?"

"Nope." I pressed my lips together, eyeing the coffee in her hand.

"Oh here, I got one for you."

"You read my mind." Silence settled over us as we backtracked to her room.

"So this dark thundercloud over you, wouldn't have

anything to do with the cute blonde I caught sneaking out with Johnson just now?"

"You think she's cute?" I gawked at her and she smirked.

"Got ya."

"Not funny. She asked me to give Levi her number, can you believe that?"

"Girl, you wouldn't believe the things I've done for those boys over the last couple of years." She shuddered. "Some of the stuff doesn't even bear thinking about."

Her words were like a slap to the face. This was their life. Sure, it was somewhat tamer with Eva on the scene, but so long as Hudson and Levi were single there was always going to be a revolving door of girls.

Could I handle that?

Could I watch him fuck girl after girl after girl, and survive?"

Mentally I could do it. I'd been through worse. Much worse. But my heart... she was already battered and bruised and no longer whole.

"Uh oh, I don't like that look," Letty said.

"What look?" I played dumb.

"The one where you're trying to figure out if you're cut out for life on the road with the band and their immoral ways."

"I can cut it," I said with conviction. Because I had something to prove. Not only to my father, and the label, and Letty... but to myself. I needed to know I could stand on my own two feet without letting a guy get in the way of things.

"Atta girl." She beamed. "Because I've kinda got used to having you around now. We all have."

———

WE LEFT for New Orleans that night. Things in the studio had been wrapped up and the song was in the post-production stages now. Letty and Alastair wanted to give The Rock Report the world exclusive at the live interview they'd arranged for two days from now.

I'd managed to avoid Levi for most of the day, but now we were all crammed onto the Van Hool because Alistair wanted a meeting.

"Hudson, let's go," he yelled.

Seconds later, the drummer swaggered into the room, shirtless, sporting shower-damp hair.

"Really, dude?" Letty rolled her eyes.

"What? It's nothing you haven't seen before."

"And I'll say to you again. Really, dude?" She smirked and he flipped her off.

"Can we please get started?" Alistair groaned. "Believe it or not, I don't enjoy being crammed on this tour bus with the four of you."

"Hang on a minute, Ali, that's a bit sexist, mate."

"Hudson!" Everyone seemed to yell at once, and finally, he sank down onto one of the chairs.

"Now that the track is recorded, I thought it was time to address the elephant in the room." His eyes found Levi across the table. "What happened with Riley is done. She's been taken care of and as far as I'm concerned, we draw a line under that shit here and now. Got it?"

A collective of grumbles filled the bus. "The label wants you back on tour bigger and better than ever. The first show is New Orleans and we know how crazy the Die Hearts can be there. Security will be tight but that doesn't mean we won't give the fans what they want, okay?"

"We know the deal, Ali." Damon folded his arms over his chest.

"Good. Because the label and Dowager will be watching. Another wrong move and everything you've worked so hard for could come crashing down."

Silence ushered over us, tension rippling in the air.

"You didn't hear this from me, but the international leg of the tour still has the green light... but, one wrong move and—"

"Yeah, yeah, Ali boy, we got it," Levi let out a big yawn. "I'm on thin ice."

"This isn't just about you, Levi, it's about all of you. One of you goes down, you all go down."

"What Ali is trying to say," Letty added, "is that we want to look forward, not back. The track is almost ready. We have the exclusive with The Rock Report soon. This thing with Riley is in the past; let's leave it there."

"Any questions?" Alistair asked.

"Do you actually style your hair like that, or is it just—"

"Hudson!" The guys yelled again, and Letty slapped him up upside the head.

"What? It was only a question."

"Right, if we're done here. Try and not kill each other before we arrive in New Orleans. We're on the bus for the next two nights. Figured we didn't need you all getting too comfortable in hotels." Alistair got up and moved to the front of the bus.

Rafe stood up and grabbed Eva's hand.

"Now, really?" Hudson asked.

"We're just going to... rest."

"Rest? Is that what they're calling it these days."

They disappeared into one of the two bedrooms on the tour bus.

"I'm going to take a shower and then call my mom," Damon announced, leaving the four of us.

Letty, Damon, Levi... and me.

I pretended to be on my cell, answering emails while Letty flicked through the schedule for the next few days.

"I can't stop thinking about those girls from the club last night. Fuck, man, she was wild." Hudson let out a dark chuckle.

I risked peeking over at Levi. He was slouched against the backrest, eyes closed.

"Yo, Lev, you sleeping?"

"Fuck off," he grumbled.

"Next time we're in Nashville we should totally look them up. She gave you her number, right?" Hudson's eyes slid to mine, smirking.

Asshole.

Everything was a game to him.

"You and that guy seemed pretty close, Pheebs. What was his name? Douglas?"

"Dougie," I said.

Levi tensed, a dark cloud swirling around him.

"The cutie in the suit?" Letty added. My eyes snapped to hers, but she just smiled. "Did you get his number?"

Levi shot up.

"Where are you going?" Hudson asked.

"To get some sleep." He didn't meet my questioning gaze.

"Sleep? It's barely eight."

"Yeah, well, beats sitting out here and listening to you three talk shit."

"Me?" Hudson frowned after Levi disappeared down the hall. "What the hell did I do?"

"How are you feeling?" Rafe approached me as I watched the production people rush around on set.

In fifteen minutes, everyone expected me to sit on that chair opposite Kinney Gretchen, one of The Rock Report's top interviewers, and bare my soul about the events of the past couple of weeks.

"Like I want to go and find a dealer and score some of his best shit."

Rafe bristled, inhaling a sharp breath.

"Relax," I said. "I'm joking."

For the most part I was anyway.

"You know, I never apologized—"

"Not this shit again?" My eyes slid to his. "What's done is done. We've got to look forward, right?"

It was what everyone kept saying. Look forward. Move on. Put the past behind you.

There was just one glaring fucking problem with that— my past wasn't behind me. It was embedded in my DNA, a dark stain on my soul that, no matter what I did, what heights of success the band reached, would never go away.

"Yeah, but I shouldn't have acted like that. I was just shocked that after everything, you'd go there with her."

I couldn't even remember the full details of *that* night. There had been an argument about Eva. I'd just found out that Rafe had been seeing her behind the band's back... behind *my* back.

"It could have been anyone." I jammed my fingers into

my hair and scraped them over my skull. The bite of pain was soothing.

"Yeah."

Silence settled between us. Letty and Eva moved into our line of sight, talking to Kinney. I watched my brother out the corner of my eye, as he watched his girl.

He was a lucky son of a bitch. He'd found it. Found *the one*. The girl put on earth to love him and him alone.

I didn't believe in soul mates. But watching the two of them called everything I'd ever believed into question. Rafe wasn't like me; he wasn't screwed up, constantly losing a battle to alcohol and drugs, but he still had his own demons. Demons that Eva was more than happy to stand at his side and slay. Together. As a team.

It was hard not to be bitter and jealous. It was hard not to drown in the void of self-loathing and hatred I so often found myself in.

Our mother had always called Rafe her angel. He was worthy of her love. Worthy of Eva's love. But not me.

Never me.

"All set?" Letty came over to us, and I nodded. "Just stick to the script and everything will be fine."

She'd spent all morning briefing me on questions and answers. It wasn't my first rodeo, but I had a history of screwing up.

"We'll do the interview first, and then they'll play the track—"

"Actually," Kinney appeared over Letty's shoulder. "We were thinking, you could do an acoustic performance of the track."

"Kinney, that's not what we agreed." Letty stepped aside, giving her a hard look.

"I know. But since Eva is here, and I know you guys don't travel anywhere without your guitars, we thought—actually, I thought, it could be kind of epic."

Everyone looked at me and I wanted to disappear. To disintegrate into nothing but particles in the air.

"Whatever," I grumbled.

"Okay, we're going to need time to set up." Letty jumped into action, pulling out her cell phone. "Eva, with me."

The two of them disappeared, leaving me with Rafe and Kinney.

"As sneaky as always," Rafe said. A few weeks ago, he and Eva had done an exclusive interview with The Rock Report, and she'd gone above and beyond the questions agreed with Letty.

It happened all the time, they would try to scratch under the surface, digging for every scrap of information they could. Always hoping to uncover their next big story.

"Hey, no hard feelings." Kinney smirked. "Besides, it looks like you and Eva are still going strong."

"We are, no thanks to you." He sulked off, leaving the two of us.

"He knows I was just doing my job, right?"

"He knows." But she'd tried to come between Rafe and his girl. That was unforgivable as far as he was concerned.

"Sorry about blindsiding you. We just thought the live performance would really give everyone something to talk about."

Phoebe entered the room, immediately catching my eye.

"Levi?" Kinney said.

"Uh, yeah?" I forced my eyes back to hers.

"I was just saying, I hope you didn't feel blindsided. It's nothing personal. We want to give the fans what they want, and this could be good for you and all the media frenzy around what happened."

My spine stiffened.

"You know, if you ever need to talk..." She plucked a card from her pocket, and all I could think was what interviewer carried a card in their back pocket?

One that was looking at you with 'come fuck me' eyes apparently.

Kinney stepped closer, taunting me with her card. "Take it." Challenge sparked in her eyes. "No strings."

What the fuck was happening right now?

I felt Phoebe's eyes burning into me, but I couldn't look at her. I'd already fucked up once.

"Okay, awkward," she let out a strained laugh, "I just thought—"

I plucked the card from her fingers and shoved it in my pocket.

"I hope you'll use it." She gave me a heated wink, before turning and walking straight into Phoebe.

"Oh, sorry, I didn't see you there." Kinney moved around her.

"I just came to tell you they're ready for you." The tightness in her voice made me internally wince.

"Thanks. Listen, Phoebe, that wasn't—"

"Not my business." She smiled around the words before turning her back on me and walking away.

———

THE HARSH GLARE of the light was blinding. I could barely see Kinney as she threw question after question at me. My palms were slick, the rapid beat of my heart in my chest nauseating.

I needed a stiff drink or a line of coke or even some Molly. Anything to make it all go away.

"So you're fessing up?" she asked. "It was you on that video?"

"I think we all know it was me, Kinney." I forced a smirk. "I'm just a guy at the end of the day. I make mistakes like everyone else."

"But there are a lot of people out there that would argue the point and say you should know better."

"And they're right, I should know better. But sometimes in the heat of the moment, when life throws a curveball at you, you don't have time to weigh up the pros and cons of a decision. You just make it. Even if it's the wrong one." My chest heaved with the weight of my words. "Haven't you ever messed up, Kinney?"

"Of course I have."

"Because you're human. And we're not designed to be flawless."

I silently prayed that would be the end of it, relieved as fuck when she changed tack.

"I'm sure everyone will appreciate your candidness. Now, what can you tell us about the new track? I think listeners have been dying for a collaboration with Eva since you first brought her out on stage in Charlotte. I've heard it, and I have to say, it gave me chills."

"I aim to please." I gave the camera a wolfish grin, flicking my tongue over my piercings in typical Levi Hunter fashion.

Kinney fanned herself. "Indeed." She chuckled. "But you're sidestepping my question." One of her thin brows arched.

"What can I tell you about *Drown?*" My eyes found Phoebe's across the room. She was wedged between Letty and Alistair, barely visible in the shadows. But I saw her.

I always fucking saw her.

"Listen to the lyrics and I'm sure you can figure it out." I shrugged nonchalantly.

"So it *is* about a woman? Because if it is, hearts will be breaking all over the country today."

"Don't worry, Kinney," her name rolled off my tongue seductively, "there's plenty of me to go around."

She clutched her heart, gasping dramatically. "Oof, there you have it, folks. Black Hearts Still Beats new track *Drown* maybe or may not be a love song."

The word slammed into me.

It was about Phoebe, yeah. But a love song?

No fucking way.

I didn't know how to love.

I wasn't *worthy* of love.

I just knew I felt something for her, something I hadn't ever felt before.

I'd thought I'd felt it with Eva at one point, but I could see that for what it was now. She was the first person in a long time to see past all the darkness shrouding me. Eva dug herself in and refused to leave, and her light—fuck, her light and purity and soul-deep goodness—was addictive.

"Thank you for talking the time to talk to us, Levi. It's always a pleasure." I nodded and she went on, "Friends, fans, and listeners, please welcome on stage Levi Hunter and Evangeline Walker with their new track, *Drown*."

The camera panned to Eva sitting on a lonely stool. I got up and made my way over, giving her a sly wink. Her lips curved as I took my place in front of the mic stand. The guys stood in the small audience, watching. I saw the pride in my brother's eyes, the raw unfiltered love he felt for Eva as he watched her intently. She was his Starshine, his redemption. And although I was so jealous some days that I wanted to gouge out my own eyes, I was also so fucking happy for them.

Silence ushered over the room as Eva gave me a questioning nod. I returned it and she strummed the open notes of the song. The second the music hit me, all the tension melted away. I clutched the mic stand like it was my lifeline, my oxygen, bleeding my words into the mic.

I felt Phoebe watching me and I couldn't resist meeting her awed expression. Our eyes locked, intense and unwavering as I revealed my truths, caressing every lyric like it was the soft curves of her skin.

She said we were a mistake. That we needed to keep things strictly professional, but I didn't like the rules. I liked to live free. Wild and recklessly. Because when the chaos stopped and everything was still, that's when the monsters found me.

Eva's soft voice took over as she sang the new

lyrics. Phoebe looked away and I was almost sure I saw a tear roll down her cheek. I didn't want to make her sad, I wanted her to realize what she meant to me. What our limited time together meant.

The bridge came and I belted out the words, my gravelly tones softened by Eva's pitch. It was a fucking perfect performance. The audience's applause filled the room as people began moving, eager to jump into their next tasks. But one person remained.

Phoebe.

She was watching me again, her thumb pressed to her plump bottom lip. Fuck. I wanted to run my tongue over it and drag it between my teeth. I wanted to make it hurt and then soothe the sting with my tongue.

"You should try and talk to her." Eva moved behind me.

"Nah, that ship has sailed, Angel."

"I might not know much about relationships, Levi, but I know longing when I see it."

Was Eva right?

Could Phoebe be longing for me even though she'd pushed me away?

Women were fucking confusing creatures. Usually, I picked a girl, fucked her into oblivion, and moved on with my life.

But not her.

Not the girl with braids in her hair and ink on her skin.

She'd latched onto my soul and buried herself deep in my chest.

Eva gave a little sigh of resignation before patting me on

the shoulder. I knew she was only trying to help, but this wasn't something she could just fix.

It wasn't something anyone could fix.

Some things just were. Like the sky being blue or the grass being green. I'd gotten off my face and fucked Riley. I'd done that.

Me.

I couldn't take it back or erase it or slap a Band-Aid over it.

So no matter how much I wanted Phoebe to give me another chance, for the first time in my life, I could see the other side of the coin. And I didn't blame her.

I was a fuck-up.

An addict.

A selfish asshole.

I probably always would be.

"What's up, N'awlins. You're looking sexy tonight."

The crowd roared, the noise reverberating deep inside me as I watched from the wings. Levi strutted across the stage as if he was made for it, and the fans lapped it up.

The exclusive with The Rock Report has been a huge success. In the last twenty-four hours, *Drown* had already been streamed almost five million times, with a unanimously positive reception. Levi's fans were all over social media, supporting their tortured idol, stamping out every piece of negative press. It was the perfect storm to cover up his mistake. People were no longer talking about the sex tape; they were taking about the song.

They were talking about *my* song.

Deep down, I think I'd known the first time he'd sung *Drown*, at Damon's birthday party, that it was about me. But I hadn't wanted to believe it then. I still hadn't wanted to believe it when I heard him sing it in the studio a few days ago. But hearing him yesterday, after the interview, I'd had no choice but to face the truth.

Levi had been performing for the show, for the hundreds of thousands of fans that tuned into Kinney's interviews. But he'd been *singing to me*.

I'd felt every lyric right down to my soul. There had been a moment the words had hit me so deeply, so profoundly, that a tear had rolled down my cheek.

The truth of it was, Levi Hunter had the power to wreck

me with a single word. Imagine what he could do if I gave him my heart?

No, I had to be strong. I had to resist the connection I felt to him. I'd tried to fix one addict, I couldn't do it again. Because when you gave so much of yourself to a person, eventually there was nothing left.

I was in a good place. I had my job at Razorsharp Records. I had new friends. Direction. I had focus.

"He seems better," Letty said from beside me, just as the band broke into their opening song.

"Yeah," I murmured, my hand drifting to my neck. Levi looked the part. He carried himself with poise and power, owning all twenty-thousand hearts here tonight. But I knew it was the mask he made himself wear. That's how it was for addicts. They showed the world one thing while hiding their truths beneath fake smirks and smiles that didn't quite reach their eyes.

"The guys want to celebrate tonight on their bus. Nothing crazy, just a few drinks."

"I don't think that's a good idea."

"You should be there. You're a part of this team, Phoebe. Besides, he'll want you there."

I inhaled a deep breath, unable to tear my eyes off Levi as he screeched into the mic. Most of their lyrics were so dark and haunting, watching him was like witnessing an exorcism. A purging of sins. My body hummed with awareness, of something otherworldly unfolding before me.

"I'll think about it," I said quietly, more to myself than Letty.

If I rode on their bus, it would mean sleeping on it. They

had bunks, but I had struggled to sleep down the hall from Levi, let alone right next to him.

"Everything will work out, Phoebe." Letty squeezed my arm. "You'll see."

I wanted to believe her.

But I knew history had a way of repeating itself.

———

"HOLY FUCKING SHIT, THAT WAS EPIC." Hudson bounded past me. "I feel like I could fly."

"Let's *not* try that," Damon grumbled, stalking off down the hall.

"We're showering on the bus, right?"

"Yeah, Duke wants to get on the road ASAP." Letty appeared. "We have a long road ahead."

The next show was tomorrow in Phoenix. That was almost a nineteen-hour ride. Sure, the band would be asleep for most of it. But for the road crew and security, it meant a long night ahead.

"I hope you stocked the liquor cabinet, Letty, baby, because I feel like getting fucked-up." Hudson grinned at her.

"Is he high?" she asked Damon and Levi. He'd creeped up on us. But now he was close, I became hyperaware of him, my skin tingling.

"High on life." He waggled his brows. "Didn't you hear them? They almost blew the roof off the place. They love us, baby. They fucking love us," he yelled, tearing off his t-shirt and lassoing it in the air.

"Fucking moron," Levi muttered beside me and our eyes caught.

"You were great," I said, quietly.

"Thanks." His expression was indifferent. My stomach sank, but then he added, "The guys want to celebrate later, you should come."

"Okay."

God. I wasn't supposed to say okay. But the pull was too strong. I could go and hangout with them without falling into the Levi Hunter trap, couldn't I?

"See you there, Intern." A faint smile traced his lips as he slipped past me, his hand brushing mine.

Heat flashed through me. But then I remembered him at the club, the blonde leaving his room the next morning, and the butterflies in my stomach turned hard, crumbling to dust.

"Phoebe, are you okay?" Eva touched my arm. I was still standing there, while everyone else disappeared down the hall. Rafe lingered but she gave him a look and he took off after his bandmates.

"The show was great," I said around a weak smile.

"Thank you. Do you want to talk about it?"

"About what?" I played dumb, but she gave me a knowing look.

"You're not foolin' anyone."

"I'm not trying to. I just..." A soft sigh slipped from my lips. "How do you do it?"

"Do what?"

"The fangirls and groupies and craziness?"

She shrugged. "It wasn't exactly what I had planned for

my life. But when I met Rafe it was like somethin' shifted, ya know?"

I did. It had happened to me twice now.

"Love makes you crazy." The corner of Eva's mouth kicked up. "It makes you take risks and push yourself out of your comfort zone. At least, it has for me."

"Yeah," I agreed because she was right.

Love did make you crazy.

And if you weren't careful, it made you lose sight of who you were.

"Come tonight. It's just us and the guys. Besides, we'll be on the tour bus." She smiled. "What's the worst that can happen?"

———

COMING HERE WAS A BAD IDEA.

I was wedged between Hudson and Letty with a glass full of tequila in front of me.

"Your turn, Pheebs." Hudson handed me the dice.

"Okay," I breathed, tipping it out of my hand onto the table. "Six. So, what now? I roll again?"

"Or hold until your next turn. I can't believe you've never played Pig before." Hudson snorted.

"Hmm. I'll go again." Scooping up the die, I rolled it a second time. "Six again."

"Beginners luck." Rafe smirked.

"You're just jealous you got a one, bro." Hudson chuckled.

He'd had five good rolls in a row before rolling a one and having to down his drink.

"What's it gonna be, Intern?" Levi cocked a brow at me, challenge glittering in his dark gaze. He'd been quiet since we all crammed in around the table on their tour bus. He wasn't playing, but he seemed happy enough watching the rest of us.

"I'm feeling lucky. I'll go again." Anticipation trickled up my spine. I was unsure about coming, knowing that I'd be stuck on the bus until Duke made a pitstop. But I couldn't deny it felt nice to be accepted among them.

"Now we're talking. Roll it, baby." The point of the drinking seemed lost on Hudson, who was getting through his Jack and Cokes quicker than he could make them.

"You might want to slow down." I eyed his half-full glass.

"Relax, *Mom*. It's a celebration. Besides, there wasn't time to fuck a groupie, so I need something to take off the edge. Unless you're offering to go above and beyond your assistant duties." His eyes narrowed, blazing with hunger.

"Hudson," Rafe warned.

"Joke." A wolfish grin tugged at his mouth. "I'm joking." His eyes slid to Levi's, the two of them locked in some kind of silent conversation.

Desperate to cut through the heavy tension, I rolled again. "Four. That's sixteen. I'm gonna go again."

"You're tempting fate now, girl," Letty said.

"I think I've got another roll in me." Feeling confident, I rolled, letting out a frustrated groan when it landed a one.

"Now you gotta drink." Hudson pushed my glass toward

me. "Three turns so you gotta take three drinks. Or you could just drink the entire thing."

Rolling my eyes, I brought the glass to my lips, overpowered by the bitter smell.

"Down in one, baby."

I poked my tongue out at Hudson before downing the entire glass.

"Holy shit, a girl after my own heart."

The liquor burned, making my eyes water, but I sucked it up. I wanted to prove to them—and myself—I had what it took to be here.

To be around Levi without skulking in the shadows. To be one of them.

"Something tells me Halstead has been holding out on us." Hudson winked at me.

If only he knew.

"Letty, you're up."

Everyone took their turn. Letty got to thirty-five before she stopped and smugly handed the dice to Eva. She rolled a one and only had to sip her drink. By the time we'd all done another three turns, I was beginning to feel more than a little buzzed.

"A-ha." I slammed my hand down on the table, snorting at Hudson's one. He'd gotten greedy rolling seven times before finally hitting a one.

"You gotta down it, rock star. Every last drop."

"I don't think I like drunk Phoebe."

"I'm not drunk, I'm just... chill."

"Keep telling yourself that." He chugged down his drink, wiping his mouth with the back of his hand.

"This has been fun and all, but I think we're going to call it a night," Rafe said.

"Noooo! The night is young. We still have all those bottles of liquor to get through." Hudson tipped his head toward the counter.

"Are you okay, man? You're acting a little weird."

"Who, me? Couldn't be better." He helped himself to a refill. "The show was great. The band was great. You and Eva are great. Pheebs is great. Everything is fan-fucking-great."

"Err, dude, that's not a word."

"Well, it is now."

I studied Hudson's eyes. He talked a good talk, but he seemed kind of... sad.

"You know you can fix this." Eva gave him a long hard look.

"Fix what? Didn't you just hear me, everything is fan-fucking-great." He downed half of his new drink.

"Let me guess, Molly finally decided to quit your ass and move on with her life?"

The air shifted at Levi's insinuation.

Molly was Eva's best friend from back home, and from what I'd gathered, she and Hudson had had a thing. Only, he also had a thing with a new girl in every city we visited.

"Fuck you, man." Hudson jabbed his finger at Levi. "Fuck you."

"Molly called me earlier," Eva said around a sad smile. "She has a date."

Hudson mumbled something to himself.

"What's the big deal?" I shrugged, liquid courage flowing

through my veins. "It's not like the two of you are together, right?"

"We're not anything." His eyes narrowed. "Like I said everything is fan-fuck—"

"Yeah, yeah, we got the memo." Damon stood up. "Come on, Hud, I think you've had enough."

"I don't need a babysitter." He flipped his bandmate off. "I'm celebrating."

"We're going to bed," Rafe said, leading Eva away. She gave me and Letty a small wave, mouthing, "Goodnight."

"And then there were five." Hudson rolled his eyes.

"Four," Damon said. "I'm gonna turn in."

"Whatever, D. New Girl, get another drink. It's you, me, and Letty, if she thinks she can handle the heat." He slid a bottle of Jack toward me.

"I'm sitting right here, asshole," Levi growled.

"Yeah, but you're no fun tonight."

"Sorry for trying to keep my shit together for once."

"New Girl, let's go."

"I'm not sure I should mix my drinks." I already felt a little light-headed, my blood warm from the buzz.

Peeking over at Levi, I found him watching me intently, his dark eyes drilling holes into my face. He looked pissed, disapproval etched into the lines of his face.

Hudson snatched the pack of playing cards off the table. "Three card draw. Lowest card drinks."

"I think the party's over, Hud," Letty said with resignation.

"It's not over until the last person is standing."

"Well, I'm out. It's almost two."

Two?

We'd been drinking for longer than I thought. But time seemed to stand still on the tour bus.

"You coming?" she asked me, "or are you—"

"Staying," Hudson was slurring now, "she's staying."

"Okay, Hud." Letty grabbed the bottle from his hand. "I'm cutting you off."

He lunged for her, but she took off down the bus with him stumbling behind.

I stared at my glass, knowing I would regret it if I drank anymore. But the heat from Levi's stare was too much to bear.

"Phoebe," he said quietly. "Look at me."

My eyes lifted of their own volition.

"You need some water?"

Did I?

Water would sober me; it would pull me from the lingering buzz I felt. But part of me liked it here, it made everything *less* somehow.

Zephyr. Levi. My father... liquor made everything float away into the distance until they couldn't reach me.

"I think I'm good," I said, downing the remainder of my drink. His eyes shuttered, and I'm sure I heard him cuss under his breath.

But Levi didn't care about me.

Not in the way I wanted him to.

LEVI

PHOEBE WAS DRUNK. I'd watched for hours as she played drinking games with the guys. It had been sweet torture watching as she sipped her glass, caressed it with her lips. I could write songs for days about the way Phoebe Halstead drank liquor.

She stared at me, the air crackling with anticipation. It was the first time we'd really been alone since Nashville. I'd tried to talk to her, but she was pushing me out.

Because I was a fuck up.

Because when things didn't go my way, I liked to play games and hurt those closest to me.

Hurt myself.

It wasn't something I did consciously, I was usually too high or wasted or lost to care.

But tonight, I'd stayed sober. All for her. And she had no fucking clue.

Her head rolled on her shoulders slightly as she stared at me.

"You're drunk," I deadpanned.

"Am not." Her nose scrunched up. She looked so fucking adorable, my chest tightened.

Fuck, this woman.

She was like no one I'd ever met.

"You slept with her." I frowned and she added, "the blonde from the club. I didn't think you'd do that. I mean, I knew you would, you're Levi freakin' Hunter, but part of me hoped you wouldn't." Phoebe let out a resigned sigh and it cracked my chest wide open.

Fuck. I'd fucked up that night. But seeing her with that Suit, it had done all kinds of shit to me. I'd wanted to hurt her, to make her feel even an ounce of the jealousy I felt coursing through my veins like molten lava. It was fucking childish, but that was me.

Levi Hunter: Manchild and asshole, incapable of talking about his feelings.

"I didn't sleep with her."

She snorted at that, and fuck, it stung that she'd written me off so easily.

"It's the truth. We got back to my room, drank some more, and I passed out." It wasn't one of my finest moments, but I really didn't give a shit where the blonde was concerned. She was a means to an end, nothing more.

Something sparked in her eyes. I wanted to believe it was hope but all I saw was doubt.

"But you took her back to fuck her, didn't you?"

"I..." What the fuck was I supposed to say to that? I'd been blind with jealousy and the need to hurt her. And Blondie had been ripe for the taking.

"God, I hate you, Levi Hunter. I hate you so much." Tears pricked the corner of her eye, each one like a jagged knife to my stomach.

I didn't want her to hate me. But I didn't know how to let her love me either.

"If it makes you feel any better, I would have hated myself for sleeping with her."

"Why?" The tears flowed freely down her cheeks. "Why would you say that to me?"

"You know why, Phoebe."

"It doesn't matter." She took a shuddering breath, wiping her eyes.

"Stop saying it doesn't matter." My teeth ground together. "It fucking matters, and you know it."

"Levi, I can't..."

"You're scared. I get it. I'm a fuck-up. I'll probably always be a fuck-up. But you make it quiet. You make it all quiet." I scrubbed my face, slipping my hand over my head to rub the back of my neck.

"I'm tired," Phoebe whispered, her eyes heavy with the weight of the liquor and my confession.

"Come on." I stood, offering her my hand. She stared at it like it was contagious. Like if she touched me, she'd be infected with the same soul-eating darkness that lived inside me.

My insides quivered with anticipation. If she rejected me, I didn't know what the fuck I would do. I was already on edge, walking a fine line between locking myself in the bedroom at the back of the bus or draining the contents of all the bottles of liquor.

"I'm not going to sleep with you." She huffed indignantly, defiance burning in her eyes.

"I can keep my hands to myself, promise."

Phoebe gazed up, studying me. "Fine. But this doesn't mean anything. I'm just really drunk and I'm not sure I can deal with one of the bunks tonight."

"Yeah, yeah, Intern." I smirked. "Keep telling yourself that."

———

THE SMALL ROOM was steeped in darkness as we stepped inside. I went to flip the switch, but Phoebe said, "Leave it, please."

I stood back, watching her as she stared at the bed.

"How many girls have you brought in here?"

"Don't ask questions you won't like the answer to."

"Right, of course." She shrunk into herself. "Maybe this is a bad idea."

It was absolutely a bad idea, but I wasn't exactly known for my excellent decision-making skills.

Moving behind her, I ran my fingers up her spine, sliding my hand over her collarbone. "I told you I wouldn't touch you, I meant it. It's late, we should sleep."

"Sleep... yes. We should do that." She gulped.

Fuck. I couldn't resist dipping my head and pressing a kiss to her shoulder. My lips lingered, as I fought the urge to claim her. To sink my teeth into her soft skin and mark her.

"Levi?" Her voice quivered. "I'm scared."

I sucked in a harsh breath. I was a mess. A fuck up. An asshole. I'd made women cry, kids cry, I'd even made grown ass men cry. I'd fought my friends, my brother, the press... myself. I'd done some heinous things, abused my body, and more than once in my life, I'd wanted to die. But hearing Phoebe whisper she was scared of me, it twisted something inside me.

This woman—this beautiful, strong woman—had the power to completely disarm me.

Me.

A guy who had only ever given one woman the power to hurt him.

"I don't want to hurt you." My lips brushed Phoebe's ear, my hand splaying around her throat, gently coaxing her face to mine.

I hadn't planned to kiss her. I hadn't planned on doing anything, but I always was a weak man unable to avoid temptation. She was standing there, and I couldn't resist.

"Levi," she whispered as our lips met in the faintest of kisses.

"Ssh, Phoebe. Just let yourself feel." My tongue slipped past her lips and curled around hers, massaging and licking. She tasted like all my favorite things wrapped up in one irresistible package. Thoughts exploded in my head of me dripping liquor on her body and licking it off, getting lit on both her *and* the alcohol. I could vividly imagine cutting lines on the flat of her stomach and snorting them off or fucking her long into the night high on Molly.

I wouldn't because she deserved more.

Phoebe deserved better.

But it didn't stop dark thoughts from infiltrating my mind.

"Why does this feel so right?" She broke the kiss, blinking up at me with her big honey eyes.

"Because maybe it is. Maybe we just both have to take a chance."

"I can't do it again. I can't watch someone I..." She

stopped herself, letting out a heavy sigh. Part of me was relieved. I didn't want to ever hear those words. "I'll never be the most important thing in your life. I deserve that, Levi. I deserve to come first."

Her honesty shook me to the core. Phoebe had scars. The deep kind. The kind I knew I couldn't fix. The kind I knew I would only rip open if I pursued this thing with her.

But I couldn't walk away.

I couldn't do it.

So long as she was on tour with us, we would continue to go around in circles until one of us cracked. Or I fucked things up for good.

Touching my head to hers, I breathed her in. "I'm not a good guy, Bee, but I'd try to be good for you."

A shiver ran through her as she swayed gently. She was drunk. Maybe more than I'd first thought.

"Come on," I said, guiding her toward the bed. "You should get some sleep."

Phoebe began stripping out of her clothes with haste, as if they were suffocating her. "Stupid shirt," she groaned as she tried to yank it over her head.

I stood back, smothering the laughter rumbling in my chest. "Need some help?"

Her eyes snapped to mine, glittering in the dark. "I can manage."

After a couple more failed attempts, I crouched down and nudged her hands away. "Here, let me." My fingers brushed her bare skin, and she whimpered again.

My dick strained against my jeans, desperate to feel her

again. But the next time I was inside her, I wanted Phoebe to know exactly who she was fucking.

I pulled back the cover. "In you go."

"I can't believe this happening," she mumbled. "How embarrassing." Phoebe buried her face in the pillow.

I made quick work of stripping down to my boxers and climbed in bed beside her. She tried to roll away, putting as much space between us as possible.

But fuck that.

I hooked my arm around Phoebe's waist and pulled her back against my chest.

"Levi, we can't snuggle..."

"Why the fuck not?" I tangled my legs with hers, fighting the urge to press my hard length right up against her ass.

"Because I'm your assistant and you're..." She let out a little huff of frustration.

"It's okay, honeybee," the nickname rolled off my tongue as easy as breathing, "you can say it. I'm the best sex you've ever had." I breathed against the shell of her ear.

Her sweet laughter filled the small room. "You're definitely the biggest ego I've ever had."

That sobered me.

I didn't want her to see me as the guy everyone else saw.

Rock god.

Sex symbol.

Wild reckless addict.

I only wanted her to see *me*.

"Levi?" My name pierced the silence. "Are you okay?"

"Yeah, I'm okay."

What other choice did I have?

I tucked her closer. "Get some sleep."

Silence enveloped us again and I lay there, waiting for her to fall asleep. If I'd have been someone else, I would have told Phoebe how this was a first for me. I would have looked into her eyes and showed her how grateful, how fucking relieved I was that she didn't push me away again.

I would have told her that while I wasn't capable of love, this came pretty damn close.

But I wasn't that guy.

Maybe I never would be.

WHEN I WOKE UP, Phoebe was gone. But I wasn't surprised. She'd been drunk. She'd let her guard down and let me slip through the cracks.

I'd laid there for hours, listening to her sleep. The gentle rise and fall of her chest, the soft inhale and exhale of every breath. It was like a quiet melody, finally lulling me into a deep sleep.

Stretching my arms, I reached over to check the time. It was a little after eight. Hunger pangs ripped through me, but I knew my stomach wasn't hungry for food. It was hungry for something else entirely. A deep-seated thirst I wouldn't allow myself to quench. Not today. Not tomorrow. Or the day after that.

Sitting on the edge of the bed, I focused on my breathing. *In and out. In and out.* I needed a cool shower, one of Damon's weird ass smoothies, and some breakfast. That would keep the urges at bay. At least until the show tonight.

But the second I stepped out of the room, and spotted Phoebe sitting at the table, nursing a mug of coffee, another kind of hunger carved through me.

Her eyes lifted as if she felt me watching her. She didn't speak, she didn't need to. Everything she had to say was right there in her eyes.

Gratitude. Understanding... Regret.

I didn't like that last one. Even after last night, she was still going to fight me on this. She was going to deny us.

Deny me.

My fist clenched and before I realized, it flew into the wooden paneling.

"What the fuck?" Damon glowered at me.

"My bad," I said thinly, sliding my eyes to Phoebe.

Realization washed over her, and the blood drained from her already pale face.

"You want some?" Damon asked, dragging my attention away from her. But out the corner of my eye, I was almost certain I saw her breathe a sigh of relief.

Anger burned through me like acid.

"Levi?" he asked again, and I blinked, trying to rein in my emotions.

"Uh, no. I need to take a piss and then I'm going to take a shower." A cold one at that.

"Okay." He frowned, concern in his eyes. "Everything okay?"

"Why wouldn't it be?" I glared at Phoebe again, but she didn't meet my eyes.

Damon glanced over at her and back at me. "Ah, I see."

"Hmm." It came out tight.

"You good?" He lowered his voice, and I knew what he was asking me.

"I will be," I said.

For now.

PHOEBE

THERE WAS something different about this show. I couldn't quite put my finger on it, but the fangirls—the Die Hearts as everyone called them—were here in droves.

The second we'd stepped off the tour buses, their high-pitched shrieks and screams of 'I love Levi' and 'fuck me hard, Hudson' had filled the air like a siren's call on the sea. It was eerie, and strangely uncomfortable to hear a bunch of teenage girls and young women whine like that. Ear splitting, blood curdling screams of sheer adoration.

Security was increased due to the swarms of fans gathering outside the Talking Stick Resort Arena.

"This is crazy," I said to Letty as we peeled out of a window, watching the lines grow below. The fans wouldn't be let in for another hour, but I was beginning to wonder where everyone was going to go.

"The local PD are standby," she added.

"What's special about Phoenix?"

"Happens sometimes." She shrugged. "Everything has blown up since the track started streaming. Website hits are up. Ratings. Downloads. It's all pointing in the right direction."

"Your plan worked."

"It did." She gave me a smug smile. "They don't pay me to look pretty."

"I can see that." I was learning so much from Letty. She handled herself with confidence and composure in what was a typically male-dominated world. It was really something to behold.

"Come on, we should go see how soundcheck is going."

I followed Letty out of the small meeting room at the top of the arena and down to the stage. They were mid-song, Levi teasing the empty arena with his gravelly and intense vocals.

"He's something, huh?"

"Yeah," I agreed.

"Do you want to talk about what happened last night?"

"Nothing happened." My cheeks flushed.

"Funny," she smiled, "because when I got up in the night for a pee, only three out of the four bunks were occupied."

My cheeks turned a shade darker as she looked over at me. "I stayed with Levi, but nothing happened."

Except the fact he'd held me all night, wrapped around me like a spider monkey.

She gave me a pointed look, as if she saw straight through me. "He's different. You should know that. I know he messed up, and he'll mess up again before the tour is over. But last night he sat and watched the rest of us get toasted. That's pretty huge for someone like Levi, and I'm guessing he didn't do it for me or Hudson."

"Maybe."

"He's trying. Give him some credit."

"You know my ex, Zephyr, was an addict." She nodded. "Well, he used to *try* a lot. He'd manage to go weeks without drinking or getting high. Then something would happen, and it'd push him over the edge, and I'd lose him. And every time it happened another little piece of me died. I can't be that girl again, Letty."

"I get it, I do." She offered me weak smile, one full of apology and pity. "But sometimes people need the right reason to change. Maybe you weren't enough for Zephyr, but you might be enough for Levi."

She took off toward the stage, joining Alistair as he watched the band.

Levi found me across the arena, but the moment our eyes collided, he looked away.

I deserved his wrath. He'd been different with me last night. Soft and tender. It had caught me off guard, my confusion not helped by the liquor swimming in my veins.

He'd touched me like I was precious. Fragile. He'd held me like I was everything. His lifeline. His reason.

But when I'd woken up cocooned against his hot body, sheer panic had overridden the contentment I felt.

Levi wanted something from me, that much was obvious.

But I wasn't sure I had anything left to give.

———

THE ENERGY of the crowd pulsed through me. It was frenetic, the air charged and the atmosphere electric. The standing area seemed to surge forward like an undulating wave as Levi sang song after song.

"It's crazy out there," I yelled over to Letty and she nodded, her eyes alight with concern.

"What?" I asked.

"Hopefully, it's nothing." She didn't look convinced though. "I want extra security at the VIP meet and greet."

"You think something could happen?"

"Experience tells me when the crowd is this wild, it's better to be prepared." She ran her eyes over the clipboard again.

After the show, the band was hosting a meet and greet with over fifty contest winners, all girls, all aged between fifteen and twenty-five.

Darkness fell over the stage and the crowd ushered into silence. A ripple of energy shot through the air as the opening beats of *Drown* played out.

My heart lurched into my mouth.

"He didn't tell you?" Letty squeezed my arm.

"No one did."

"Phoenix, give it up for Miss Evangeline Walker," Levi's gravelly voice came over the speakers making every hair along the back of my neck stand to attention.

A single spotlight found Eva across from us, the other side of the stage. She walked out, guitar in hand, waving at the crowd. They went wild, screaming her name, professing their undying love for Levi. They had the Hunter-Walker magic all right, and everyone loved them for it.

The stage lights went up just as Damon kicked in the beat and Levi sang the first lyrics. I was paralyzed by his voice, hypnotized by the intensity in his words. The longing. Every time I heard the lyrics, I found new layers to their meanings.

Eye so deep I fall and fall
Can't escape, and I can't feel
These feelings crash over me
Until I'm numb inside and cut free

But I'm broken now, I'm dead inside
She can't save me no matter how hard she tries
But I'm broken now, I'm dead inside
She can't save me no matter how hard she tries

HE MIGHT HAVE BEEN BROKEN, but one thing was clear...
I was pretty sure I was falling for Levi Hunter.

———

THREE SONGS LATER, the band came off stage, high on adrenaline and what I considered to be one of their best performances to date.

"Water," Hudson said. "I need water."

He'd been back to his usual self today, and no one had uttered a word about Molly and her date.

Rafe pulled Eva into his arms, the two of them falling against the curtain in a tangle of limbs and lips.

"That was... wow," I said as Levi approached.

"Thanks." He barely looked at me, moving past us to take off down the hall.

Dejection burned through me, but I'd earned it. You

couldn't reject someone like Levi and expect him to fight for you.

"Okay, guys, thirty minutes until the first VIPs arrive."

"Is there food?"

"Isn't there always?" Letty gave a Hudson an amused look.

"Lead the way."

"We'll be there soon," Rafe's muffled words drifted over to us. I glanced back, wishing I hadn't, when I saw their intimate embrace.

I ended up walking back to the dressing rooms with Damon.

"How are you holding up?" he asked.

"Me? I'm okay."

He gave me a warm nod. "You'd be good for him, you know. But I sense you have some baggage of your own."

"You could say that."

"Levi is complicated, Phoebe. The most complicated guy I've ever met... but I think, deep down, all he wants is to feel worth something more than all this."

I didn't get chance to ask what he meant because Damon took off down the hall, disappearing into the band's dressing room. The meet and greet would be in a separate room, bigger, with a few shaker tables, a complimentary buffet table, and a temporary bar.

I tried not to dwell on Damon's words as I went to help Letty make sure everything was set. I would oversee giving out the VIPs their exclusive goody bag and directing them for photos.

But by the time the band entered the room—well,

everyone except Levi because of course he was late—the words were still stuck in my mind.

Everyone seemed to be on Team Levi. It was almost as if they wanted me to give him a chance. But what I couldn't figure out was if it was because they thought he deserved a shot at happiness, at love...

Or if it was because they'd exhausted all avenues and I was their last hope to fix him.

———

THE VIP FANS were a mixed bunch. Half of them seemed happy to bask in the thrill of being within looking distance of their favorite band, while the other half were overexcited and more than a little drunk.

"Travis," I said to Eva's bodyguard. "Keep an eye on the group with the black and red t-shirts."

"Noted," he said, whispering something into his hidden wrist mic.

A couple of other bodyguards edged closer to the rowdy groups of girls. Two in particular had made a scene when they arrived, shouting inappropriate things to Hudson. He'd laughed it off, but some of the younger fans, accompanied with their parents, had complained.

"Okay," Letty shouted, waving her hand in the air. "If I can have everyone's attention. Levi is going to be along any second and I wanted to quickly explain how this is going to work. We'll get group A lined up first for photos and autographs and then dish out goody bags. Group B will receive their goody bags first and then do photos, sound good?"

A chorus of cheers echoed off the walls.

When Letty had spotted the rowdy girls, she'd switched things around so we could get the younger fans in and out quicker.

But the second the door open and Levi stepped into the room, all hell broke loose.

"Ohmigod, there he is," someone yelled as some of the girls broke forward.

Security flanked Levi, warding them off, but he stepped forward, laughing. "Relax," he smirked, "there's enough of me to go around."

Letty ushered for me to intercept the girls on my side. I jumped in front of them, hands outstretched. "If everyone could just wait in their area, we'll get—"

"Levi, I love you," a shrill voice pierced the air. "I love you so much."

"I can't believe it's him," another voice said, as the horde of overeager fans began to swarm. Security tried to hold them back, but they were a force to be reckoned with, pushing up against our human wall.

"Shit," Letty grumbled. "Someone call for back up. If everyone could just calm down."

"Listen to the lady," Levi chuckled. "She might be small, but she is mighty."

There was something off about his tone. Anyone else might not have noticed it, but I wasn't anyone.

My head snapped around, studying his face. Sure enough, I saw the slight glaze to his eyes.

Levi was high.

Un-fucking-believable.

"Letty," I caught her attention and flicked my head to where Levi was standing.

"Okay, ladies, if you could all form an orderly line we can get started—"

A handful of the older girls broke free, charging at me and Travis. "You need to stop," I yelled. "Stop, no—"

Someone shouldered me out of the way, an elbow clipping my cheek. Pain exploded along my face just as I lost my footing and began to fall.

"Phoebe," someone yelled my name, but the world tilted, agony piercing my hip as I collided with the edge of the merchandise table. My body folded into itself as I landed with a resounding *thud*, my head cracking against the hard floor.

"Shit, someone call medical," another voice yelled, but everything was spinning, my skull pounding, making everything foggy.

"Phoebe, can you hear me?" A panicked voice hovered on the edge of my consciousness as everything began to go black.

"Do something," he yelled, so full of pain and anguish. "Somebody, do something."

LEVI

"Why isn't she waking up?" I asked the nurse for the tenth time. The constant itch under my skin was right there, whispering to me. Calling to me like a siren on the wind. It was only made worse by the fact I was in the medical center, surrounded by readily available drugs and medicines that would carry me away from this nightmare.

"Give it time. It was quite the bump your friend had."

Friend.

I almost snorted at that. Phoebe wasn't my friend. She was the North Star in my dark, dark skies.

"Anything?" Letty entered the room.

After all hell broke loose at the meet and greet, she'd had to stay behind to deal with the disgruntled fans. The guys had tried to get me to stay at the arena, but I'd hopped into the ambulance with Phoebe before they could stop me. Johnson and Stalter had followed behind, dealing with the staff at the center.

I didn't care about any of that. I only cared about the girl lying in the bed. She looked like an angel lying there. A sleeping angel dreaming peacefully with the devil standing over her shoulder.

My fingers began drumming against my knee, lyrics forming in my head.

Oh, pretty angel gives me your eyes
Come back to me, I need you right here

Oh, pretty angel show me your smile
Come to back me because I can't be without you

You're the light to my dark, the star in dark skies
You're the voice that I hear, when things don't go right

The angel on my shoulder, I can't let you go...

"Levi?"

"Huh, what?" My eyes snapped to Letty's, and she frowned.

"Are you okay? You look—"

"Fine. I'm fine." I scrubbed my jaw. "She still hasn't woken up."

"But they said that's normal right?"

"Yeah..." I chewed my thumb. The skin was beginning to crack around my nail.

"Maybe you should go—"

"I'm staying."

Letty's expression softened. "She's going to be okay, Levi. It was just a bump to the head. She's got a concussion and a nasty bruise where she collided with the table, but Phoebe is going to be fine."

"I know." I did. But I really needed her to wake up, so I could see for myself.

"Do I need to be worried?" There was no judgment in Letty's expression. I guess that was the thing about working with unstable rock stars, you got used to all their personal shit.

"Honestly, I don't know."

"What can I do?"

"Keep me away from the nurse's trolley, the one full of pain pills." I laughed but it came out strangled. "Too soon?"

Letty rolled her eyes.

"I'm joking. At least, I think I am."

"You going to be good if I check in with Alistair and get coffee?"

I nodded.

"You want anything?"

"I'm good." I was too restless to eat or drink, unless it was a bottle of Jack, and something told me the staff here wouldn't take too kindly to me drowning myself in whisky.

My leg jostled up and down, my fingers digging into the leather covering the arm of the chair. Phoebe would wake up soon and everything would go back to normal. Except, that meant she would be still pretending not to care. At least now, *I* could pretend. I could imagine that when she woke up and realized l was here, she would finally give in to the connection we shared.

I knew she was scared. I knew her ex had done a real number on her. Why else would she be so against us getting close?

Because you're not worth it. You'll never be worth it.

I screwed my eyes shut, trying to ignore the little voice. But it only got louder. Hunger swam in my veins. A raging ravenous inferno, it burned so bright I could practically taste the high.

I'd smoked a blunt earlier, before the show. Weed wasn't usually my go-to poison of choice, but I'd needed to take the edge off. I'd needed something to douse the feelings.

"L- Levi?"

My eyes flew open, her voice instantly grounding me. The hunger melted away leaving nothing more than a faint pulse of need.

"Phoebe, thank fuck." I leaned forward, brushing the hair from her eyes.

"What happened?" She lifted a hand to her head, groaning. "Levi?" The fear in her voice made me flinch.

"I should get the nurse." I stood up, but her voice gave me pause.

"Don't go. Not yet."

Glancing back, I caught her eyes and she smiled. Phoebe was awake... and she was smiling.

"Yeah, okay." I dropped down in the chair.

"I'm in the hospital?"

"A local medical center. You hit your head pretty hard, knocked yourself clean out." I winced at the words, remembering the moment I'd watched as she went down.

Powerless.

That's how I'd felt. Completely and utterly powerless.

"How embarrassing." Phoebe let out a little sigh.

Heavy silence filled the room. She watched me intently through cloudy eyes. I stared back, a hundred things running through my mind. Things I wanted to say. To tell her. But nothing would come out.

Finally, she broke the tense atmosphere. "Are you okay?"

Fuck.

There she was, lying in a hospital bed, asking me if *I* was okay.

There was so much wrong with that.

"I am now," I confessed, dragging my chair closer to the side of her bed.

Her breath caught at the honesty in my words. Or maybe it was the fact, I'd reached for her hand, closing mine around it. Phoebe didn't reject me. She didn't pull away like I'd burned her.

My eyes widened.

"I'm sorry... for how things have been between us," she said. "I should have talked to you like an adult instead of just... I'm sorry."

"You're scared of me," I deadpanned, trying to pretend the words didn't affect me the way they did.

She let out a tense chuckle. "I'm not scared of you, Levi. I'm scared of how much I care about you."

Her words slammed into me, shooting me straight through my dead rotten heart.

"Shit, Bee," I glanced away. "I don't really know what to—"

"Hey, it's okay." She squeezed my hand. "It's okay, Levi."

Nothing about any of this was okay.

Her. Me. The Die Hearts. The fact I couldn't walk into a room without girls wailing and screaming my name. My life wasn't normal.

I wasn't normal.

I hadn't been normal long before promises of record deals, endorsements, and world tours.

"Levi?"

"You're right to be scared, Intern." My chest tightened as I ran my thumb down the curve of her hand.

"You're going to choose right now to finally push me away?" She smiled sadly.

My brow lifted at that. "What are you saying?"

"I'm tired of fighting this thing between us, Levi. I'm so tired." Her eyes flickered shut and I gripped her hand harder.

Phoebe chuckled again, her soft laughter like music to my fucking ears.

"Why?" I asked. I had to know, I needed to know.

"Because you're trying. You're here and you're trying. That has to count for something, right?"

"Yeah, I think it does." At least, I hoped it did.

"Can I ask you something though?" She peeked over at me. I nodded. "Were you high tonight?"

Fuck. She knew.

Of course she fucking knew.

Ever since she'd arrived on tour with us, Phoebe had been able to see me in a way most people didn't.

"Yeah," I admitted. "But it was only a little weed. I just needed something to take the edge off. I swear—"

"Levi, it's okay. I trust you."

She was high. That was the only explanation. Woozy on the cocktail of drugs they were giving her.

She trusted me?

I don't think anyone had ever said those words to me.

And even though they meant more to me than anything else, I wanted to tell her that she was making a giant fucking mistake.

I couldn't be trusted.

What addict could?

But I didn't.

Like a child starved of attention, I latched onto her words and let them sink into me, filling up the emptiness I felt every day of my life.

I would fuck up again. I knew it, and deep-down Phoebe knew it. But right there, in that moment, neither of us wanted to acknowledge it.

———

"How's our favorite patient?" Letty breezed into the room sometime later clutching a disposable coffee cup.

"She feels like someone took a tire iron to her skull," Phoebe groaned, and I leaped up.

"Are you okay? Do I need to get the doctor?"

"Levi, relax. I'm okay." She smiled and fuck, if it wasn't like sunshine on a rainy day. "I figure the pain meds are starting to wear off. What time is it?"

"Late," Letty said. "A little after two."

"And they allow visitors this late?" She cocked a brow.

"Hmm, Levi—"

"What?" I shrugged, not liking the way Letty was looking at me. "They said someone could stay with her."

"After you threatened to get the poor nurse fired."

"Levi!" Phoebe looked at me with a strange mix of surprise and horror. "You did that?"

"They said I wasn't family." I shrugged.

Something in her expression softened. "I can't believe

you did that." She was smiling now. "Can I get out of here soon?"

"I think we're stuck here for the night, sorry. You have a pretty bad concussion, so they want to monitor you overnight."

"Ugh, great."

I squeezed her hand gently, and Letty raised a brow. "Something you two want to tell me?"

"I... uh," Phoebe flushed trying to pull her hand away, but I wouldn't let her.

"I'm staying," I said.

"Levi, no," Phoebe blurted. "You should go and get some rest."

"You really think I'll be able to sleep knowing you're in here? Yeah, not happening." I gave her a pointed look.

"Johnson and Stalter are right outside. The place is fairly quiet now so you should get some peace. You need to rest." Letty looked at Phoebe. "And you," her eyes slid to mine, "try not to threaten anymore staff. They're here to help, okay?"

"Yes, *Mom*," I grumbled.

"If you two don't need anything else, I'm going to call the guys and let them know you're all right."

"Thank you."

"Yeah, thanks," I said. "For everything." Letty didn't get enough credit for putting up with our brand of crazy.

"I'll see you both in the morning." She gave us a small nod, her mouth tipped in a knowing smile.

The second she was gone, Phoebe turned to me. "You need to get some rest too."

"No, I need to be here, with you."

"At least try to sleep. Maybe they can wheel in a cot for you—"

"Ssh." I pressed a finger to her lips. "I'll be fine. In fact," I brought her hand to my mouth and kissed her knuckles, "I'm going to sleep right here."

Laying my head on her arm, I closed my eyes. Phoebe's soft laughter washed over me like a warm blanket.

How did she do that?

How did she make my heart squeeze until it felt like I couldn't breathe?

Phoebe Halstead might have been scared of me...

But I was fucking terrified of her.

PHOEBE

I woke disorientated. There was a dull ache in my skull, and when I opened my eyes, the stream of sunlight was too harsh. But it wasn't my head that worried me. It was the fact I could barely feel my arm. I glanced down to find Levi curled around it, holding on like it was his life raft, while he slept peacefully.

Memories of the night before slowly unfurled in my mind. The show, the meet and greet after. The out of control fangirls. The world tipping on its axis as I crashed into the table and fell.

Oh God.

How freaking embarrassing.

I could imagine the headline now: **Intern PA get gets trampled on by Die Hearts stampede.**

I let out a quiet groan. I'd known something felt different about the show in Phoenix. I just hadn't expected I would end up in hospital with a concussion.

Gingerly, I tried to retrieve my dead arm from Levi's death grip. He made a small whimpering sound, and I froze. Was he dreaming? It didn't sound like a dream, more like a nightmare.

"Levi," I whispered, stroking his hair with my other hand. "Levi, wake up."

"Huh?" He shot up, rubbing his bleary eyes. "Oh, hey."

"Hey."

Silence descended over us as we both took in the gravity of the situation. I was in the hospital and Levi was here.

He'd been here all night, glued to my bedside, after threatening the staff who tried to make him wait outside.

Jesus.

I really hoped Letty and the security team had locked staff into airtight NDAs because the last thing the band needed was this getting out.

"How are you feeling?" I asked him.

"Shit, Bee, isn't that supposed to be my line?"

"I'm okay."

"None of this is fucking okay," he ground out, his eyes glittering dangerously.

"It was an accident, Levi. I'm fine, I promise."

He reached for my hand, tangling our fingers together. "I don't think I've ever been so scared as I was watching you fall. It was like I just froze. The whole world slowed down around me."

The vulnerability in his voice gutted me. He didn't look at me, but rather stared past me as if he was lost in his memories.

"Levi," I said softly. "Come back to me."

"Shit, sorry." He dragged his other hand down his face.

"Where'd you go just now?"

"It doesn't matter." A faint smile traced his lips, but I saw the pain in his eyes. And I knew that whatever Levi had just been thinking about, wasn't nothing.

"Thank you," I said, stuffing down the emotion clogging my throat, "for being here with me."

"Phoebe, I—"

"Good morning." Letty breezed into the room looking far too cheery for eight in the morning. "Good news.

You're free to leave once the doctor has done his final rounds."

"Thank God." Relief settled into my bones. I didn't want to be here any longer than necessary.

"You've got to take it easy for the next couple of days. Which means you're on vacation."

"She has to leave?"

Letty and I both looked at Levi. "She doesn't have to *leave*," she reassured him. "But no more late nights or drinking games on the bus. At least not until your headache is gone."

"No fun." I chuckled. "Got it."

"We've got the show in San Diego tonight, so Alistair has given the all-clear for us to check into a hotel tonight, so you'll be a little more comfortable."

"Oh no, he doesn't need to do that. I'll be fine on the tour bus."

"It's already taken care of. We roll out as soon as you're free."

I relaxed back against the stiff pillow and let out an exasperated breath.

"I could always see if they can keep you for another—"

"No, no." I shot Letty a desperate look. "I just don't want to cause any fuss. I feel so silly."

"It wasn't your fault. I should have known the second those Die Hearts turned up drunk that shit was about to get messy."

A low growl rumbled in Levi's chest.

"Down boy," Letty said. "It's our job to keep the fans happy, remember?"

"It's bullshit if you ask me. She was hurt, that isn't—"

"Levi, stop." I squeezed his hand, aware that Letty could see us holding hands. But I didn't pull away, I couldn't. Levi's touch was too calming, too nice.

Dammit. I was so screwed.

Part of me was hoping he would mess up again. It would have made it a whole easier to keep him at arm's length. But he was here. Levi was right here beside me acting so territorial and possessive it melted the ice around my heart.

"Okay, I'm going to try to get things moving with your discharge. Levi, you—"

"Staying," he said with complete conviction. "I'm staying."

"Fine. But we need to figure out how to get you out of here without causing a scene."

"Johnson will figure it out. That's what we pay him for." Levi closed his eyes, letting his head roll back.

"Okay?" Letty mouthed, and I nodded.

"Go, we'll be fine."

She left, closing the door behind her.

"Levi?" I whispered, gently squeezing his hand.

"Yeah?" His eyes flickered open, settling on my face.

"You don't have to stay. You heard Letty, I'll be out of here soon enough."

"Ssh, honeybee," he leaned forward, resting his chin on my arm. He looked so adorable like this. "I'm not going anywhere."

"No?" My brow lifted.

"No, you're stuck with me now, whether you like it or not."

It sounded like a promise.

One I really wanted him to keep.

TWO HOURS LATER, I was free. Levi had insisted on wheeling me out of the medical center to the familiar black SUV. Johnson and Stalter had arranged with the staff to sneak us out of the back entrance reserved for emergencies only. Much to everyone's relief, there wasn't a fan or any paparazzi in sight.

"I bet everyone's fed up with waiting," I said as we piled inside. My head still felt a little tender, but overall, I felt okay. I had strict orders to take it easy for the next couple of days.

"Actually, they went ahead." Letty checked her cell phone. "We're going to meet them there. You should try to rest." She gave me a knowing smirk, sliding her eyes to Levi who was beside me.

"I'm okay," I said as the air inside the SUV turned thick with tension.

Levi's mood had turned significantly darker since this morning. He was still careful with me, treating me like fragile glass. But he was closing down right in front of me, and I didn't know how to reach him.

In the hospital, inside the privacy of my room, it had been easy to let our guard down. But the second we stepped outside, his walls went up.

"Hey." I reached for his hand, aware that Letty was pretending not to watch. "Are you okay?"

"Yeah, just tired." He pulled his hand away, leaving me cold.

A shudder rolled through me. Letty tried' to catch my attention, but I rested my head against the tinted glass and closed my eyes.

I couldn't sleep, not with the whir of the engine beneath me, and Letty's constant stream of calls. First, Alistair, and then someone at the label. It went on and on. Until her voice became muffled white noise in my head.

Somewhere into the three-and-a-half-hour journey, my neck begin to ache, and the bass drum in my head began getting louder again.

"Hey, are you okay?" Letty asked, concern etched into her expression as studied me.

"I'm just tired and uncomfortable."

"Here. Try some water. It isn't time for your pain meds yet."

"Letty," I let out a strained chuckle. "I'm fine. I just need to lie down when we get there."

"Maybe we should make a pitstop—"

Levi grumbled something under his breath. Unclipping his seatbelt he turned inward slightly, beckoning to me. I frowned and he rolled his eyes. "Come on, honeybee, I don't bite." He grabbed his jacket and rolled it into a cushion, placing it on his lap.

"I'm not sure—"

"It might help," Letty said, a knowing smirk on her face.

Another bolt of pain rippled through my skull and I smothered a whimper.

"Get over here," Levi barked.

My eyes flickered to his and he gave me a weak smile. "Please," he mouthed. It was then I noticed his clenched fists, the slight set to his jaw.

"Okay." I unclipped my belt and gently lowered my body down, resting my head on his lap. Levi slid his hand around the back of my neck, massaging the skin there. It was heaven, his warm fingers acting as a natural pain reliever. But there was also something possessive about the way he held me, as if he wanted to take my pain as his own.

By the time Letty's call ended, I was barely lucid.

"You holding up okay, Hunter?" Her voice teetered on the edge of my consciousness.

I wanted to know what he was thinking, what his reply would be. But the fingers of darkness were too hard to resist.

––––––––

"Phoebe, wake up. We're here."

My eyes cracked open slowly as I tested their reaction. Letty's face filled my line of sight. "Welcome back," she said.

I sat up, taming the flyaway hairs out of my face. "What time is it?"

"A little after two. We stopped for gas, but you were out for the count."

"Where's Levi?" I asked. He was gone, but his jacket was still rolled up beside me.

"He went ahead to get some rest before soundcheck."

"Oh, okay." I swallowed the dejection flooding me.

She gave me a sympathetic glance but didn't say anything more about it. "Come on, you must want to lie down on something a little more comfortable than Levi's lap." Her chuckle was lost on me as we climbed out of the car. We were in the basement parking lot of the hotel.

One bodyguard flanked us as we rode the elevator to the top floor. Usually, the band had the penthouse and we stayed on the floor below.

"The band have the suite," Letty said as if she could hear my thoughts. "We have the adjoining annex."

The doors pinged open and she led me down the private hall. I could hear the guys on the other side of the door, mostly Hudson's raucous laughter.

"You want to go say hello?"

"Actually, I think I just want to sleep."

"It's probably for the best." She stopped at the final door. "This is us. Take your pick of bedrooms."

"If I get some rest now, I'll probably be okay for the show tonight."

"Nice try but you're staying put. Doctor's orders, remember? I need you healthy for the rest of the tour. Take some time to rest. We'll manage for one night without you."

I didn't want to stay here alone, knowing they were all at the Viejas Arena. But she was right. My skull felt like it had been through a meat grinder.

"You'll come say goodbye before you leave?" I said.

"Of course. Now go get some rest. I'll bring you some water and pain pills in a minute."

"Thank you."

I made my way to the back of the suite, taking the bedroom closest to the floor-to-ceiling windows. There was a big wraparound balcony that I was hoping ran the entire length of the suite.

Sure enough, when I stepped inside, I was greeted with an amazing view of the city. But the constant *thud* in my head made it impossible to focus.

In that moment, I wanted only two things: To sleep for a week.

And a backstage pass to Levi Hunter's thoughts.

LEVI

"HEY, YOU OKAY?" Rafe approached me as I hovered in the wings watching Eva do her thing. The crowd was hanging onto her every word, the atmosphere a lot quieter than last night. Thank fuck. I didn't want to relive that anytime soon. Every time I thought about Phoebe being thrown out of the way by those crazy fucking fangirls, my blood boiled.

She was okay, but it could have ended a lot differently.

"Yeah, I'm good," I forced out the words.

The truth was, I was losing the fight to stay calm. Ever since waking up, wrapped around Phoebe's arm, I was waiting for things to go back to how they were before—with her ignoring me.

She'd been different in the hospital. Receptive to my touch, relieved even. I'd been so fucking dumbstruck, I didn't think to ask what it meant, and she'd given me no sign that it changed anything.

We were stuck.

At least, that's how it felt.

I just wanted a sign. A tiny sign that she wanted more...

Instead, I'd held her the entire way from Phoenix to San Diego as she slept off her headache. Letty had watched me, a mix of understanding and trepidation on her face. She didn't say anything, she didn't have to.

The second the car had pulled into the underground basement, I'd gotten the hell out of there. I didn't want to listen to Phoebe wake up and tell me it was better for us to remain friends. As if we could ever be that. I'd been inside her for fuck's sake. I knew the sounds she made when she came. I knew how sweet she tasted, how tight she was.

Fuck.

Fuck.

Fuck!

I tried to think about anything except Phoebe naked and ready underneath me.

"She's going to be okay, you know?" Rafe clapped me on the shoulder, making me startle. I slid my eyes to his and gave him a stiff nod.

"It's okay to care," he added. "We were all worried about her. About you. But you held it together, man. You're here and you're okay."

Okay wasn't a word I'd have chosen to describe myself. I was barely in control. If he looked closely enough he'd see the slight quiver to my hands, the struggle in my eyes. I wanted nothing more than to fuck off the show and go find a bar or back alley and score some blow. Usually I was desperate to feel something, chasing a high that would drench me in ecstasy. But Phoebe, she had the opposite effect. She made me feel too much. She made me want things I had no right wanting.

"You can talk to me, Levi. I know things haven't been right between us," he said over the roar of the crowd as Eva finished up her set.

"Things are fine," I said flatly.

"Levi, come on... I want us to—"

"Hey." Eva bounded over to us, her cheeks flushed and eyes sparkling with that post-show high.

She threw her arm around Rafe's neck and leaned up to

kiss him. I looked away, something twisting deep inside me. I wanted that... fuck, I wanted it so much. But I knew if I had it, I wouldn't be able to keep it. Everything I touched turned to ruin.

Myself included.

I moved away, giving the two of them some privacy, and myself a chance to breathe. I stared out at the stage, watching as the road crew began moving instruments and speakers into position for our set. Anticipation crackled in the air, rippling up and down my spine like a warm current. It was all for us: the sold-out show, the fangirls, the constant screams of appreciation and adoration. I was one of the most popular, most revered, and celebrated singers of the moment. Levi Hunter wasn't just a name to watch, it was fast becoming the name to remember. It had once meant everything... it had been the validation I'd needed. I was a broken, tormented soul, but when I stepped out on that stage, I became somebody else.

I became larger than life, a god to worship, immortalized and revered.

But something was missing.

The vast jagged hole inside me was no longer filled by the screams of tens of thousands of excited fans. Maybe it never had been. Instead, it craved something else. Connection. Intimacy. It craved her.

Phoebe Halstead.

My honeybee.

And she wasn't here. She was holed up at the hotel, alone, recovering after being hurt... because of me. Because of the craziness of my life.

My fists clenched.

"Levi?" Eva touched my arm and I flinched. "What is it? What's wrong?"

"Angel," I sighed, "that is such a loaded question."

What wasn't wrong?

Fuck, I needed a hit. I needed something to calm the storm raging inside me. Hunger carved through me, making my skin itch. I tried to focus on my breathing, but it was difficult. It was—

"You should see this." Eva thrust something under my face.

Her cell phone.

I frowned, trying to make sense of the words.

PHOEBE: Is he okay?

"WHY ARE YOU SHOWING ME THAT?" It came out tight.

"Because she cares, Levi. And I know you're finding it hard being here when she's there."

"How did you—"

Eva smiled, her eyes full of understanding. "I know things. You should call her."

"I'm not sure that's a good idea." We had a show to do. If I heard the pain in her voice, I wouldn't be able to focus.

"Levi," Eva said more firmly, "call her." She handed me her cell phone.

I stared at it for a couple of seconds before taking off down the hall to find somewhere a little quieter.

Phoebe answered on the second ring. "Eva, what is it? What's wrong?"

"Bee," I breathed.

"Levi?"

Relief slammed into me and I dropped my head against the wall. "You're okay."

"I'm okay." She chuckled. "Going out of my damn mind being stuck here while you... while you're all there. Good luck with the show."

"Bee, I don't care about the fucking show. I only care about... you."

Her breath caught. "Levi, I—"

"Levi, dude," Hudson yelled. "We're on like now."

"You should go," Phoebe said.

"Just give me a second. There's something I need—"

"Levi, let's go!"

"Fuck, fuck." I ran a hand down my face. "I need to—"

"Go. You need to go. Break a leg." Her soft laughter filled the line but then she quickly rushed out, "Actually, don't. The label would kill me."

We hung up but I didn't move, I couldn't. I didn't want to be here, I wanted to be there, with her.

I wanted the girl, the relationship, the happily-ever-after...

Even though I knew there was no fairy tale ending for a guy like me.

———

Sweat rolled down my back. My t-shirt clung to my slick skin as I strutted up and down the stage, screeching the lyrics into the mic. Adrenaline pumped through me like cocaine. I was high on the music, high on the crowd singing the lyrics back to me, high on Hudson's heavy beat reverberating through me.

I hear the voices, inside my head
Whispering things of sorrow and sin
I hear the voices, inside my head
They taunt me, telling me to just give in
To succumb to the pain, to let go and fall
But I don't wanna relent, I don't wanna fade

It feels so good, but it hurts so bad
This high that I'm riding, don't want it to end
I don't wanna come down, don't make me come down
'Cos I'm chasing... I'm chasing nirvana

It feels so good, but it hurts so bad
This high that I'm riding, don't want it to end
I don't wanna come down, don't make me come down
'Cos I'm chasing... I'm chasing nirvana

But I don't wanna die

"THANK YOU, San Diego. You've been amazing, we'll see you again soon." I punched my fist in the air and inhaled a ragged breath, dragging air into my lungs.

The crowd roared, the noise deafening. Hudson was whooping behind me, Damon and Rafe grinning like fools either side of me. The lights started to dim, darkness closing in around me, and like after any good high, I began to crash.

A war raged inside me. The happy chemicals trying to stave off the negative ones. Serotonin duking it out against monoamine oxidase A.

But unless I chased the high—swallowed, snorted, or smoked something to increase my dopamine and norepinephrine—I knew it was a battle I couldn't win.

After the high, always followed the low.

Always.

It was about the only thing in life I could count on.

"Holy shit, that was intense." Hudson clambered down off his podium and leaped onto my back, hugging me. "We rocked the shit out of this place."

The three of them walked off stage, jostling each other, but I remained, staring out at the emptying arena. There would be no meet and greet tonight, no rabid fangirls lying in wait out back by the tour buses, security had made sure of that, there was just the deafening quiet and the promise that, in two nights, we got to do it all again.

"Yo, Levi," Hudson called. "You coming? I could eat a small cow."

He was always thinking with his stomach or dick.

"Yeah. I'm coming." My eyes lingered on the dark arena again. This was all I'd ever wanted so why didn't it fill me up?

Why wasn't it enough?

As I walked off stage to follow my bandmates, my family in all the ways that counted, I tried to ignore the little voice in my head.

You know why.

———

THE GUYS WANTED to get pizza. Well, Hudson did, but there was only one place I wanted to be.

"What do you mean you're not coming?" He frowned. "You have to come."

"Hud," Damon warned.

"I'm not hungry." I shrugged.

"Not hungry for pizza you mean." Hudson leveled me with a knowing smirk.

"Fuck off."

"No, but you're about to get fucked. I bet Pheebs likes it nice and—"

I'd fisted his shirt and yanked him forward before I knew what was happening.

"Whoa, man, relax," he stuttered. "I'm just busting your balls. I like Phoebe. You know that."

"Levi, let him go."

My teeth were ground so tight I felt pain shoot into my gums. Anger vibrated under my skin as I narrowed my eyes at Hudson, daring him to say another word.

"Levi," Rafe said again. "Let him go."

Shoving him hard, Hudson stumbled back. His hands

shot up. "Shit, man, I was joking. It was a joke. I didn't realize you—"

"*Hudson*!" Damon glared at him.

"Yeah, okay. Shutting up now."

Tension rippled between us.

"What's going on?" Eva approached us, glancing from me to Hudson and back again.

"Nothing," I let out an exasperated breath. "I need to get out of here."

Before I did something really fucking stupid.

"You're going back to the hotel?" she asked.

I nodded. My bandmates watched me. I felt their states of curiosity lick up against me. I didn't like it. Being treated like an animal at the zoo. Caged. Wild and unpredictable. But I understood their motivations.

They were worried.

They were always fucking worried.

Being the reckless one, the one who marched to the beat of his own drum, had never bothered me much before. Probably because I was always too wasted or high to care. But I was sober more than high these days, and I saw myself the way they saw me.

And I didn't like my reflection.

"Come on, we can ride together."

"You're not coming for pizza?" Hudson asked her.

"No, I'm exhausted." Her eyes flicked to Rafe. "Someone kept me awake half the night."

"I... uh..." He blushed. My baby brother actually fucking blushed as he ran a hand over his hair. "See you later?"

"Of course." Eva went over and kissed him, then she turned to me and smiled. "Let's go."

"Guess we'll see you later then?" Hudson said.

Things weren't right between us still. We all knew it. But as I walked away from them with Eva, I couldn't find it in myself to care.

I woke with a start. Rubbing my eyes, I sat up and gave my eyes time to adjust to the darkness. My head still hurt but it wasn't as bad as earlier.

"Letty?" I called out to the shadows. Something moved over by the door and I could just make out—"Levi?"

"Sorry, I didn't mean to wake you." He stepped closer. He looked like shit, dark circles ringing his eyes.

"What happened?"

"Nothing... nothing happened. The show was great, everything was fucking great..." Pain bled from his words, infecting the air around him. I could sense it, like a bad storm on the horizon.

Slipping out of the covers, I went to him. His eyes glittered in the shadows, tracking my every step. My heart thumped in my chest, racing wildly as I reached him. "Do you want to talk about it?"

I could do this. I could be this person for him.

"I really, *really* don't want to talk." A sigh rumbled in his chest. It was such a defeated sound, full of pain and sadness. It made my heart ache.

"Oh, Levi." I cupped his face, wishing I had the answers, wishing so much that I had the power to fix him. I knew I couldn't, not until he fixed himself. But it didn't stop me wanting it.

"Honeybee." He sank into my touch, the tension melting out of his shoulders. "I shouldn't be here... I should go before I fuck everything up."

Levi started to pull away and panic washed over me. "Don't," I said, snagging his wrist. Because I knew if I let him go, if he walked out of here right now, he'd walk straight into the arms of a bottle of liquor or a line of coke or anything he could get his hands on to quiet whatever demons were in his head.

"Stay."

"You don't know what you're asking," he breathed the words as if it took all his willpower to say them.

His eyes burned into mine, holding me captive. I knew that one day, I would look back on this moment for what it was—the moment I gave Levi Hunter my heart.

The moment I willingly handed him the power to ruin me.

"It's okay," I said, pushing down every doubt and fear. "I'm right here, Levi. I'm here." Leaning up, I touched my head to his. Our lips were so close I could feel the warmth of his breath.

"Phoebe..." My name was a pained whisper on his lips. His body shook as we stood there, kissing but not kissing, touching but not touching.

Slowly, I lifted my hand back to his cheek, the strong ropes of my resolve slowly unraveling. "Kiss me, Levi," I whispered, letting my lips trace the outline of his.

His eyes shuttered, a deep growl vibrating in his throat.

For a second, I was scared he wasn't here with me. Still as a statue, I wasn't even sure Levi was breathing.

"Le—"

He grabbed the back of my neck and kissed me hard, plunging his tongue deep inside my mouth. I couldn't breathe. Every slide of his lips, every drag of his teeth, the dig of his fingers around my hip as he held my body to his— it was possessive and all-consuming. Dirty and desperate. It was Levi crawling into the cracks of my heart, forcing himself into my veins, scratching himself onto my bones.

It was everything.

"Fuck, honeybee," he rasped. "Do you have any idea how hard you get me?" Levi grabbed my hand and smashed it to the bulge in his jeans.

A whimper spilled from my lips as he leaned in and sucked on my neck, soothing the sting with his tongue. "I could get high on just the taste of your skin."

One of his hands dropped to the hem of my oversized band t-shirt. I'd pulled it on earlier after taking a hot bath. He roughly gripped my thigh, whispering into my ear. "Skin like silk, eyes like honey, this girl will rip out your heart before you can blink."

His fingers brushed higher, grazing my panties.

"Levi..." I sucked in a sharp breath, fisting his t-shirt as I waited for him to touch me there.

But he teased me, rubbing his knuckle over the soft cotton. "Beg, Bee, I want to hear you beg."

"T- touch me, Levi... please."

Without warning, he yanked the material aside and thrust two fingers inside me. My body bowed into him, pleasure saturating my veins.

"Oh God, yes..."

Pressing his thumb hard against my clit, Levi finger fucked me with skilled finesse. I tried to bury my face in his shoulder as I drowned in intense waves of ecstasy, but he pressed his brow to mine, pinning me in place with a dark look.

"I want to watch you fall apart," he drawled. "And when you're nothing but broken shards of skin and soft moans, I'll piece you back together and do it all over again."

I pressed my lips together, suppressing the urge to cry his name. A wildfire swarmed in my stomach, burning me from the inside out as he continued working me with his fingers.

"Almost there?"

I nodded, delirious on the sensations coursing through me. His other hand slipped between us and I heard the telltale sound of a zipper.

"I need inside you, Bee... tell me I can—"

"Yes, God, yes." I was so close, just another—

Levi pulled his fingers out of me and stepped away. "Turn around and put your hands flat on the bed," he ordered, his pupils blown with lust. A shiver zipped up my spine at the dominance in his voice. I turned slowly and moved to the bed, my body swaying with lust.

"Hands," he said gruffly.

I folded my body over the bed and placed them down, my skin tingling with anticipation. Levi stepped up behind me, running one of his hands up my thigh. He hooked his fingers into my panties and inched them down. My heart fluttered in my chest, my breath hitching as he slid himself through my wetness. We both groaned.

"I can't be soft," he rasped. "I don't know how."

"I don't need soft, Levi. I only need you."

He slammed inside of me making my body lurch forward. A garbled cry got stuck in my throat as he pulled out and slammed back inside. His hands clamped around my hips as he rode my body with powerful, unrelenting strokes. Whatever demons he was fighting, whatever darkness he was trying to outrun, he used my body to purge his sins.

"Fuck, Bee... you feel so fucking good." Levi changed the angle slightly, going deeper. Moans spilled from my lips as I tried to stay in the moment, but pleasure was firing off inside me like tiny bolts of electricity. One of Levi's hand trailed up and down my spine, slipping under my t-shirt to find my breasts. He squeezed and pinched, making me cry out.

It was too good.

Too much.

Too everything.

"Come, honeybee, give it to me..." His fingers found my clit, strumming me like a guitarist plucked his strings. It was enough to push me over the edge, my body quivering with bone-deep pleasure.

"Yes, fuck... fuuuuuck." Levi stilled, jerking inside me. It was only then, when I felt the trickle of warmth, that I realized he hadn't worn a condom.

He slowly withdrew from me, making me whimper again. Everything was so sensitive, I felt wrecked.

I glanced back at him and our eyes collided, and he knew.

"I'm sorry, I didn't think... fuck..." Guilt swam in his eyes as he ran a hand down his face.

"I'm on birth control." I reminded him as I stood up to face him.

"I'm clean," Levi said, swallowing hard. "I swear I haven't been with anyone else since we…"

"Okay." I nodded, refusing to let this be the reason either of us pulled away.

"Yeah?"

"Yeah. I need to go clean up. You good if I just…" I motioned to the bathroom.

Levi's eyes darted to the door and back to me. He looked ready to bolt.

"I'd really like it if you were here when I came back," I added, feeling emotion wrap around my throat.

He didn't reply, his expression an indecipherable mask.

I waited another couple of seconds and when it was apparent he wasn't going to answer me, I slipped quietly into the bathroom, and cleaned up. Afterwards, I splashed some water on my face. My skin was flushed, my eyes bright with desire. I looked thoroughly fucked, felt it too, a delicious ache between my legs.

I'd broken my promise. I was no longer treading dangerous shores with Levi, I was swimming in deep waters without a life raft.

I knew the pitfalls of loving an addict. I couldn't fix Zephyr and deep down, I knew I couldn't fix Levi. But I also knew I couldn't continue working with the band and fighting the simmering connection between us.

It was either walk away and go cold turkey or throw caution to the wind and hope my heart was strong enough to survive.

When I returned to the room, my heart skipped a beat

at the sight of Levi laid out on the bed. His hooded eyes found mine.

"You stayed," I whispered.

"I never was very good at making the right decisions."

"You wanted to leave?" Sitting on the bed, I folded my legs in front of me and gazed down at him. He'd pulled off his t-shirt and left his jeans unbuttoned, a trail of dark hair disappearing inside.

"Will you hate me if I say yes?"

"I'd rather you be honest with me than lie." Even if it did hurt to hear him say the words.

"I didn't want to leave you." He wrapped a hand around my ankle. "I wanted to escape the way you make me feel."

"How do I make you feel, Levi?"

"Like I can't breathe," he admitted. "But at the same time, I've never been more alive. It's as weird as fuck. I want to drown in you, honeybee. Drown in you and never come up for air."

"And that worries you?"

He nodded. "You could be my new favorite addiction."

His honesty was like a gunshot to my heart. I'd danced this dance before.

"Tell me about him."

"Who?" I frowned, surprised by Levi's question.

"Don't play dumb, Bee. I know you better than that. The guy, the... ex, who hurt you."

"His name was Zephyr."

"God, I really fucking hate that name."

I threw my head back, laughing until my cheeks hurt.

"What was he like?"

My eyes slid back to Levi's. "A free spirit. He didn't conform to the rules. I guess you could say he was a bit of a rebel."

"You have a type." Levi grinned, but I saw the flash of jealousy in his eyes.

"My mom always said I had a thing for fixing broken things."

"You mean she's gone?"

I nodded, emotion clogging my throat. "She died when I was fifteen."

"Shit, Bee, I'm sorry."

"It's okay; it was a long time ago."

"So it's just you and your dad?"

I grimaced. "Well, he's alive, if that's what you mean."

"He got you this job, right?"

"Have you been digging for dirt on me?" My brow lifted.

"I may have asked around." Levi smirked, his hand creeping higher along my calf. His touch was hypnotic. Magical and dangerous.

"Levi..." I didn't know if I was warning him or begging him for more.

"Yeah, Intern?"

God, he made it sound so dirty. Like I was the student, and he was the teacher, and he was going to enjoy every single second of our lessons in seduction.

He hooked my legs and crawled over me, pressing me flat into the mattress.

"I thought we were talking," I said, fighting a smile.

"We were. But the time for talking is over, Bee." He slid his hands between our bodies and grasped himself, working his length inside me. I gasped, my sensitive walls rippling around him.

"Fuck, Phoebe," he groaned. "You feel incredible." Levi rocked forward a little, making us both cry out. "Hold on," he whispered against my lips, slowly increasing his pace.

It was deeper like this, more intense. Every bump of his pelvis against mine sent sparks of pleasure shooting through me.

Levi kissed me, slow deep licks that mirrored the way he fucked me. It felt good, really good.

It felt a lot like making love.

LEVI

Phoebe slept soundly in the crook of my arm. I couldn't remember the last time I'd done this. If ever. Usually, I was too wasted or high to cuddle, passing out the second it was over, leaving my bedmate to fend for herself.

But not Phoebe.

This was the second time I'd woken up with her in my arms, and the second time I hadn't wanted to run.

She transfixed me. Captured my attention in a way no girl ever had. And the more I learned about her, the more I wanted to know. I was like a puppy desperate for any scraps I could get.

"Hey," she said, her voice thick with sleep. "What time is it?"

"Early," I replied.

Phoebe pushed up onto her elbow and gazed down at me. "You're still here."

"I am. It would seem you tired me out, Bee."

She smiled before leaning up and brushing her lips over mine. "I think you've got that muddled around."

I cupped the back of her neck, anchoring her to me. Kissing Phoebe was fucking delicious, and I already knew I'd never get enough. I could feel her snaking into my chest and weaving herself into my DNA.

"What?" She eased back to look me in the eye.

"I'm addicted to you, Bee."

"Levi..."

"What? It's true. I already want more." *And more... and more.*

I wanted to lose myself in her completely. Fuck her so deep she forgot where I ended and she began. I wanted us to meld together and become one.

I wanted... God, I wanted so many things. Things I couldn't tell her for fear that she would run.

I was a complicated guy; my emotions ran on a higher wavelength than most. I was either bouncing off the walls or in a heap on the ground, clawing my way through every minute of the day.

"We talked about me," she said around a small yawn. "I want to know about you."

My spine stiffened as she trailed a hand up my stomach, tracing my abs. I caught her wrist, bringing her fingers to my lips and kissing their tips. "What do you want to know?"

"Everything." Phoebe smiled again but I didn't return it, a pit of dread swarming my stomach. "But I'll take whatever you want to tell me."

My shoulders relaxed a little. She wasn't going to push. But she wasn't going to let me off the hook either. Did I really want to do this? Let someone in after all these years of keeping people out?

Not even Damon and Hudson knew everything. I'm not even sure Rafe knew the whole story and he'd been right there in that hell hole with me.

I inhaled a shaky breath, raking a hand over my hair. "My childhood isn't sunshine and rainbows, honeybee."

"You think I don't know that?" Her hand glided up my

chest and settled on my jaw. "I see the darkness in your eyes, Levi."

I snorted at that. "It's not the darkness in my eyes you need to worry about, it's the darkness in my soul."

"You don't scare me," Phoebe whispered, her tone contradicting her words.

"I should." My hand moved around the side of her neck so I could brush my thumb over her cheek.

Silence settled between us. It was barely sunrise, the first hint of sunlight just beginning to peek in through the thick, heavy hotel drapes. A new dawn. A fresh start.

Another day of trying to keep my demons at bay.

"What are we doing, Levi?" The uncertainty in Phoebe's voice hit me like a wrecking ball.

"Do we need to label it?" I didn't work well with labels.

Idol.

Singer.

Worthless.

Evil.

Fuck up.

"No, I guess not." She held my eyes. "But I have some lines. Lines I expect you not to cross while we're... doing whatever this is."

"You have lines?" I snorted. "Of course you do."

Phoebe glowered at me, but it was too fucking adorable to be threatening. "Number one, no drugs, *at all*. That's a dealbreaker for me."

I'd expected it but it still felt like a noose around my neck. There would be times when I couldn't control it, times when I needed to relax or forget or feel something.

"Number two?" I asked, changing the subject because I really didn't have an answer to her first point.

"No groupies. No waitresses or bar staff or assistants or fangirls... do I need to go on?" Her brow lifted.

"I think I got the point." I stroked my jaw, smirking. "You're saying while you're riding the Levi fun train no one else can." My dick jerked at the image of her riding me, her thick hair cascading down her back, her honey eyes blown with pleasure.

Phoebe swatted my chest. "You want this, you play by the rules."

"You'll be the only girl sucking my dick, don't worry."

Her lips parted on a soft gasp, doing nothing for the dirty images running through my mind.

"Was there a number three?"

"We don't tell anyone."

"The fuck?"

Her cheeks turned pink as she held my confused stare. "I need this job, Levi. For more reasons than one."

I didn't want to be anyone's secret. I'd spent too much of my life being the kid that nobody wanted.

"Are you ashamed of me?" The words flew from my lips before I could stop them. Regret filled Phoebe's eyes as she crawled over me, straddling my hips.

"No, no. It isn't like that." She touched my face. "You know the label will frown on it, they have those kinds of rules for a reason. I'm not a famous rock star, Levi. I don't have an endless bank account and my dad hasn't financially supported me since I turned eighteen. I can't lose this job. I just can't."

"Can the band know?"

What the fuck was I saying? I didn't want to put a label on us, but I didn't want to sneak around like a dirty little secret either.

"Levi..."

"They already know something happened between us, Bee." I curved my hand around her neck and pulled her down to me. "They can be discreet. We're on tour; there isn't a lot of time to be alone. I don't want to keep this from them."

Her hand slid over my shoulder as she touched her brow to mine. "Don't break my heart, Levi. I'm not sure I'd survive it."

Guilt punctured my chest. Phoebe knew me. She knew guys like me. She knew I couldn't offer her that and yet, she asked me anyway. Because sometimes it was better to live in the lie than survive the truth.

I kissed her hard and said, "I promise."

I STAYED until the sun came up, and then snuck out of Phoebe's room like a thief in the night. Except, my stealth clearly needed some work because I walked straight into Letty as she sipped her morning coffee.

"Want one?" she asked, as if the fact I'd just left her intern's bedroom was no big deal. "There's a fresh pot."

"Hmm, no, I'm good."

"Relax, Levi. I'm not Alistair. I'm not going to remind you of the label's policy on fraternizing with—"

"Yeah, yeah, Panem, save it. I'm well aware of the risks."

"Is she okay?"

"Yeah, she's still sleeping." After I'd fucked her in the shower, Phoebe had climbed back into bed and passed out.

"I'm sure she is." She smirked, and I flipped her off.

"Come on, sit, have coffee."

I eyed her with suspicion. "Is this the part where you grill me and then warn me not to break your girl's heart?"

"I think we know there's no use in that. You've obviously both decided to throw caution to the wind and... well, whatever this is." She waved her hand around.

"We're not putting a label on it."

"Of course not. Wouldn't want to pretend it means more than it does."

I flipped Letty off again, and she chuckled. "You're both adults, Levi. And you'll do whatever you want to do anyway. All I'm asking is for you to be careful. Phoebe is..."

"Yeah." I didn't need Letty to tell me she harbored some dark shit. I saw it every time I looked at her.

I was beginning to wonder if that's why I was so drawn to her.

"From what I can gather, things ended badly with her ex. Has she talked to you about him?"

"A little." My shoulders lifted in a small shrug.

I didn't like to think about Phoebe with another guy. In fact, I fucking hated the idea. But I was weirdly obsessed with knowing stuff. Did *Zephyr* make her moan the same way I did? Did he know exactly how to touch her to make her shatter?

Did he love her?

If he had, why did it end?

Why on earth had he ever let her walk away?

"Look, you're both adults, you can make your own decisions. And for some ungodly reason, Phoebe seems to like you." Letty poked out her tongue, and I flipped her off... again. "Just take it slow."

"Relax, it's not like I intend on putting a ring on her finger. It's just a bit of—" I swallowed the words, because it wasn't just a bit of fun.

It wasn't that at all.

"Yeah," Letty gave me a sad smile, "didn't think so."

Heavy silence settled over us as we drank our coffee. In the early days, when we'd done our first tour, mornings had been a damn sight different to this. Letty usually had to drag us out of bed, hungover and exhausted. Our hotel rooms were always full of people: roadies, crew, fangirls, the clingers-on all looking for their next meal ticket. It had been the perfect distraction from my demons. The never-ending flow of attention and liquor and drugs was like a balm to my dirty black soul.

But it wasn't sustainable.

What was it they said? The higher the climb, the further the fall?

Well, I fell.

Over and over, I clawed my way to the top, and time and time again, I plunged into new depths of self-loathing and pain and emptiness.

It was a bitter cycle. One I didn't ever think I'd break. Eva had gone some way to breaking the chain though. We didn't party so hard these days or burn the candle at both ends the way we'd used to. She was like a natural sedative, tamping down our wild ways. Now she had my brother as good as wifed up. Damon had a reason to ride us even more than usual. And Hudson... well, he was still Hudson. But overall, the band was in a better place.

I was the loose cannon, I always would be. But even I was getting ground down by the life.

I let out a bitter laugh.

Letty frowned. "Something funny?" she asked.

"Twenty-one and I'm already jaded."

"The industry will do that to you." Concern glittered in her eyes. "Do I need to be worried?"

"Nah, I'm good. I need this." I needed music like I needed my next breath. It was my anchor. The thing that tethered me to this existence.

"Maybe you should talk to—"

"If you're about to suggest I see a shrink, save it. I tried that shit, it didn't work." I didn't want to revisit my past, to unpick my deep-seated mommy issues. That only led down one street... and no one wanted to meet that Levi anytime soon.

"Okay," she held up her hands, "it was just a suggestion."

"I'll be okay." But even as I said the words, I felt the lie snake through my chest.

It wasn't even nine and I'd already told two lies this morning.

But it saved people from facing the truth...

That I was, and always would be, a screw up.

PHOEBE

WE WERE BACK on the road, traveling to San Francisco. It was a seven-hour journey, but Letty wanted to spend the time going over the plans for the European leg of the tour that she'd received from the label.

"Paris, Madrid, Barcelona, Rome, Budapest, London... wow, this is—"

"Pretty awesome, right?" She shuffled through the papers.

"It looks intense. Do you think they're up to it?"

"Phoebe, it's a world tour. A *world stadium* tour, that's... well, it doesn't get any better than that." She sat back and let out a soft sigh. "But yeah, it'll be intense. Here we have the tour bus. It gives you a certain level of normalcy. This," she motioned to the schedule, "is going to mean a lot of overnight flights; a different city every day. It'll take its toll."

"Do you think they're ready for it?"

"Is anyone ever truly ready? They're the rock band of the hour. Their fan base is growing quicker than we can keep up. Now Eva is on board, things have the potential to blow up even more. Everyone wants a sprinkle of Hunter-Walker magic. I've got a ton of interview requests to go through. The press opportunity is huge."

"I can help with those."

"I was hoping you would say that." She shot me a knowing look. "We need to vet each request, make sure the station is legit. Dusty wants to get the major stations pinned down in each country. I'll handle those. You take the smaller ones: independents, local broadcasters, online streaming services."

"Got it." My eyes widened at the list she handed me.

"There's still a few months," Letty chuckled. "We have time. Have you ever visited any of these places?"

"No, have you?"

"I went to Italy once with my Nonna. But I was only twelve."

"You're Italian?"

"My mom was... I mean, she is..." My brows knitted, and Letty added, "She's alive. We're just not on good terms right now."

"I'm sorry."

"Don't be. Families are there to test us, right?"

"There's only me and my dad," I said.

"Oh God, Phoebe, I'm sorry. I didn't even—"

"Relax. It's fine." I offered her a reassuring smile.

"Are you close?"

"God, no. My father is... he's very business orientated." The words were like ash on my tongue.

"He works in the film industry?"

"He does." I began highlighting the stations I needed to go away and research. "After Zephyr, my ex; our relationship was at breaking point. I told him I wanted to turn things around, and he knew someone at the label. It seemed like a good opportunity."

"What happened with him... your ex, I mean?"

Pain washed over me, but it didn't cripple me the way it used to. "He—"

The bus lurched to a stop.

"Sorry 'bout that," the driver, a heavy-set man called Gareth yelled.

"What's going on?" Letty got up and moved down the bus. I followed her, glancing out the window to see what they were both looking at.

"The Van Hool blew a tire."

"Shit," Letty grumbled. "This is all we need. How far out are we?"

"Just shy of two hours. It's a long walk." Gareth placed the toothpick back in his mouth and waited for instructions.

"Come on, let's go chat with Duke." We filed out of the bus. Security pulled up behind us, and Johnson and Stalter came around to inspect the tire.

"Must have hit a jagged stone. She's torn right through."

"Already called for assistance." Duke clambered off the bus. "It'll take them a little while to get to us."

I scanned the road. We were in the middle of nowhere, only the barren land of the San Joaquin valley visible as far as eye could see.

"Well, would you look at that." Hudson joined us.

"Back on the bus," Letty ordered. "Right now."

"Relax, Let. We're in the middle of nowhere."

"What the fuck happened?" Levi sauntered toward us. He looked disheveled, his hair sticking up all over the place and his eyes ringed with dark circles.

I frowned, watching him. He caught my eye and winked.

"Tire blew," Duke and Stalter said in unison.

"Can you fix it?"

"Not without help. Got someone on their way but it'll take time."

"Great, so we're stuck out here?"

"We can all ride on the second bus," Letty said. "Then Duke can catch up with us later."

"Or," Hudson chimed, "we could go check out that place." He pointed off into the distance. I hadn't noticed it before, but he was right. There was a diner up ahead.

"I'm not sure that's a good—"

"Relax, Letty. I've got this." He took off in that direction. Stalter cussed under his breath, something about, 'moronic rock stars' and went after him. Damon, Rafe, and Eva had all gotten off the bus to see what was happening.

"I could eat," Damon said, surprising all of us.

"Sounds good to me." Levi glanced at me and I felt myself grow hot all over.

"Fine." Letty threw up her hands. "Looks like we're going for lunch. Johnson, have a car follow us. Gareth, bring the bus."

Johnson nodded and whispered something into his mic, while Gareth climbed dutifully back on the second bus.

"I'll wait with Duke," Travis suggested.

"There's no need for—"

"I'll wait." He gave Letty a stiff nod, and she took off after the guys.

"Intern?" Levi yelled, turning around and walking backward. "You coming or not?" the corner of his mouth kicked up and I saw the amusement glitter in his eyes.

Jesus.

What had I gotten myself into?

———

SECURITY CHECKED the place over before any of us stepped inside. The diner was virtually empty, save for a couple of truckers. I'd spotted their vehicles in the parking lot around the back of the building. They didn't pay us much attention as we all piled into a booth. The security guys were happy then to hold back, one remaining at the door and the other perching on a stool at the counter.

"Don't get many famous folks passing through," a woman with a head of frizzy blonde hair said.

"Our bus broke down. We're waiting for the recovery truck. We were hoping to get some lunch." Letty approached her. "We'd appreciate your discretion."

The woman narrowed her eyes at us. "Y'all don't look familiar. Should I know who you are?"

Hudson snorted and Damon jabbed him in the ribs. Letty shot them a hard look before returning her attention back to the woman.

"Could I speak to you for a minute, in private?" She eyed the two truckers. They seemed completely disinterested in us, poring over the newspaper, sipping their strong coffees.

The two of them disappeared to the far end of the diner. I knew Letty would be briefing her about the need for absolute discretion. When they were done, the woman went into the kitchen. She returned with two brown paper bags and two disposable coffee cups and dropped them down on the counter in front of the truckers. "Jerry, Kingston, I'm gonna need y'all to be on your way. Here's a little something for the road. The kind lady over there settled your bill." She motioned to Letty.

With little resistance, the two men got up and left as we

watched on. Johnson flipped the open sign to closed and pulled down the blind.

The woman approached our booth with a wide smile. "I'm Jeanette, and I'll be your server today. What can I get y'all?"

"What's good?" Hudson asked, giving her a cocky smirk. Jeanette blushed, but she didn't let the attention from a gorgeous rock star intimidate her.

"We do a mean burger. It comes with bacon, cheese, pickles and my fella's special sauce."

"Sounds amazing, I'll take two."

A chorus of snickers filled the air.

"Greedy fucker," Levi murmured. He caught my eye again, holding my stare. He was right opposite me. There was no escaping, and by the time Jeanette reached me for my order, I could barely string a sentence together.

"Loaded fries please," I managed to choke out. "Extra cheese, and I'll take a strawberry shake."

"Good choice, hon. We'll get those right out to you. If you need anything, just holler."

"I like it here." Hudson mused. "It's got spunk."

It was a quintessential roadside diner. Checkerboard curtains and tiles, plain Formica tables, and red, fake-leather booths. But the coffee smelled good, and Jeanette seemed nice.

"Everything okay?" I asked Letty as she studied the window.

"Yeah. I just don't like getting caught out."

"Hopefully the tire will be fixed soon, and we can get

back on be road," I said. "And if it isn't, we can go back to the original plan of all riding on the second bus."

"Yeah, you're right. It's fine." Despite her words, her shoulders didn't relax.

I got it. Alistair had handed her the reins while he attended to business in Atlanta. He was joining us in Sacramento in two days' time. She didn't want things to go wrong on her watch.

Something nudged my foot under the table and my eyes snapped to Levi. He smirked, dirty thoughts glittering in his eyes. "I need to take a piss," he announced.

"Restrooms are through that door and down the hall," Jeanette called over.

"I'll be back." His eyes lingered on mine a fraction too long. I felt Hudson watching me. Noticed Damon watching Levi.

Damn him.

I wasn't ready for our... whatever we were, to be out in the open. Not even to his bandmates.

Jeanette arrived with our drinks, so I used everyone's momentary distraction to slip past Letty and go to the bathroom. Levi was just coming out of the men's bathroom.

"What are you doing?" I hissed.

Levi started at me intently, crowding me against the wall. He leaned in and ran his nose along my jaw. "They're my friends, Bee. My brothers. You think they don't know that I was balls deep inside you last night? And again, this morning?" You think they don't look at me and know I'm thinking about all the ways I want to make you come undone?"

"Behave, Levi," I breathed, trying to calm my racing pulse. "You said we could be discreet."

"I know, but I can't help it if every time I lay eyes on you, I want to get you naked." His hand slipped between our bodies finding my center. He cupped me there, pressing the heel of his palm right up against my clit.

"Oh God," I whimpered, biting down on my lip. "Levi, we can't..." My eyes flickered down the hall to the door. No one could see us, but anyone could walk in at any moment.

"But it feels good, right? I make you feel good?" He dipped his head to look at me, his eyes hooded, hunger simmering there. But there was a vulnerability in his voice that floored me.

"You know you do." I swallowed a gasp as he rubbed me harder. Levi slipped his hand lower, grazing my bare thighs.

"Fuck, I love bootie shorts." He grazed his pinky back and forth, making me shudder.

"We should stop... we should definitely stop."

He nuzzled my neck, licking and sucking the sensitive skin. "Or," he breathed. "I should see how quick I can get you off."

"Lev—" I pressed my lips together, smothering a moan as he plunged two fingers deep inside me.

"Just feel it," he whispered against the side of my throat. "Just let go."

LEVI

I couldn't help myself.

The second my eyes landed on Phoebe, I knew I had to have her. Just a small taste. Something to tide me over until I got her alone and naked again.

Her head rolled back, hitting the wall. "God, it's…"

"Yeah, Bee, I know." I worked my fingers, curling them and rubbing deeper, watching with rapt fascination as she began to fall.

"Levi, fuck…"

I wanted to fuck her. I wanted to drag Phoebe into the bathroom, push her up against the wall, and sink deep inside her. But I wouldn't. Not yet.

I wanted her desperate for me, the way I was desperate for her.

"Feel that," I slid my fingers back and forth. "Imagine it's me inside you, fucking you." *Loving you.*

The words hit me straight in the stomach. That wasn't what this was though… it couldn't be. I wasn't capable of *that*.

Shaking the words from my head, I circled her clit, unwilling to stop until she came all over my hand.

"Levi, God…"

"Just let go… let go, Bee." I whispered the words against the corner of her mouth before plunging my tongue past her lips. Phoebe came hard, her body pulsing around my digits.

She sucked in a ragged breath. "That was… so reckless." Her eyes flicked down the hall as I pulled my hand away and brought my fingers to my lips, making a show of sucking them clean.

"You can't do stuff like that." Her cheeks were flushed, her eyes bright and burning with lust.

I wanted to tell her I was Levi Hunter, that I could do whatever I wanted, whenever I wanted. But she wasn't some fangirl looking for a repeat ride. Phoebe was so much more.

I kissed her slowly, letting my tongue tangle with hers. Phoebe hooked her arm around my neck and kissed me back. There was no better rush than the way she made me feel. I felt ten fucking feet tall.

"Stop," she breathed, tearing away. "We have to stop."

I smirked. "Or we could—"

"Don't say it." She pushed a finger against my lips. "I'm trying to the responsible one here." Her tone was light, playful even.

"They all know, honeybee. Does it really matter if—"

"It matters to me, Levi. I'm not ready to be under the spotlight, not yet." Her expression slipped and I didn't like what I saw there.

Fear.

Uncertainty.

Pain.

I was asking a lot of her, I knew that. If word got out that Phoebe had caught my eye, her life would turn to shit pretty quickly. She wasn't Eva. She wasn't the sweetheart of Country. And even if she was, Eva still got her fair share of hate. Fan mail, trolls on social media, even scrutiny from the press. Not everyone was team Hunter-Walker. But a lot of people were because Eva was somebody. She was a star in her own right. In a world that chewed up and spit out rising talent, it gave her credibility and status.

Phoebe didn't have that buffer. As far as *they* were concerned, she was no one, but to me, she was someone. And that would be a problem.

A huge fucking problem.

"Yeah," I conceded. "Okay." Stepping back, I put some distance between us.

"Okay?" She frowned. "You mean you're not going to fight me on this?"

"What can I say, Bee? I'm growing."

Her lips curved, and silence fell over us.

"I should probably go," I finally said. "Don't want anyone to think I'm back here doing very bad things to you."

"Levi..." Her breath caught. "I'll hang back. I need a minute."

"Don't take too long, or I'll have to come looking for you." I winked and stalked out of there with a huge fucking grin on my face.

"Yo, what took you so long?" Hudson asked as I reached the table.

"Seriously, bro?" I arched a brow as I slid into the booth. The food still hadn't arrived, and my stomach grumbled.

"Where'd Pheebs go?"

"To take a call, I think," Letty said without hesitation.

I felt Eva and Rafe's eyes burn into the side of my face, but I played it cool. Maybe Phoebe was right, maybe it was best for us to keep things between us quiet for now. Although as I watched my brother whisper something to Eva, jealousy licked my insides.

"Here we go, folks," the server appeared with our food. "I hope y'all are hungry."

I was... but not for the burger she placed down in front of me.

Just then, Phoebe returned, sliding in next to Letty.

"Everything okay?"

"I..."

"With the call?" Letty prompted.

"Oh yes, the call. It was fine." Phoebe chose the exact moment I picked up my burger to look my way. I grinned as I took a big bite, only causing her cheeks to flush a deeper shade of red.

"Here you go, hon." Jeanette pushed a basket of loaded fries in front of Phoebe, but I noticed she barely touched them.

I frowned. Why wasn't she eating?

The small thought festered as I devoured my burger, growing into something bigger. By the time we were done, and Jeanette had cleaned away our plates, I wanted nothing more than to pull Phoebe to one side and ask her what was wrong.

"Can I get you anything else?"

"I think we're good here. I'll come settle the bill." Letty nudged Phoebe to let her up.

"I'll come too," she said, trailing after our assistant.

"She seem okay to you?" I asked no one in particular.

"Who, Letty? Yeah, why wouldn't—"

"Not Letty, asshole," I said to Hudson. "Phoebe."

"Phoebe, why would you think—"

"She barely touched her fries."

"Maybe she wasn't hungry." Eva offered me a reassuring smile, but it did little to the many thoughts running through my head.

"I'm sure it's nothing, man." Rafe frowned, trying to give me a questioning look, but I was too busy watching Phoebe as she hovered next to Letty.

Was she avoiding me again?

I frowned again. I needed to relax. Nothing had changed.

"Okay, we're good to go," Letty said as she reached us.

"Let's hope Duke's got that tire fixed," Damon said.

"If he hasn't, we'll have to all ride on the second bus."

"I'll ride with Stalter and Johnson in the SUV," Hudson said. "In fact, I call shotgun."

"Never gonna happen, dude," I said. "Stalter doesn't give up shotgun for anyone."

"We'll see about that." He shot me a cocky smile, and for the first time since finding out Riley had screwed me over, things felt okay between us.

———

THE VAN HOOL wasn't fixed, so the seven of us crammed onto the second bus and rode the rest of the way to San Francisco together. Damon, and Eva and Rafe decided to take a nap in the bunks. Hudson was upfront talking Gareth's ear off, and Letty was busy doing whatever Letty did. That left me and Phoebe.

She was quiet, sitting at the table reading some emails. I sat and watched her work. Every now and then her eyes flicked to mine. Eventually, she placed down her cell and let out a heavy sigh. "I can feel you watching me," Phoebe whispered.

"Just enjoying the view."

Letty snickered and I flipped her off.

"You didn't eat your lunch?"

Phoebe's brows knitted. "I wasn't hungry."

Shuffling along the bench, I closed the space between us. This bus was smaller than ours, less luxurious, but it was still functional as a tour bus. When my leg pressed up against Phoebe's her breath caught.

"Stop," she warned. "Somebody might see."

"No one is watching except Letty," I said quietly, "and she knows I've been inside you."

Wetting her lips, Phoebe swallowed hard. "You're not making this easy, Levi."

"Who said I want to make it easy?" Leaning in, I ran my nose along her jaw, reveling in the soft moan that escaped her lips. Taking one of her hands, I pulled it under the table and pressed it over my rock-hard dick.

"Maybe I want to make it really, *really* hard." My eyes dropped to hers, and Phoebe's lips parted on a silent 'O'.

I massaged her hand over me, not caring that Letty was a few feet away. It was the wrong fucking move because now all I could think about was getting inside her. Burying myself so deep that she forgot her own name.

"Levi, stop," she whisper-hissed, pulling her hand away. My soft laughter filled the bus.

"How long do think you can keep this up, really?"

Indignation flashed in her eyes. "This isn't a game." She pinned me with a hard look.

"No, it's not. It's inevitable."

A faint smile traced her lips. Lips I wanted to devour, to slide my dick between and—

"Hey, what's going on here?" Hudson poked his head around the wall. I'd never seen anyone move so quickly. Phoebe darted away from me and pretended to be reading something on her cell.

"Just being my usual annoying self," I said, feeling a lick of irritation up my spine. I knew Phoebe wanted to keep us a secret, but I didn't like thinking she was ashamed of me.

Of course she is, the little voice whispered.

A dark cloud descended over me. If anyone noticed, they didn't say anything. I couldn't escape to the bedroom, this bus didn't have one, so I leaned my head back and closed my eyes. The darkness wasn't a friend, it never had been, but knowing Phoebe was close, knowing she was almost within touching distance, settled something inside me.

Even though she'd hurt me just now, I still took comfort from her proximity.

I still let her presence fight my monsters.

———

"Come here you little brat." Mom grabbed my hair and dragged me out of the bedroom I shared with my brother. "What did I tell you about always playing that crap?"

"It's just music, Mom," I cried, my head burning where her fingers pulled my hair.

"It's the devil's work, boy, that's what it is. Just like your dirty black soul. You're just a kid." She shoved me hard and my underdeveloped body crashed against the counter. I knew I was smaller than other kids my age because last week at the store we'd run into Mrs. Dexter and her kids. Charlie was nine like me, but he had more meat on his bones, and he was taller. Asshole.

I wanted to be big and tall and have muscles. Then Mom wouldn't be able to push me around. Then I'd be able to take my brother Rafe far away from here.

"What do you possibly know about rock and roll?"

"I like Jagger's voice. Everyone says I sound just like him."

She cackled, revealing her rotten dirty teeth. "You sound like a rock star? Don't be so ridiculous. You're a kid. Nothing but an evil little cunt."

"Mama," I shrieked, clutching her arm. Rafe would be close by, he always was, and I didn't want him to hear her cussing.

"Get off me." She backhanded me across the face, and I crumpled to the floor, tears burning my eyes. I tried to swallow them down, but it hurt. It hurt so bad.

"You ruined my life. Do you know that kid? Your father left because he didn't want you, Rafe's daddy left because he couldn't stand to look at you, and now I'm stuck with you."

"They didn't leave me because of me," I screamed. "They left because of you. You're mean and you say mean things."

Her eyes turned black and I knew I'd messed up. I should have just kept my mouth shut. But sometimes I got so mad. I wasn't a bad person, I wasn't.

"What did you say to me?" She fisted my hair again, yanking me up to my feet.

"N-nothing, Ma'am. I'm sorry, I sorry. I just—ow!" Her

overgrown fingernails split open my skin and I felt a warm trickle of blood.

"You're nothing, boy, nothing. And one day, I'll be rid of you forever."

"LEVI." Soft fingers stroked my hair. I leaned into their touch, moaning. "Hmm..." Laughter drifted over me and I finally cracked an eye open.

"You fell asleep." Phoebe's smile greeted me.

My hand shot out, fisting her t-shirt, and I pulled her down to me, capturing her lips.

"Levi," she protested, pressing her hands firmly against my chest. But I was too strong, and I needed her too fucking much.

"Just one little kiss, honeybee." I didn't know where we were, my head swimming with confusion. I'd been dreaming. Dark desolate dreams that made me feel hollow and weak. Opening my eyes to see her face was like a rainbow after a brutal storm. I wanted to soak it up, drown in her light.

I just wanted her.

The realization was that strong, I hooked my arms tighter around Phoebe, crushing her to me.

"Levi, what has gotten into you?" she chuckled, trying to slide her hands back to my chest and get leverage to look up at me.

"Just let me have this," I murmured, my lips going to the shell of her ear. "I just need... fuck, Phoebe..." *You, it's you.*

She held me, staying still with me in that moment. It was everything... yet, nowhere near enough.

I hadn't had a nightmare, not in the traditional sense of the word. No, my monsters liked to hide in my dreams. To pounce when I least expected them. I could still see *her* face. Her twisted smile and taunting eyes. Her snarl as she berated me. *You're nothing, boy, nothing.*

"You're shaking," Phoebe said, finally getting enough leverage to look into my eyes.

"I'll be okay," I murmured, sheer exhaustion creeping into every muscle.

"What happened?"

"Trust me, Bee, you're not ready to know all my secrets."

A frown crossed her expression. "I want to help."

"You do," I said with conviction. "This, you being here with me, it helps."

We sat there for a little longer. I didn't ask where everyone was, and she didn't tell me. I was just relieved to have her there.

After a little while, Phoebe untangled herself from my arms. "We should probably..."

"Yeah," I swallowed, "okay. Just give me a minute."

"Of course, I'll be right outside." Phoebe kissed my cheek before leaving me. I watched her disappear down the hall and heard her exit the bus.

Running a hand down my face, I took a shuddering breath. The pit in my stomach was bottomless, making me feel nauseous. It would have been so easy to grab a bottle of liquor and try to drown my monsters. But I'd made a promise to myself—and Phoebe—to try.

After inhaling another deep breath, I went to join my bandmates. The second I stepped off the bus, I saw them all watching, waiting. But I only had eyes for Phoebe. She looked up, her worried gaze meeting mine and before I knew what I was doing, I marched toward her and pulled her into my arms. She let out a little gasp of surprise as I hugged her tight. But to my relief she hugged me right back. We stood there, in the middle of the fucking parking lot, holding each other.

Someone finally cleared their throat and I jerked away, snapping out of the spell I'd found myself under.

"Something you want to tell us?" Damon asked, not even a hint of judgment in his voice.

I glanced at Phoebe and tried to snatch my hand from hers. But she held it tighter, smiling at me.

"Yeah?" I asked, trying to understand what this meant.

Phoebe nodded, heat creeping into her cheeks.

"Okay, yeah…" When I turned back to my bandmates to explain, Hudson took one look at us, and smirked.

"About fucking time."

"I... UH..." It was adorable watching a world-famous rock star stutter over his words.

I stepped forward slightly. The urge to shield him, to protect him from his bandmates' scrutiny coursed through me.

Watching Levi whimper and startle in his sleep was one of the most heart wrenching things I'd ever witnessed, and I'd seen Zephyr OD more times than I could count.

"Is this going to be a problem?" I stared at the four of them, knowing that Eva was already on our side.

"No problem here," Damon said.

"The only problem I have is that I'm disappointed you chose Hunter over me, Pheebs." Hudson offered me a cocky wink.

"Rafe?" I asked but his eyes weren't on me, they were staring right past me to his brother.

"This is a bad idea," he said.

Levi tensed, trying to pull his hand from mine again. But I held on tighter, glancing back. The two of them were locked in some kind of silent conversation though.

"You think I don't—"

"I'm a big girl," I said, demanding Rafe's attention. "I can look after myself."

His expression hardened. "It isn't you I'm worried about."

The air crackled with tension. I felt Levi's eyes drilling

holes into the side of my face. But I didn't take my eyes off Rafe.

"We'd appreciate it if you kept this between the six of us for now."

"Seven." Letty appeared around the corner, shooting me a warm smile.

"It's new and I don't want it—"

"Yeah, we got it. We know the deal."

I bristled at Damon's curt reply but quickly realized why he'd interrupted me.

"Ali, boy," Hudson said. "This is a surprise."

I snatched my hand from Levi's and inched away from him.

"Yeah, well things got done quicker than I imagined so I decided to head down and meet you here." He jammed his hands in his pockets. "Everything okay?" Concern filled his eyes.

"We survived without you, if that's what you mean?" Letty raised a brow, and he chuckled, the heavy atmosphere finally dissipating.

"I never had any doubt you could steer the ship in my absence. I'm glad to see you're okay, Phoebe." His eyes settled on me.

"These things happen." I shrugged.

"Yes, well they shouldn't. We'll be making some changes going forward. What's the plan today then?"

"Oh, you know, braid each other's hair and do some face masks." Hudson scoffed. "What do you think the fucking plan is? We're going to rock the shit out of this place." He took off toward the arena.

"He's as Hudson as ever, I see."

"Actually," Letty said, approaching Alistair with her cell in hand. "I wanted to discuss some things with you. If you have time…" The two of them took off after Hudson.

"I'm going to give my mom a call," Damon added. "Catch you guys inside." He disappeared inside the building, leaving the four of us.

Eva gave me a reassuring smile. "Why don't we all grab some—"

"Actually, I'm going to go find Hudson." Rafe dropped a kiss on her head. "I'll see you later." He barely looked at Levi or me as he took off.

"He can be a real fucking dick sometimes." Levi blew out a strained breath.

"He'll come around," Eva said. "He's just worried."

"I don't know what the fuck he wants from me. I'm here, I'm trying…"

"Hey," she went to him, bracing his arms, "we know you are, and we're all so proud of you. He just cares, Levi. Too much sometimes."

"Yeah, whatever."

"I'll talk to him."

"If anyone needs me, I'll be on the bus." Levi stalked off, disappearing onto the bus.

"You should go after him," Eva said.

"I'm not sure that's a good idea."

"He needs you, Phoebe." She gave me a knowing smile. "You know, he was worried about you earlier, at the diner."

"Worried …about me?"

"You didn't eat anything."

"I wasn't hungry." I'd told Levi that already.

"I know that, and you know that, but Levi's default setting is to think the worst. He's a complicated guy," Eva let out a small sigh, "more complicated than you or I will probably ever know."

I glanced back at the bus, her words tugging at my heart strings. I'd promised myself not to end up here, yet here I was. Fallen completely down the Levi Hunter rabbit hole.

"If you ever want to vent or talk, I'm here. I know how hard it can be to care about someone like Levi."

Yeah, because she cared too.

"Thanks, I appreciate it." The knot in my stomach tightened.

"Go." Eva nudged her head to the bus. "We'll see you later."

Inhaling a deep breath, I left her and went in search of Levi, telling myself everything would be okay.

That I wasn't about to let history repeat itself.

"Levi?" I called out. He wasn't sitting at the table, so I moved deeper down the bus.

"You should go, honeybee." He sounded so defeated, so lost.

Pulling back the bunk curtain, I took his hand in mine. "Tough luck, rock star. You're kind of stuck with me."

He inhaled a shaky breath, his eyes shuttering. "You stood up for me." Two dark orbs, as black as the night, stared back at me.

"Yeah, I guess I did. Don't make me regret it."

"Shit, Bee, you think—"

"Relax, I'm joking." My lips curved. "Do you think there's room for a little one?"

Levi shuffled back as far as he could go, and I climbed in beside him. It was a risk with Alistair around, but I hoped Letty and the guys would keep him occupied for the time being.

I curled into his side, shivering when he wrapped his arm around me and pulled me closer. "Want to talk about it?"

"What is there to say? Rafe is just waiting for me to fuck everything up again. You... the band... myself."

"He's just worried."

"You think I don't know that?" Frustration coated his words. "You think I don't know he's spent his entire life worrying about me. Sometimes I swear he was only born to watch over me, which is really fucking ironic considering our mom named him after an angel."

"What?"

"Yeah... Raphael. Her beloved little angel." He almost sneered the words. "Fuck, she loved him. Doted him on like he was her saving grace. Furnishing him with love and attention while I was left to watch from the sidelines like some fucking leper.

"I tried real fucking hard to hate that kid. From the second he was born, and I was old enough to understand that he was everything our mom ever wanted, while I was some... some monster. I tried to hate him. But he had this way of worming himself under your skin. He was so fucking cute. Like a little puppy following me around, all big desperate eyes and broken speech." Levi's chest heaved with the weight of his words. I didn't say anything. I didn't want to interrupt. He needed this. He needed to confide in someone, and part of me was honored he'd chosen me.

"Looking back, I think he knew I needed him, even then. He'd waddle up to me after one of mom's tirades and wrap his tiny arms around me and hug me tight. I was his big brother, yet, in his own way, he always took care of me."

"I'm sorry you had to go through that." I peeked up at Levi.

"It is what it is." His shoulders lifted in a half shrug.

"No, it isn't. No child should ever feel unloved by their own mother."

"She didn't *unlove* me, Bee, she hated the very bones of me. Sometimes I'm surprised she didn't try to drown me in the bath or lace my cereal with cyanide."

His brutal words sent a shiver down my spine. How could anyone do that... to their own child? Their flesh and blood? He was just a boy. An innocent, helpless boy.

"Levi, that's... oh my god." Bile washed in my stomach as my heart shattered for him.

"Don't be sad, honeybee, she did me a favor." But as he said the words, I saw the doubt in his eyes.

The fear.

Levi and Rafe's mom had emotionally and psychologically damaged him. Attachment issues, substance abuse issues, depression, trust issues, his chaotic personality, it all pointed to a history of deep childhood neglect and abandonment. Now he was stuck in a cycle of negative behavior because somewhere, deep down inside himself, he truly believed he wasn't worthy.

"You're wrong, Levi," I whispered, hugging him tighter, trying to swallow the rush of emotion I felt for this beautiful broken boy.

"Yeah, well, it's too late now," he said with heartbreaking resignation, as if he'd already written himself off and accepted his fate.

I wanted to grab him by his arms and shake him, but I knew enough to know that it wouldn't make a difference. Levi had to see his worth, he had to believe it. Ultimately, it had to come from inside himself, not from now much I or anybody else wanted it for him.

"I'll break your heart," he whispered. "You know that, right? I'll try to be good, but something will happen, and I'll screw up. It's just what happens. It's who I am."

His words were like a knife to the heart. I knew he was right. I knew that there was no way we would come out of this whole, but it was too late now. We were here and I wasn't going to be the one to walk away.

Steeling my spine, I met his piercing gaze.

"I really hope you prove yourself wrong."

THE SHOW WAS INCREDIBLE. Despite the dark cloud hovering over Levi after our heart-to-heart earlier, he managed to pull off a near perfect performance.

I watched the whole thing with butterflies in my stomach. He was something else. Raw, rugged, and real, he strutted up and down the stage, stopping to sing with his brother or hop up on the podium to watch Hudson play a solo. The crowd was electric, the guys were amped, and no one outside our circle would have known anything was wrong.

"He's on fire," Alistair said from beside me. "It's like he's got something to sing for again. The guy should count himself lucky the label didn't ship him off to rehab after that PR disaster and—"

"Excuse me, I need to use the restrooms." I shouldered past him, almost running straight into Letty. She took one look at me and said, "Is everything okay?"

"It will be." I nodded, taking off down the hall.

Slipping into the bathroom, I splashed some water on my face and ordered my heart to calm down. It was just Alistair being Alistair. He was a good manager, one of the best. But hearing him talk about Levi like that had caught me off guard. I'd always felt this innate need to protect Levi but now we'd acknowledged our feelings about each other, I felt like a mamma bear protecting its cub.

The rumble of the crowd overhead signaled the end of the show. The band would return on stage to play an encore and then we needed to be on our way.

By the time I returned, the band was just wrapping up their final song. Levi bellowed into the mic, his voice so gravelly and seductive my stomach clenched as I imagined him whispering the lyrics into my ear as he fucked me into submission. But my naughty thoughts were quickly erased by the realization that we would be travelling on separate buses.

Now Alistair was back, there was no way we could sneak around so obviously.

"Hey, what's up?" Letty nudged my shoulder.

"Nothing." I forced a smile. "We all set?"

"Yup. We need the band out of here pronto. They'll have to shower and eat on the bus. Duke wants to get a head start."

"Got it."

The band started filing off stage and the road crew leaped into action. It was hard to believe that in less than an hour it would be like we were never here.

"Hear that, Pheebs?" Hudson slung his arm over my shoulder. "That is the sound of sweet success. What did you think Ali, boy? We rocked it, right?"

"Nobody likes a bragger, Hud." He checked his wristwatch. "We need to be on the road in thirty. Don't make me wait." Alistair marched off down the hall.

I shirked out of Hudson's sweaty arm and wiped myself. "Gross."

"Naw, don't be like that, baby."

A low growl came over my shoulder and I glanced back to see Levi shooting daggers at Hudson. He chuckled, holding up his hands. "Can't help it if the ladies can't resist me, Hunter."

"I'll give you a ten second head start," Levi deadpanned. "One... two..."

"Lighten up, Lev—"

"Hud!" Damon shook his head.

"Hey." I moved beside Levi, the urge to reach out and touch him almost too much to bear. Eva and Rafe were already tangled up in each other, making out up against the wall. Just the sight of them made my heart ache.

"Hey," Levi said, letting his hand drop to his side and brush my fingers. I smothered a whimper.

"This is harder than I thought it would be," I admitted, letting my hand linger against his.

"Yeah." It came out tight.

Earlier on the bus, nestled in the bunk together, it was like we'd carved out our own little world. But right here, surrounded by his bandmates and my colleagues and the crew, we were back to being boss and assistant. Rock god and mere mortal.

"Try and get on my bus tonight." Levi kept his eyes forward despite the rough demand to his voice.

He didn't want me to try, he wanted me to find a way to make it happen.

"I'm not sure I can." Disappointment flooded me.

Before we reached the dressing room, he snagged my hand. Our eyes collided and I found myself lost into two pools of ink. Heat flowed through me. I could feel his desperation for me... his bone-deep need.

"If you don't find a way," he whispered, but he might as well have growled the words. "I will."

LEVI

"Surprise." Hudson's amused laughter filled the bus. "Look who I found." He pulled Phoebe in front of him.

"What the hell?" Her eyes were wide with disbelief. "He just..."

"Kidnapped you?" Hudson grinned. "You can thank me later."

"Seriously, man." Rafe shook his head. "That was a bum move."

"Lighten up, *Dad*. Our boy Levi was sulking about not being able to spend the night with his girl and I really didn't want to listen to his bitching so... I fixed it." He shrugged, moving past Phoebe to help himself to a drink. The bus rumbled us and began moving.

"Oh, look at that," he smirked, "too late to send her back."

"What did you tell Alistair?" Damon asked.

I still hadn't taken my eyes off Phoebe. Her cheeks were flushed, her eyes darting between the four of us. She reminded me a lot of Eva in the early days, like a fish out of water. But my girl was less pure, a little more jagged around the edges.

My girl?

Fuck.

I liked the sound of that... too much.

I'd never opened up to anyone the way I'd opened up to her earlier. Not a therapist or Eva, not even my brother. Of course, he knew stuff. He was there for a lot of it. But he didn't *know*. He couldn't. Because our mother's hatred, her venomous tongue and cruel touch, was never once directed at him.

In the end, she'd neglected him too, choosing her beloved vodka over being any kind of mother to us. But he didn't know.

Not really.

"Well, don't just stand there, Pheebs." Hudson teased. "Come in, make yourself at home."

Phoebe let out a resigned sigh and traipsed over to me, dropping down beside me. "Hi." She peeked up at me.

"Hi." The corner of my mouth tipped. "I didn't expect to see you here."

"Neither did I. Alistair is going to—"

"Relax." I curved a hand around the back of her neck, stroking the skin there. Phoebe relaxed under my touch. "He knows the kind of shit we get up to."

Just then, Damon's cell started ringing. "Talk of the devil." He answered. "Yeah, she's here. No, she's fine. Yeah.... Okay." Damon hung up. "The boss says under no circumstances are we to corrupt the intern. Alistair wants to talk to you," he pointed at Hudson, "tomorrow."

"Uh oh, I'm in trouble." Hudson waggled his brows, downing another beer.

"Maybe we should ask Duke to stop and—"

I pressed my mouth to her ear. "You think I'm going to let you go now you're here?" I couldn't resist grazing her lobe with my teeth.

"Oh, Jesus." Damon groaned. "I'm gonna hit the sack."

"Where's Eva?" Phoebe asked Rafe. He barely looked at her as he answered.

"She wasn't feeling too good, so she went straight to bed. In fact," he stood, "I'm going to join her."

"He hates me, doesn't he?" She let out a defeated sigh, dropping her gaze to her lap.

"Honeybee, look at me." I slid my finger under her jaw, tilting her face to mine. "He doesn't hate you. He hates me. He hates that I'm going to let this happen even though I shouldn't."

"Don't keep saying that. I'm a grown woman, Levi. I can make my own choices. I know what I'm getting myself into, but it's too late to stop now." Her big honey eyes gazed up at me.

Jesus, this girl.

This strong, resilient, foolhardy girl.

I flicked my tongue over her bottom lip, before sucking it into my mouth.

"Aaaand, that's me done. Party for one in my bunk again. Unless you two would be down for some—"

"Fuck off," I murmured against Phoebe's mouth, flipping Hudson off to the side. His strained laughter was drowned out by the roar of blood in my ears.

"Levi," Phoebe whispered.

"Yeah, Bee?"

"Kiss me."

"I thought you'd never ask."

———

WE STUMBLED into the tiny bedroom at the back of the bus in a tangle of limbs and laughter. Fuck, the sound did something to me. *She* did something to me.

"Hurry," Phoebe drawled, peeling off her t-shirt.

"Strip for me, Bee." I stepped backward until I hit the door, watching her through hooded eyes.

Slowly unbuttoning her shorts, she pushed them off her hips and let them fall to the floor.

"Fuck, you are perfection." My gaze ran over the curves of her body, lingering on the swell of her hips. There was some slight bruising, finger marks. It shouldn't have affected me as much as it did.

"I like my mark on you," I said roughly, toying with my snake bite piercings.

Phoebe gave me a coy smile but there was nothing pure about the heat in her eyes, as she hooked her bra open and let it slide off her arms.

"Your turn, rock star," she breathed, letting her hand trail down between the valley of her tits.

"Get on the bed," I commanded, my voice thick with lust. My blood was like molten lava in my veins as I watched her inch backwards, dropping down seductively on the edge of the bed.

"Open that pretty little mouth, honeybee." I snapped my belt and unbuttoned my jeans. My dick strained painfully against its confines as I prowled toward her. A predator about to claim its prey.

By the time I reached Phoebe, I was fisting my dick, aching to get inside her. But first I wanted her to suck me.

Her eyes were fixated on my Prince Albert piercing as I

wound a hand around her hair and guided her mouth to my length. "Suck," I growled, almost coming on the spot when she flicked her tongue over the steel barbell, twirling it around in her mouth.

"Christ, Bee, that feels so fucking good." My grip on her hair tightened as I thrust up into her mouth, barely able to contain myself. Her fingers dug into my ass as she took me deeper, licking and sucking like she couldn't get enough.

My balls drew tight, that familiar tingle creeping up my spine. I was so fucking close to exploding. "Shit, Phoebe..." She started jacking me with her hand all while sucking me harder.

"Fuck... fuuuuuck," I came without warning, but she didn't let up, swallowing me down like a fucking pro.

Red hot jealousy burst in my veins. I didn't want to think about Phoebe with other guys. She was mine.

Mine.

I tore off my t-shirt and shoved my jeans down, kicking out of them. Then I was on her, crawling over her body and pressing her into the mattress. Phoebe wound her legs around my hips, drawing me into her body. I felt her shudder beneath me and froze.

"You good?" I ran my nose along her jaw, kissing her.

"Yeah, just a little nervous." She traced the profile of my face with her fingers. It was such an intimate action, I was paralyzed. No one had ever touched me like I was precious before. Rare and special.

"You Hunter brothers sure have some good genes." She kissed me tenderly, slow and lazily as if we had all the time in the world.

"But I'm the better-looking brother, right?" My brow quirked up, making her chuckle.

"Oh, I don't know... if Rafe wasn't taken, maybe I would—"

I rocked into her in one smooth stroke, replacing her sassy words with throaty moans. She arched her back, stretching out beneath me as I rode her, slow and deep. My lips latched onto her neck, licking and sucking, dipping lower to circle her nipple and draw it into my mouth.

"Levi," she breathed, gasping for breath as I sunk my teeth into the soft flesh.

But I couldn't hold back, I couldn't be soft and gentle... not when I felt like I wanted to rip out of my skin and crawl inside her.

Grabbing her thigh, I went harder... faster... driving into her over and over, until sweat coated us and the room filled with nothing but the sounds of skin on skin, moan after moan.

"I can't... it's too much..." Phoebe panted, pushing me away, pulling me closer.

I slipped a hand between us, finding her clit and pinching hard. Her orgasm hit like a wrecking ball, making her cry out as she clung to my body, riding the intense waves of pleasure.

But I wasn't done. I kept pounding into her, chasing the release I so desperately needed. My fingers gripped her hips tighter as the endorphins rushed through me. I was close. So fucking close to ecstasy. To that one moment of sheer bliss when all the shit faded away.

"Levi, God..." she gasped, already drowning in sensation again.

I buried my face in her neck, smothering my groans as I came.

"Bee?"

"Yeah?" Her voice was muffled with exhaustion.

"You make me want to try," I confessed, the words coiling through my chest and taking hold.

"Levi?" she said a couple of seconds later.

"Yeah?"

"You make me want to try too."

THE NEXT MORNING, I woke to an empty bed. Phoebe's smell was all over my bed sheets, giving me a serious case of morning wood. I rubbed my eyes, and sat up, the smell of strong coffee and bacon drifting through the crack in the door.

Climbing out of bed, I pulled on some jeans and went in search of breakfast and my girl.

I didn't expect to find her at the small cooktop with Hudson.

Leaning against the doorjamb, I watched them as they laughed and joked, while Phoebe monitored the pan.

"So come on, Pheebs, tell me what you really see in Hunter. Is it his stellar personality or that whole The Crow meets Edward Scissorhands vibe he has going on?" Hudson smirked in my direction, and I flipped him off.

Phoebe's head whipped around and she smiled. "You're awake."

"Edward Scissorhands, Hud, really?" I raised a brow.

"You're so fucking pale, man. You need some tanning lotion, you know, the fake stuff."

I flipped him off again, striding towards Phoebe. Her eyes were too busy checking out my ink to see the hunger in mine.

Hooking an arm around her waist, I leaned down and ghosted my lips over hers.

"Good morning," she murmured.

"Ugh, oh God, I'm think I'm gonna—" Hudson started fake-retching. Phoebe buried her face in my chest, her soft laughter tickling my skin.

"Fuck off, Ryker. Go play with yourself in the shower or something."

"Oh, thinks he's something special now he's got a woman." He went and sat at the table.

"Hey, what's going on?" Eva slipped out of the other bedroom. "So, it's true then?" Her eyes went to Phoebe. "Hudson kidnapped you onto our bus."

"Something like that."

"Well, I'm glad you're here."

"Rafe?" I asked.

"He's still sleeping."

"Of course he is," I grumbled, tightening my arm around Phoebe as she continued cooking the bacon.

"I missed you." Dropping my chin on her shoulder, I inhaled deeply.

"Did you just... smell me?"

"I can't help it if you smell so good. You should have woken me up."

She tilted her face to mine. "You looked so peaceful, I didn't want to disturb you."

It was true, I had slept well. There had been no twisted dreams, no nightmares... nothing.

"It's you, honeybee," I whispered. "You make it all go quiet."

Emotion glittered in Phoebe's eyes, but she didn't say anything. I felt Eva watching us, and I lifted my eyes to hers. She smiled warmly.

"I can help Phoebe," she said.

"No," I replied. "I've got this." Leaning closer, I kissed Phoebe's cheek, and said, "What do you need me to do?"

FOR THE NEXT FOUR DAYS, Levi and I found as many ways as possible to be together. It wasn't easy, being on the road and getting any quality time together. But somehow, we made it work.

He'd followed me into arena bathrooms, pulled me into dark corners of the stage. He'd even managed to sneak onto my bus this morning and make me come in the shower before anyone else woke up. We were completely infatuated with each other.

People noticed the difference. They saw glimpses of a guy who began to smile, to ask people how they were; a guy who laughed.

God, his laugh was something else. It reverberated inside me and made me all giddy. I was in love with the sound, craved to hear it like an addict craved their next high.

I knew I was swimming dangerous waters, letting myself fall deeper and deeper.

But I couldn't stop myself.

There was only one problem: I was pretty sure Alistair thought something was going on between me and Hudson.

"Hey," I said to him as I approached.

We were in Portland with back-to-back shows at the Moda Center, and then an intimate gig at The Cellar, a club downtown that was partnering with Masterpiece on their live music events. It was the band's first performance outside the tour since the Riley scandal and everyone was feeling the pressure.

Hudson looked up and grinned. "Pheebs, to what do I owe this pleasure?"

"Can we talk for a second?"

"Is that code word for like get each other off backstage? Because I've been waiting for you to—"

"Stop, for the love of God, stop."

"Sorry, my bad. I'm just really fucking horny."

"Yeah, what's up with that?"

Usually Hudson had a different girl in every city we visited, but I'd noticed a severe lack of fangirls lately—since the night Levi hooked up with Blondie, actually.

"Don't ask," he gritted out. I sensed a story there, possibly one starting and ending with Eva's best friend Molly. But I didn't ask. I already had one rock star's baggage to deal with. I didn't need another.

"Anyway," I said. "I wanted to ask, has Alistair has said anything else to you?"

"Ali?" He frowned.

"Yeah. I get the feeling he thinks there's something going on... between us."

Hudson ran a hand through his hair, offering me a nervous smile.

My stomach twisted with dread. "Oh no, Hudson, what did you do?"

"It's all good, I promise."

"Hudson... tell me you didn't—"

"I was protecting you... well, Levi." He gave me a sheepish shrug. "If Ali boy knows the two of you are... he'll blow a gasket, Levi will go into nuclear meltdown, and everything will turn to shit."

"Ugh." I groaned. This was bad. Really fucking bad. Things were good between me and Levi, really good. But if he realized Alistair thought I was hooking up with Hudson, or worse, Alistair mentioned it to anyone... the fallout would be huge.

"You should have told me."

"I didn't want you to worry. Alistair isn't going to say anything. I told him we'd hooked up a couple of times but that it was just sex."

"Hudson!"

Great, so now Alistair thought I was just another fangirl, unable to keep her legs closed for the band.

"What? It's better than the truth. Ali knows that girls find it hard to resist all this." He swept a hand down his body.

I rolled my eyes. "You know, if you want Molly to give you a shot, maybe you should try not acting like a self-absorbed asshole for two minutes."

"I don't... that's not... fuck, you're a real bitch sometimes."

"Takes one to know one." I winked at him.

Hudson's shoulders shook with laughter, but then something caught his eye behind me and he paled.

"Phoebe, a word, please?"

Shit.

I turned slowly to see Alistair standing there, a scowl painted on his face.

"It's better for the band, remember?" Hudson whispered, and I waved him off, making my way over to Alistair.

"I haven't wanted to say anything because quite frankly,

this band has had enough to deal with lately, and I know how well you've fitted in here. But this thing between you and Hudson. Do I need to be concerned?"

Heat crept into my cheeks, but I forced myself to meet his concerned gaze. "It's not like that between us."

"Right answer." He gave me a stiff nod. "The last thing we need is another inter-band relationship."

My stomach sank. Hudson was right, Alistair would never accept me and Levi together. Which meant if the truth came out, I would have to choose... Levi or my job.

I pushed those thoughts out of my mind. Alistair didn't know. He thought I was hooking up with Hudson, the last person in the band expected to catch feelings.

"Okay, well, I'm glad we cleared that up." Alistair loosened his tie. I didn't quite know why he always wore the damn things given the amount that he tugged and pulled at them.

I went to walk, but he wasn't done. "You know, Phoebe," he said. "I've worked with these guys since the beginning and if I've learned anything about them, it's they're careful about who they let into their inner circle. After Riley, I felt responsible for forcing someone onto them who didn't have their best interests at heart. Letty has nothing but good things to say about you; same goes for Eva and the guys. You've been given the seal of approval. I'd hate to see you do anything to mess it up."

With that veiled warning, he gave me a thin smile and left me standing there, with guilt in my stomach and a bad taste in my mouth.

———

THE MOOD after the show was tense. It had gone off without a hitch, but the guys were exhausted, a sign of four back-to-back shows. And now they had to perform to a bunch of industry people to launch their new endorsement with Masterpiece, one of the biggest sound equipment manufacturers in the world.

Levi sat beside me, clutching my hand in the dark space between us.

"You good?" I asked him, noticing the way his leg bounced up and down. He was nervous. He didn't need to say the words. I felt it.

We all did.

"You've got this," I said, keeping my voice a low whisper meant only for his ears. "We're all right here."

Eva watched us with hope in her eyes. If I'd learned anything about the sweetheart of Country, it was that she had a big heart and only saw the good in people. She wanted Levi to find healing and happiness. She wanted me to be the one to help him find it.

But for as good as things were now, I wasn't foolish enough to ignore the fact we were only ever one incident away from everything coming crashing down around us.

"So we all know the plan," Letty said, breaking the thick silence as the SUV arrived in downtown Portland. "It's an eight-song set. We'll end with Eva coming onstage and an acoustic performance of *Drown*. Any questions?"

"Will there be food?" Hudson grumbled. "I'm fucking starving.

"Yes, there'll be food. The event has been sponsored by Masterpiece; no expense has been spared."

The car came to a stop and security climbed out first. The entrance to the club was swarmed with paparazzi and fans. But it was expected. The label and Masterpiece had made no attempt to conceal the location of the intimate performance. They wanted the attention, they wanted to create a media frenzy.

They wanted all eyes on Black Hearts.

Trepidation flowed through my body like a warm current. We'd all changed after the show. The guys were in cleaner, crisper versions of their usual jeans, but were all wearing black dress shirts in various stages of undress. Damon had his fully buttoned, his sleeves rolled up to his elbows. Rafe's was open at the collar revealing the tip of the impressive tattoo running down his shoulder. Hudson had his shirt completely open, a gray and black skull tank underneath, and Levi had gone for shirt open with nothing underneath, displaying his inches upon inches of taut inked skin.

The second he'd stepped out of the band's suite, the air had been sucked clean from my lungs at the sight of him.

He smoothed his thumb over the curve of my hand as he looked at his feet. This was a big night for him. The pressure and expectation. I wanted to support him, but I couldn't help but feel like my presence was only going to aggravate him. It was an industry party. There would be liquor and dancing and lots of conversation.

It was my job as Letty's intern to work the room and network. I'd dressed for the occasion in a fitted black dress that hit my knee but scooped low in the front and even lower in the back. I'd paired it with ankle boots with a thin chain and a matching clutch bag. My hair was braided off one side of my face and left loose and wavy over the opposite shoulder. Big black lightning bolt earrings hung from my ears and my lips were the shade of Black Hearts red.

Levi's reaction was something I would never forget. The way his eyes lit up, slowly trailing down my body and back up, and the possessive hungry smirk he gave me. The silent promise in his dark gaze to do dirty things to me at the first opportunity he got.

Whenever that would be.

I let out a little sigh, and Levi instantly went rigid. "What is it? What's wrong?" He gazed down at me, his brows furrowed.

"Just thinking it might be a while until we can be alone."

He leaned in close, brushing his lips over the corner of my mouth, sending shivers sparking through me. "I'll be inside you before sunrise."

God, his voice was so rough and full of wicked intent.

Someone cleared their throat and we both looked up to find Rafe watching us.

"What?" Levi hissed.

"Didn't think you'd appreciate all of them seeing you like that." He shrugged right as the door opened and the flashes started going off.

"Rafe, Rafe, over here."

"Levi, we love you."

"Ohmigod, ohmigod, I see them. I see them."

"Fuck me, Hudson."

The wail of fans hit me like a freight train. Levi had already released my hand. He waited for Eva and his brother to climb out before he followed, being swallowed by the frenzy.

"Showtime," Letty said as she ushered Hudson and Damon out. "Ready?" Her attention was solely fixed on me now.

"Honestly, I'm not sure." This felt different. Like I was stepping onto that small red carpet and living a lie.

Every night, I got to be with their rock star, their idol. There wasn't an inch of skin on my body that Levi hadn't touched with his fingers or tasted with his tongue. He'd fucked me more times than I could count in the last few days, made love to me almost as many times—not that he would ever admit it. But when it was just the two of us, and his walls came down, it was a wonderful thing.

The brooding damaged lead singer of Black Hearts Still Beat was whip smart and funny, not to mention a lyrical freakin' genius. He was so much more than the guy they knew and worshipped. But I couldn't tell anyone. I couldn't stand and shout it from the rooftops because this... *this* was our reality.

A whirlwind of fangirls and a sea of paparazzi.

"Come on." Letty nudged me forward and I spilled out onto the sidewalk. But no one was there waiting for me. There were no flashes or screams of my name.

Because I was no one.

I was the girl in the shadows, and right now, watching as Levi and the guys were swamped by security and a rabid horde of fans and press, I was the girl falling in love with a guy from afar. Except, he wasn't just any guy. He didn't only belong to me. Levi Hunter belonged to the entire world.

No matter how much I loved him—and I did, I was in love with him—no matter how much I wanted him, part of him would always be theirs.

It was the price of being with a rock star.

A price until this moment, I'd told myself I could pay.

LEVI

I COULDN'T FOCUS. As I stood on the small stage, the lights beating down on me, the steady beat of Hudson's drum vibrating inside me, and my brother's riff running through my veins, all I could see was her.

Phoebe looked sensational. The black dress molded to her curves like a second skin. Her boots, her hair, those sinful red lips... I was rock hard the second my eyes had landed on her in the hall earlier.

And I was still hard now.

Thankfully, lack of focus didn't affect my ability to regurgitate lyrics I knew better than I knew myself. Song after song we seduced the crowd until I had them eating out of the palm of my hand.

My eyes tracked Phoebe as she worked the room. I knew it was part of her job, to mingle and chat. But every time I saw some overweight Suit put his hand on her, my mood grew darker.

She was mine.

Etched onto my bones, woven into my soul. The more time we spent together—and it wasn't nearly enough lately—the more I wanted. Her smiles and laughs, her kisses, and her pouty lips wrapped around my dick, sucking me the way no one else could. Fuck. I needed her.

But I was on a strict warning from Alistair and the label not to put a single foot out of line tonight. This was launch event for our endorsement with Masterpiece. It was everything we'd ever wanted.

Somehow, I didn't think finding me balls deep in Phoebe in the bathroom or some darkened corner of the club was exactly the kind of press they had in mind.

It was going to be a long fucking night until we got back to the suite and I could finally find peace inside her.

She was fast becoming my favorite place to be. And it wasn't just the sex either. I loved lying with her, listening to her talk about anything and nothing. I'd never wanted to open up to a girl before, except Eva. But I didn't feel even an ounce for Eva what I did for Phoebe.

I wanted to tell her my truths, to slowly shed my armor and give her my black ruined heart.

But that terrified the shit out of me.

What if she decided she didn't want it?

What if she decided I was too much to handle?

What if she decided I wasn't worth it?

Every day, I tried to stave off the little voice inside my head whispering evil twisted things. And every day, the only thing that could quiet it was her. The second Phoebe looked at me, or touched me, or kissed me, it all went away. She was both my curse and my cure. And I didn't know if she knew it, but she held the power to both save me...

And completely ruin me.

It was a scary fucking place to be.

"We're going to take a quick break," I drawled into the mic. "But we'll be back soon with some more of our favorite songs, and we might even have a little surprise guest for you." I winked at Eva and the whole room seemed to find her in the crowd, applauding.

Letty greeted us at the side of the stage, handing me a bottle of water. "That was perfect. Dowager loved it."

"He's here?"

She grinned. "Flew in specially to see you in action. He's just meeting with Alistair and a couple of his PR guys. But he'll want to see you later."

I nodded, my eyes sweeping the room for Phoebe.

"You can't," Letty said quietly, touching my arm. "Not here, not tonight."

"I'm not a fucking idiot," I snapped. "I know the score."

"You're tense." Concern glittered in her eyes as she pulled me to one side, letting the rest of the guys go find a drink. "What's wrong?"

"I'm fine." I scrubbed my jaw.

"Levi, talk to me. I can't help if you don't talk to me."

"I don't like her out there being groped by fat old men thinking they can touch what's mine. There, better?"

Her lips twisted into a knowing smile. "You're jealous."

"No shit," I muttered, feeling it snake through me, coiling around my heart like barbed wire.

"You know she's crazy about you, right?"

"She's talked to you about me?" My brow went up.

"Not really, but I'm a woman. We know these things. But you need to be careful, Levi, especially with so many eyes on you tonight. I don't think either of you are ready to have this out in the open."

I wasn't.

The idea of sharing Phoebe with the public freaked me out. I didn't want them to take her from me, to make her run.

But I hated being sidelined. I fucking hated not being able to storm over there and claim her as mine.

"I need a drink," I said.

"Levi, I'm not sure—"

"Just something to take the edge off, unless you want me to drag Phoebe to the nearest bathroom and get her to help me unwind?"

Letty let out an exasperated breath. "I know you care about her, but don't let her become your crutch, Levi. She deserves more than that."

I didn't appreciate the hard look she gave me. Letty was supposed to be on our side.

"I'll be at the bar." I brushed past her and avoided making eye contact with anyone. If I didn't look at them, maybe they would leave me alone.

I managed to make it to the bar un-accosted. A bartender rushed straight over. "Nice set, man," he said.

"Thanks, can I get a Jack and Coke on the rocks?"

"Sure. Coming right up."

I felt Rafe before I saw him. "Come to bitch me out?" I drawled.

"Actually, I came to ask if there's anything I can do."

I leaned back against the bar, lifting my eyes to his. "You care now?"

"Shit, Levi. I always care. I'm just worried. Getting close to Phoebe is—"

"Don't, just don't."

A couple of people approached but I caught Stalter's eye and he intercepted them, giving me and Rafe privacy. This conversation, although I'd been hoping to avoid it, was long overdue.

"Talk to me, Levi. You never talk to me anymore."

"I like her. Is that what you want to hear?"

"You think I don't know that." He ran a hand through his hair as he exhaled a long breath. "But getting closer to her... if things don't work out—"

"Because I'll screw it up? That's what you mean, right?" Disappointment swelled in my chest. I knew I'd given him every right to think so poorly of me. Time and time again, I'd let him down. Let myself down. But Rafe was my brother. The one person who knew me better than anyone else in the world. Wasn't that supposed to count for something?

"That's not..." A heavy sigh escaped his lips. "There are a hundred reasons why it could go wrong."

"Jeez, thanks for the vote of confidence."

"Did you know her ex was an addict?" His expression softened.

"Yeah, I know." My jaw clenched, and I reached for my drink, downing it in one. I held the empty up to the bartender and he started making me another one.

Rafe eyed my fresh drink the second I picked it up. "You're drinking, why?"

My gaze darted from his scrutiny, immediately finding Phoebe in the crowd. She was in a small group of men and women, talking and laughing. But there was a guy standing a little too closely, his eyes flicking repeatedly to her tits.

Rafe noticed and gave me a sad smile. "It drives you crazy, doesn't it?"

"Yeah, I want to rip his fucking arm off." If he touched her one more time, there was every chance I would.

"Now you know how I felt." He pinned me with a hard look. Guilt flashed through me. I'd been a dick when Eva had first joined the tour. I hadn't exactly made a play for her, but I had made her a pawn in some twisted game to punish my brother.

To punish myself.

"I was an asshole."

"Yeah," he said. "You were. But it all worked out in the end. I got my girl."

"I'm happy for you both, ya know?" I didn't always show it, but I was. If anyone deserved a girl like Eva, it was Rafe.

"I know." His expression softened. "So, you really like her, huh? Do you think it could be... *more*?"

"Do you think I'm capable of more?" Because I sure as fuck wasn't... but I wanted it.

Damn, I wanted her.

In any and every way I could get her.

"It isn't for me to tell you what you're capable of, Levi."

"Could have fooled me," I grumbled, the burn of liquor in my veins not nearly enough to take the edge off. Flagging the bartender down again, I ordered a double.

"I'm just worried. We all are. When things are good, they're really good. But when things go bad—"

"If... *if* they go bad." Oh, who the fuck was I kidding? They would go bad.

They would go bad and it would be all my fault. Just like it always was. A flashback flickered through my mind.

"What the hell happened in here?" Mama yelled as she entered our small living room.

Rafe had found a marker pen and decided to decorate one of the walls. His dark swirls and circles looked were better than the peeling paper and black moldy patches, but Mom didn't look impressed. In fact, she looked livid.

"I..." He trembled, the pen hanging between his fingers.

"Levi! Explain yourself now." She scowled at me.

"Me? But I didn't—"

"He's just a child. He wouldn't do something so naughty if he didn't have you whispering in his ear all the time, would you, Raphael?"

"I- it was me, Mama," Rafe cried. "I did it. The walls look so tatty and I just thought—"

"Enough!" She grabbed my arm and yanked hard, so hard I was surprised my shoulder was still in its socket. "There'll be no tea for you tonight, Leviathan. Go to your room and think about your actions. Raphael is such a good boy, do you really want to infect him, ruin him with your evil ways?"

Rafe caught my eye and his bottom lip wobbled. I shook my head gently. Don't say anything else. There's no use in arguing with her. She could have caught him red-handed and it would still be my fault.

"Straight to your room and don't come out again until I tell you, do you understand?"

"Yes, Ma'am." I moved to the door, glancing back at the last second, wishing I hadn't when I found her consoling Rafe. Hugging him. Doting on him.

Loving him.

"Levi?" my brother's voice pulled me from the memory.

It was one of many. My childhood was steeped in memories of her favoring Rafe, loving him when she so vehemently hated me.

"I'm okay."

"You sure?" His eyes narrowed, searching mine for answers.

I managed a small nod.

"You're right, I'm sorry," he said. "But I'll always be your brother, Levi, your blood. And I'll always want to protect you. It's just who I am."

"Yeah, I know. It's why I love you so fucking —*motherfucker*." I shouldered past Rafe, storming toward Phoebe and the sleazy fucker touching her as if he had a God given right to put his hands on her.

"Levi," he called after me, but it was too late.

He was touching her—he was touching *my* girl.

"What the fuck—"

"Oh no, asshole," Hudson jumped in front of me. "I know I didn't watch you just put your hands on my girl."

"Y- your girl?" The guy stuttered, glancing between Phoebe and Hudson while I just stood there, wondering what the fuck was happening.

Hudson grabbed Phoebe's hand and pulled her into his side, slinging his arm around her shoulder. "She's with me. And I'm with the band so I'm thinking you need to take a hike."

Security had closed in around us, cutting us off from the rest of the crowd.

"Babe, wanna tell me what happened?" Hudson asked Phoebe. She gazed up at him with cloudy eyes. "I... he..."

"Now, now," the guy puffed his chest out, "let's not get carried away. I was merely asking the young lady if she wanted a drink."

He had to be pushing forty, sporting a round face and thick neck. My body vibrated with anger as I inched forward, but a heavy hand landed on my shoulder. "Relax, he's got this," Damon said.

Got this?

What the fuck was that supposed to mean?

The fucker was touching my girl and I'd been sidelined by... by Hudson of all fucking people.

Phoebe cast me a sidewards glance but quickly looked away.

"Landon, what the hell is going on?" Dowager pushed through the circle with Alistair trailing behind.

"It's a misunderstanding, Tim." The asshole paled. "A simple misunderstanding."

"Hudson?"

"Ask Phoebe..."

"Phoebe?"

"Mr. Milligan..." She took a deep breath, standing taller. "Asked me if I wanted a drink. When I said no, he grabbed my ass and told me to lighten up and enjoy myself."

I saw red.

In my mind's eye, I lunged forward and wrapped my hands around his fat neck and squeezed, but in reality, Damon and Rafe steered me away from the group and pushed me across the room. Nobody seemed to notice, too busy eyeing the drama.

"He fucking touched her," I snarled. "He fucking put his hands on my—"

"Ssh, before you turn this into something else entirely."

They crowded me toward the bar, flagging down the bartender. A couple of seconds later, Rafe handed me a glass of Jack and Coke.

"You think getting me lit is a good idea right now?"

"It's better than you going back over there. We still have to finish the set. Dowager is—"

"Dowager needs to fire that handsy son of a bitch. I mean it, Rafe. I want his ass nailed to the fucking wall for touching her."

"She's fine." He stepped aside. "See, Phoebe is fine."

Yeah, in the arms of another guy.

My fucking bandmate.

"Someone remind me why Hudson is over there right now, and I'm not?" I growled, my jaw clenched so tight it hurt.

I was her guy. *Me.* It was supposed to be me protecting her, me keeping guys like Milligan away.

Jealousy swarmed my chest, threatening to pull me under.

"He's protecting you... and her," Damon said, and my eyes snapped to his.

"What the fuck is that supposed to mean?"

He ran a hand over his face, glancing to Rafe, the two of them sharing a strange look. Then he said eight words that had me reeling.

"So funny story, uh... Alistair thinks Phoebe and Hudson are hooking up."

Everyone was staring at me. Alistair and Hudson. Tim Dowager. The slimeball that had slid his hand under my dress and grabbed my ass. We'd officially stopped the party, everyone eager to see what was happening.

Hudson stood firmly at my side, his arm still hooked around my shoulder. He made it seem so easy. I still couldn't quite believe what was happening.

I'd been groped by a colleague, and Hudson Ryker, constant pain in my ass and perpetual playboy, had jumped in to save me.

Dowager and Slimeball were arguing, while Alistair and Hudson tried to express their less than impressed opinions of the situation. A hand slid into mine and I found Letty's concerned gaze.

"He's with Rafe and Damon," she whispered. "They took him to the bar." Her head tipped toward the long sleek chrome bar running one length of the room. Sure enough, Levi stood there, staring right at me. I inhaled a shaky breath, trapped in his murderous gaze.

I could imagine the million and one scenarios running through his head and knew none of them would be good. Someone had touched me, put their hands on me without permission, and now Hudson was acting like I was his girl.

Jesus, I was surprised Levi had remained so calm.

"He knows he can't lose it, not here," Letty added.

"This is bad," I whisper-hissed, "really fucking bad."

"I know. Let me go talk to him. They need to finish the set. This is too important."

"I know, please tell him this,"—I glanced at Hudson's arm wrapped possessively around my shoulder—"means nothing."

"He's just protecting you both."

"Yeah, I know." I knew Hudson's dramatics were part of his strange attempt at protecting Levi from a) himself and b) outing our relationship. If Hudson took the fall, people would write it off as nothing more than a fling. But if people knew Levi Hunter was tangled up with a girl... it would become a media frenzy.

I felt Levi's hard gaze drilling holes into the side of my face, but I couldn't meet it, not when a group of men were standing around arguing over me like I was invisible.

"Stop," I said a little too forcefully. They all turned to look at me. "Mr. Mulligan has repeatedly said it was a misunderstanding so I would like that to be the end of it. The band has a set to finish and we're drawing a crowd."

"Very well," Dowager nodded but he didn't look too comfortable about the situation. "But we'll be talking about this first thing tomorrow, Landon. Alistair, if your men would like to escort him off the premises."

"Come on now, Tim, let's not—"

"Mr. Mulligan," Stalter said. "If you'd like to come with us please."

He scoffed as if the entire thing was ridiculous, shooting me an indignant look as he passed me.

"I'm real sorry about that, Miss—"

"Halstead."

He frowned. "Peter Halstead's daughter?"

Oh God. He knew my father?

Dread snaked through me. This could not be happening.

"Penelope?"

"Phoebe." I grimaced.

"Ah, yes, that's the one. I didn't realize you were working at the label."

"I'm just interning."

"No way, she's a crucial part of the team." Hudson grinned proudly, completely unaware that he was only making things worse, his arm still slung around my shoulder.

"And this." Dowager wagged his finger between the two of us. "Could it be the infamous playboy Hudson Ryker is finally off the market?"

"Okay, Tim," Alistair clapped him on the back, steering him away. "Why don't we go and get a drink before the band come back on."

"Drinks are on me," Hudson called to their retreating form

"Oh my god," I breathed. "He knows my father."

"And that's bad why?"

"Why?" I shrieked. "Because he has no idea I'm on tour with the band. And if Dowager tells him, he'll probably mention that you and I... oh fuck." I buried my face in my hands.

"Relax." Hudson finally released me, stepping back as if he'd finally realized we weren't together. People were still watching, eyeing us with mild curiosity.

God, what a disaster.

Dowager knew my father and now had the ammunition

to crack open the truth about my job at the label. If Alistair didn't believe there was something going on with Hudson and I before, he would now. And Levi... my poor broken Levi was staring at me with such hurt and betrayal in his eyes. I wanted to rush over to him and explain everything.

But the music cut, and the emcee's voice came over the mic. "Please welcome back on stage, Black Hearts Still Beat."

"I guess that's our queue," Hudson said over the raucous applause. "Listen, about what just happened... he'll understand. I was just protecting him."

"I know," I whispered, hugging myself tight.

As the guys climbed back on stage, Letty and Eva came and stood beside me. Eva laced her hand in mine, offering me a reassuring smile. But nothing could undo what had just happened.

I'd arrived at the club a no one, but I had a horrible feeling that everything had just changed. That by publicly defending me, Hudson had created a ripple that couldn't ever be undone.

———

BY THE TIME the band finished their set, my nerves were shot. Levi had delivered another note perfect performance, the duet with Eva a firm crowd favorite. But I saw the dark cloud circling him. He was pissed. Confused at being sidelined earlier. I knew Letty, Damon, and Rafe had all tried to talk to him, but I also knew his mind would be playing all kinds of tricks on him.

As they came off the stage, I hovered in the wings waiting for a chance to talk to Levi.

"Maybe this isn't a good time," Letty whispered, but I shrugged her off. I just needed a minute to reassure him, to let him know that everything was okay.

But Levi didn't stop for me. He brushed right past me as if I was nothing to him. As if I was completely invisible.

It hurt.

It hurt so fucking much, I felt like I'd had the wind knocked from my lungs.

Eva gave me a sympathetic smile. "He'll come around," she said, taking off after Rafe. I knew Dowager wanted to meet with the band and celebrate their new partnership. There would be photos and drinks. And then Letty had arranged for the band to make a sharp exit due to their tour commitments.

I didn't want to wait until we left. I needed to make him understand *now*.

Steeling my spine, I approached Levi at the bar. He looked right through me, sending a shudder through me. "Can we talk a second?"

"I don't think now is a good time," he deadpanned. No emotion. No anger.

Nothing.

"Levi, please." I stepped closer, careful not to get too close. The party was in full swing now, the dance floor a sea of bodies all drinking and dancing.

"If you don't want me to fuck everything up," he finally met my eyes, contempt burning in his depths, "I suggest you get the fuck out of my way."

"Levi, please—"

"Yo, man." Hudson appeared, instantly grinding to a halt when he saw us locked in some kind of stare off. "Is everything okay here?"

"You tell me?" Levi gritted out.

"Relax, bro. I got your back." Hudson nudged his shoulder. "No one is any the wiser about... well, you know. Come on, Dowager wants us over in the VIP section. Pheebs." He gave me a wolfish grin before tapping Levi's chest and dragging him away.

I spun around and ordered a drink. Letty found me midway through downing the sugary sweet cocktail.

"That bad, huh?"

"He wouldn't even look at me."

"Levi is... complicated."

"I know that," I sighed, the weight of the night's events pressing down on my chest, "but surely he doesn't really think that me and Hudson..."

"Deep down he knows it. But the mind is a dangerous thing."

"So, what do I do?"

"Wait it out, I guess. This is new territory for us. Levi has never... aaand I'm giving away all his secrets."

"Are you saying there's never been another girl?" I mean, I knew there had never been a leading lady in his life as far as the press was concerned. But still. It was hard to believe he was a twenty-one-year-old guy and there had never been anyone else.

"Except Eva, and that wasn't like what the two of you share at all."

Weirdly, I didn't get jealous hearing Eva's name come up. I was glad that Levi had her. She was different to most people. Kind and compassionate and understanding. Levi needed people like that in his life.

Letty and I stood by the bar sipping our cocktails. Aside from Dowager meeting with the band, the party morphed from a networking event to a crowd of people all looking to let loose and enjoy the free bar. I watched groups of scantily clad women dance, men stalking them from the sidelines, weighing up when to make their move. Past the dance floor, I could just make out the VIP section. Dowager was seated right in the middle of the band, his expression animated, and hands exaggerated as he told them his story. He beckoned for something and a group of girls were called past the rope dividing their section with the rest of us.

"Oh, shit," Letty breathed as I watched the girls all pick a guy and sidle up beside them. Except Rafe because Eva was plastered to his side like armor.

"Uh, Letty, what is happening right now?"

Dowager had just dismissed one of his employees for groping me, but he was proffering the guys with half-naked women. Talk about double standards.

"It's a man's world, girl," she scoffed.

My eyes almost bugged out of my head when Levi hooked his arm around a slim blonde's waist and pulled her down on his lap. I saw the flash of triumph in her eyes, the blatant hunger as she slid an arm around his neck and sat there like a queen atop of her throne.

"It's acceptable to drink more, right?" The knot in my stomach twisted violently.

"I swear sometimes," Letty groaned, "he's like a child."

"Yeah, well, I'm not looking to play games."

"I'm not sure he knows how to *not* play them. It just what he does. Oh shit." She spun around and faced the bar. "See that guy coming over here."

"Eyebrow piercing with all the tats?"

"That's the one. I need you to get rid of him."

"Me, but why—"

"Hey, Letty," he said, reaching us. She ignored him. His gaze flicked to mine, and I smiled.

"I'm sorry, Letty is unavailable right now."

He snorted, running a hand over his faux hawk. "She's standing right there."

"I know, but she's still unavailable."

"I see." His teeth ground together. "I'm Miller."

"Phoebe."

"You're with the band?"

"I'm with the label, yes."

"Cool. I'm an exec with Dream Sounds. The band killed it tonight. Especially, *Drown*. That has number one hit written all over it."

"We're hoping it'll go all the way to the top."

Well, this was bizarre. Standing here talking to Letty's friend while she pretended he didn't exist.

His eyes flicked to Letty again and he released a frustrated breath. "Well, it was nice meeting you, Phoebe. Tell Letty I said when she's ready to grow some balls and hear me out, I'll be waiting." He gave me a stiff nod before jamming his hands in his pockets and walking away.

"Ugh, I can't believe he's here." She peeked up at me.

"Want to talk about it?"

"No." She grimaced. "I really don't. Ready to call it a night?"

"But don't we have to—" My eyes found Levi again across the room. He still had the blonde in his lap, his hand curved around her waist.

Damn you, Levi Hunter.

I swallowed the ball of emotion clogging my throat.

"I'll go see if they're almost done." I didn't like the pity in Letty's eyes, as if she already knew the outcome. "And then we can get out of here, okay?"

"Yeah." After the events of the night, I was more than ready to leave.

Letty downed the rest of her drink and marched over to the VIP area. Security let her past and she stood over the group. Part of me wanted them all to get up and follow her out, but I knew they wouldn't.

When she returned, she schooled her disappointment, flashing me a warm smile. But it did nothing for chill running through me.

"Come on, girl," she grabbed my hand. "Let's get out of here."

LEVI

Letty loomed down over us, giving me a disapproving look. The blonde was oblivious, running her hand up and down my bare chest. Her touch was all wrong though. Like sandpaper on glass. But I was too wasted to care. I hadn't intended on getting drunk, not until I'd seen Hudson jump in and protect my girl.

My girl?

Was she even my fucking girl after tonight? Alistair thought she was hooking up with Hudson... Hudson of all fucking people. Rafe and Damon had tried to reason with me, tried to tell me it was for my own good. But the little voice in my head wouldn't stop taunting me.

She wants him.

She wants him.

She wants him.

By the time I stepped down off the stage, my mind was swimming with a lethal mix of anger and liquor. It hummed through me, a bittersweet symphony luring me toward the darkness.

Phoebe had tried to talk to me, but I couldn't even look at her without seeing Hudson holding her, defending her. So I'd done the only thing I knew to stop myself from doing something I'd later regret—I'd headed straight for the bar and downed two more doubles.

By the time Dowager requested our presence, my eyes were blurry, and my head rolled slightly on my shoulders as I tried to listen to what the fuck he was saying.

He sure knew how to keep his guests entertained though. An open bar. Girls on tap. What more could a guy want?

Her. You want her.

"God, you're so hot," Blondie leaned in, letting her hand trail awfully near my dick. Only, it wasn't interested, shriveling inside itself.

"We're leaving," Letty said a little louder than necessary. "The cars are on standby. Should I have them—"

"Actually, Letty," Alistair jumped in. "I think we're going to stay a little longer, celebrate." He slid his hand up the cute brunette's thigh. She leaned into him, whispering something.

I didn't blame him. Riley hadn't only screwed me and the band over, she'd screwed him over too. We all knew they were banging, and rumor around the crew was that Alistair wanted more. It had to have hurt finding out she was a traitorous bitch only out to line her pockets and progress her career.

After everything that had happened, I was surprised he could even be in the same room as me, but that was Alistair, as professional and courteous as ever.

"Excellent choice, Ali." Dowager lifted his glass. "To new partnerships."

"You sure you want to stay?" I heard my brother ask Eva.

"I don't know... should we? I don't want Dowager to think we're being rude."

"Stay," I slurred. "Eat, drink, and be fucking merry."

"You need to relax." He glared at me.

No, what I needed was her.

Phoebe.

My honeybee.

But everything was spinning and when I looked over at Letty to tell her that maybe I was ready to go after all, she was gone.

Fuck.

"Here, Levi. Drink this, it's sooo good." The blonde licked her lips, bringing her glass to my lips. It was some fizzy cocktail, all sugary sweetness.

"Will it make everything disappear?" I asked her.

"It'll make you feel like you're flying," she winked, pushing it to my lips. I opened my mouth letting her feed me the drink until I'd drained the glass empty.

"I heard you like a good time." Her fingers scraped my jaw as she ghosted her lips over mine. "Well, this will blow your fucking mind."

The words spun around in my head as she smirked at me.

"What the—" I pushed her off me and she stumbled off my lap, sending glasses spilling everywhere.

"Levi?" Rafe leaped up.

"I need to go." I clambered to my feet, my muscles already heavy like lead.

"You keep making good music, son," Dowager's voice sounded stretched out and wrong.

"Levi?" Johnson discreetly grabbed my arm, guiding me away from the crowds.

"I think... she... fuck." My head began to spin.

"Levi?" Rafe caught up to me. "What's wrong?"

"I think she laced my drink."

"What the fuck?"

"I need to get back to the hotel." Before the effects of whatever she slipped me—most probably G—kicked in.

"Have the girls already left?" Rafe asked Johnson.

He touched his earpiece and said, "They're just about to leave. If we're quick, we can make it."

"Rafe," Eva called.

"Go get her" I said, my face growing numb. "We'll wait for you."

"Levi?" Letty gawked at me as Johnson pushed me inside. I stumbled onto the long leather bench.

"Some fucking bitch laced my drink."

"WHAT?" she shrieked.

I nodded, leaning my head back and closing my eyes.

"Blondie?" Phoebe asked and I nodded again, not bothering to look at her.

I didn't want to see the disappointment. Not when I could feel it heavy in the air the second I'd climbed into the SUV.

"What was it?" Letty asked.

"Probably G."

"Fuck," she hissed. "That's messed up."

"She probably thought she was doing me a favor."

"Here." Phoebe pressed a cold bottle of water into my hand, and I finally dropped my eyes to hers.

"Thanks. But it won't stop the high."

"I know." Sadness seeped into her expression. "But it'll keep you hydrated."

"Listen, honeybee, I—"

The doors opened again and Rafe and Eva piled inside.

"Alistair and the others are staying behind to deal with Dowager and the girl." My brother gave me a small nod. "We got you," he said.

"Don't fret, brother, being roofied feels damn amazing so far."

As the minutes ticked by, I couldn't feel my face, and my body started to grow hot all over. But damn, whatever it was she had slipped me was some good shit. I felt weightless, my skin buzzing with sensation.

"Isn't there anything we can do?" Eva's voice sounded all funny, like she was underwater.

"Not really. He just needs to wait for it to wear off."

"Which could take how long exactly?"

"A few hours or until he passes out."

That was Phoebe, I'd know her voice anywhere.

Someone snickered. At least, I think they did as I started to sink deeper into a warm blissed out state of mind.

"Levi," a little voice whispered. But not *her* voice. No, this voice was soft and kind. This voice made me want crawl out of the darkness and embrace the light. "Try and stay with us."

Something soft brushed my hand and I moaned. Fuck, that felt good.

"Do it again," I rasped, willing my eyes to focus. Phoebe's face filled my blurry vision. "Hey, Bee."

"Hey, Levi." She gave me a smile, but it was all sad and defeated.

"What's wrong, baby girl?" I said, reaching for her cheek, brushing my fingers back and forth. Phoebe let out a heavy sigh, gently pulling my hand away from her skin.

"We're almost at the hotel."

"We are?" I tried to sit up, my body swaying. Phoebe shuffled closer, pressing her arm closer to mine. "God, I want to fuck you, honeybee. I want to bury myself so deep inside you, you can't ever make me leave." I leaned in, running my nose along her jaw, smelling her. "Fuck, you smell good."

"Levi." Phoebe tried to push me away, but I was a dead weight against her.

"Don't ever leave," I whispered. "Everyone always leaves—"

The car lurched to a stop and the doors all opened. "He might need some help," someone said, and then hands were grabbing me, helping me from the SUV.

"I can fucking stand." I shirked the hulk of a guy off.

"Bee." I searched the underground parking lot for her. When I couldn't see her, panic coursed through my veins. "BEE?"

"I'm right here." She appeared at my side.

"Thank fuck." I grabbed her hand, lacing our fingers together. "I thought you'd left me."

"I didn't go anywhere."

We followed security toward the elevator.

"Someone's going to need to watch him tonight," she said.

"I'll do it," Rafe said. My brother. My protector. Even now, when he hated me, he still found a way to keep me safe. I owed him. I owed him so fucking much.

"Love you, man," I said, my tongue like cotton in my mouth.

Someone chuckled, but it was hard to focus. Everything —the strip-lighting, the motion of the elevator, the scent of Phoebe's perfume—called to my senses, the overstimulation a potent rush through my veins.

Phoebe's fingers brushed my hand, sending little shocks of electricity zipping up my arm. I wanted her to rub herself all over my body, to light me up from the inside out. If I could just keep my fucking head upright for more than a second.

"Jesus, he's a mess."

Somebody, Phoebe I think, pulled me out of the elevator and along the hall.

"You smell so good." I nuzzled her neck and we both stumbled against the wall.

"Levi, stop." She held me at arm's length, brushing the hair from my eyes. "You need to sleep it off."

"Stay with me." I grinned, my jaw slack and heavy.

"I don't think that's a good idea."

"Please, Bee, I need you."

Her brows pinched together.

"I'll beg. Don't make me beg."

"Fine. Just for a little while."

"Yes," I punched the air. "She loves me. Honeybee still loves me."

Phoebe sucked in a harsh breath, watching me with a cloudy expression. Or maybe that was my eyes that made her seem cloudy.

It didn't fucking matter though because my Bee was here... and she was staying.

———

"LEVI, JUST STOP, MAN." Rafe tried to wrestle the cell phone out of my hand.

"Just one more." I scrolled through the playlist, no fucking clue what I was searching for. All I knew was we needed something with a heavy beat.

"Let me try." Phoebe appeared.

"Bee, get over here." I grabbed her hand and yanked her toward me. "Let's dance."

"It's late, Levi. We need to get some rest."

"Just one more song." I spun her around so her back was pressed against my chest and tucked my chin into her shoulder. "I love this one."

"You love *Yellow Submarine* by The Beatles?" She snorted.

I hugged her tighter. I wanted her naked. To feel her skin pressed close to mine. I was already shirtless, my body temperature too warm for clothes.

"Go," she said, and I realized Rafe and Eva were still here, watching me with concerned expressions.

"You can go," I added. "Bee will look after me. Won't you, baby girl?"

"We'll be close if you need us," Rafe said, ignoring me.

"I can handle him."

"Of course you can handle me." I brushed my lips over her neck, loving the way she tasted on my tongue. My hands splayed on her stomach, desperate to feel her skin.

"Levi," she said. "I don't think that's—"

"Ssh. I need you Bee, I need you so fucking much." If I didn't get to sink inside her soon, I would die a slow painful death, burning up from the inside out. "Let's go to our bedroom."

"You're high." Her tone grew irritated.

"And you're fucking delicious." I licked and nipped her skin. I needed to look up the girl from the club and send her a thank you note because whatever she'd slipped in my drink was fucking magic. I felt amazing. Endorphins raced through me, making me feel like I could fly.

"Levi, stop... *stop*." Phoebe tried to untangle herself from my arms, but I spun us around and started walking her toward my bedroom. I needed her underneath me, naked and waiting, her perfect fucking curves on full display. Her ink and piercings and smooth as silk skin.

We stumbled through the door, and Phoebe managed to slip free of my hold. The soft *thunk* of the door closing behind us echoed through my chest as I watched her inch back.

"Don't play hard to get, Bee. You know this only ends one of two ways." I toyed with my lip piercings.

"You're high. Tomorrow you won't remember any of this."

I prowled toward her. My hands were already at my jeans, unsnapping my belt and pushing them off my hips. My dick was rock hard, desperate for her.

Starved for her.

"Skin like silk, eyes like honey, this girl will rip out your heart before you can blink," I murmured the lyrics as I crowded her against the wall. Phoebe's eyes were wide as I leaned in and kissed the corner of her mouth.

"I need inside you, baby girl."

"Don't... don't call me that." Her eyes fluttered closed as she inhaled in a sharp breath. "I'm not one of them, Levi. I'm not one of your groupie whores."

"No." I slid my hand to her throat. "You are so much more. My girl. My honeybee. My love." Her body went rigid. "Does that scare you, Bee? To know that I love you? Because I do, you know. I am hopelessly and obsessively in love with you. And now I've told you, you can't ever leave me."

"Oh, Levi," she whispered, staring right into my black soul. "What am I going to do with you?"

DEEP DOWN, every girl wanted those three little words. They were magical, seductive, and comforting. But I didn't want them like this, *never* like this.

Levi was high. Off his face on liquor and GHB. All because a girl—some deceptive little bitch—had spiked his drink to get her shot with the rock star. The thought made me sick to my stomach. It made me want to go back to the club and hunt her down. But Levi needed me here.

"Did you hear me, Bee? I fucking love you."

God, I wanted to believe him. I wanted to latch onto those words and never let go. But he didn't have a clue about what he was saying.

I knew enough about GHB to know that the right dose could make someone feel euphoric and extremely turned on. It wasn't Zephyr's poison of choice, but he'd taken it a couple of times at parties and it always ended in us fighting because he couldn't keep his hands to himself. Once, I'd found him about to get his dick sucked by some skank in a bathroom. He'd been so fucking high, he thought it was me.

Pain stabbed through me. God, I'd put up with some crap, all because I was a girl in love with a guy who loved getting high.

I'd watched Zephyr pass out, have seizures, foam at the mouth, and be carted off by an ambulance more times that I could count. Being with an addict was like being the mistress in a relationship. Because their one true love would always be chasing the high.

When I'd finally walked away from him, I'd vowed never to find myself in the same situation.

Yet, here I was. In so deep with Levi Hunter, I didn't know which way was up.

But there was something different about Levi. He didn't get high to feel good or party all night or because he could. He did it to escape his monsters.

He did it to survive.

It didn't make it any better or easier or safer... but it did go some way to explaining his addiction.

And tonight, he hadn't let himself fall into the darkness. He'd immediately removed himself from all temptation.

That had to count for something, didn't it?

"Bee, I need you." He kissed me again, just a faint brush of his lips against mine. His fingers stroked my throat, tender and teasing.

"Levi, we shouldn't—"

Resistance was futile. Levi was too high to hear the word no. Too overpowered by the chemicals coursing through his system.

"You make it all quiet, Bee. You settle my soul." His intense gaze burned into mine. His pupils were blown, the heat rolling off him in powerful waves.

"You won't remember this in the morning," I said around a sad smile.

"Wrong." He shook his head. "I remember everything about you, honeybee. I remember the way you cry my name. How hot and tight you feel as I slide inside you. I remember how sweet you taste... I'll remember, Bee. Because you're already in here." He tapped his temple.

My eyes fluttered shut, overwhelmed at his words, the situation. Levi was starved of affection. He'd never been given the unconditional love of a mother. Those early attachment bonds had never settled into place, and now his emotions were all confused, his wiring all wrong.

But when I opened my eyes and saw him watching me, I felt it. I felt his love for me punch me right in the gut.

"Levi, I—"

His mouth crashed down on mine, stealing the air from my lungs and all rational thought from my brain. His touch was desperate, needy and feral. His fingers touched and pressed and grabbed, as if he might never get this feeling again and wanted to cling onto it for as long as possible.

"Fuck, Bee, you're so fucking sexy, I can't get enough of you." His words were slurred, low and rough. He peppered my face with kisses. Hot, wet, clumsy kisses that left me breathless and wanting.

My head was screaming at me to stop him, to take the high road and stop this madness. But my body was a tight ball of sensation, all too happy to drown in his touch; and my heart, my heart was a runaway train heading straight for disaster.

"Off." He grunted, clawing at my dress. "This needs to come off." We barely broke the kiss so he could peel my dress over my head. My hands pushed his jeans down over his hips, my fingertips grazing his hardness.

"Fuuuuck, Bee. I need inside you, I can't wait. I swear to fucking God I'll die if I don't get inside you in the next two seconds." Levi grabbed my panties and tore them clean off my body before picking me up and pressing me against the nearest wall. He didn't even give me warning, just sank inside me. I whimpered, scratching my nails over his shoulders. It was too much. His touch. His punishing rhythm. The way he knew exactly how to play my body to make me cry his name.

His mouth dropped to my collarbone, sucking and kissing the skin there, leaving a trail of hickeys I knew I would regret tomorrow. But I couldn't stop myself.

I couldn't stop him.

The innate part of me that wanted to fix him, wanted him to take whatever he needed from me. If it wasn't me, I knew he'd probably have found another girl to lose himself in tonight. Maybe the blonde from the club, maybe some other girl who only wanted her one night with a rock star. Or maybe he would have continued drinking, taking more drugs, until he passed out... or worse.

A shiver ran through me, and I pulled Levi closer into my body. He walked such a dangerous tightrope, all recovering addicts did.

"Levi, it's... God..." I cried as he continued fucking me against the wall. His eyes were black, his body coated in sweat. It was like he was possessed, lost to the euphoria and soul-crushing hunger.

"I need more, Bee... I need..." He buried his face in the crook of my neck, his body trembling.

Panic rose inside me. "Levi?" I tried to nudge him back. "Levi."

"I'm okay," he murmured. "I just need..."

"Lay me down," I said, softly.

He stilled, inhaling a harsh breath. Cradling me against his body, Levi carried me to the bed and lay me down. He stood there, looming over me, his dark eyes trailing a blazing path over my body as he stroked himself.

Levi's knee landed on the bed and he crawled over me, kissing up my body as he went. He stared down at me. "Promise me, Bee. Promise me that you'll never leave me."

"Levi, I..." The words were right there, on the tip of my tongue, but I couldn't do it.

"Say it." He kissed me hard and deep, letting his tongue plunder my mouth, as he rocked slowly into me. We both groaned, the connection so powerful, it swept us in its devastation.

Desperate hands grabbed my thighs, spreading me wide as he went harder... *deeper*, trying to reach inside me and leave a mark. "Say it, Bee. Fucking say it." His words were thick, drowsy, as he continued driving inside me.

My legs ached, my body lax and pliant beneath him. But he didn't stop. He didn't stop after I clenched around him, crying out his name over and over. He kept going, chasing the high. The fall. The bittersweet climax.

Eventually, Levi let out a guttural roar, jerking inside me. His body collapsed on top of me, rolling to the side. "Fuck, baby girl," he crooned, slipping into unconsciousness. "That was... fuck."

My eyes stung with tears. He didn't know it was me anymore. I could have been any girl, any body, warm, wet, and willing.

I slipped out of bed and hurried into the bathroom to clean up. I was a mess, covered in bite marks and bruises. After I was done, I wrapped myself in a fluffy hotel robe, got a glass of water and went back into the bedroom. Levi was out cold. I rolled him into the recovery position, checked his breathing, and placed the glass of water on the side. Then I curled up in the chair and watched him sleep, knowing that tonight, I would get none.

———

"Phoebe, wake up."

My eyes flew open to find Levi frowning at me. "What are you—"

His eyes narrowed, homing in on my collarbone where the robe had fallen open. "What happened?" he gritted out.

I uncurled my legs and sat up, taming my hair over one shoulder. "You don't remember?"

"Would I be asking if I did?" I flinched at his harsh tone, and he let out a weary sigh. "Shit, I'm sorry, I just... I wake up with no memory of how I got here and you're asleep in the fucking chair... And then I see your skin covered in bruises and bite marks..."

"Someone laced your drink."

"What the fuck?" He barked again, but this time, I expected it.

"At the club. You don't remem—"

"There was a girl." His brows furrowed. "A blonde."

Fuck. It hurt to hear him talk about her.

"She slipped something in my drink?"

I nodded. "We think it was GHB. You were very... *happy*."

"I know what G does, Bee. Fuck. I don't remember. Did I... hurt you?"

I schooled my expression, locked it down tight. He

couldn't know the truth. If he did, he would lose his shaky thread of control.

"You were horny, Levi. Things got a little... wild."

"You let me... while I was high on G?"

I shrugged, my eyes darting to the floor. He kneeled in front of me, sliding his fingers under my chin and forcing me to look at him. "Tell me what happened."

"You were pissed, at me and Hudson—"

"Not that part, I remember that part." Anger flared in his eyes. "After the girl. I can vaguely remember leaving the club. You were there. Rafe and Eva too?"

I nodded again. "You knew immediately that she'd given you something. You wanted to leave before you..." I skimmed over that part. "We all rode back here together. Rafe wanted to look after you but you were getting really worked up."

"Fuck... they saw me like that?"

Another nod. "You were pretty clingy."

"I didn't say anything, did I?"

"Just the usual high off your face bullshit."

He didn't remember.

Levi didn't remember confessing how he felt about me. Or at least, how he felt about me at that precise moment.

A small dose of GHB was apparently a lot like an MDMA high. The increased levels of serotonin and dopamine had tricked Levi, messed with his emotions. Made him think things that weren't real.

My stomach sank.

"I agreed to watch you."

"That's why you were in the chair?" His thumb brushed my jaw making me shiver. "After we..."

"We had sex, yeah."

"Shit, Bee, I'm sorry. I'm sorry you had to see me... like that." Levi leaned back, rubbing a hand over his jaw.

"I'm just glad you're okay." It was the truth. Last night could have ended so differently. "You know, this thing with Hudson... he was only trying to protect you. To protect us. If Alistair finds out—"

"I know, I fucking know, okay?" Frustration drenched his words. "I watched you working the room, talking to all those guys—"

"Levi, it's my job. I was networking."

"I know that, I do. But my brain," he jammed his fingers into his hair and yanked the ends, "my brain gets it wrong sometimes. And then that fat fuck put his hands on you, and I wanted to tear him limb from limb, Bee..." Levi glanced away. "But Hudson leaped in like your knight-in-shining armor or some shit."

"He didn't want you to do something you'd regret. He was protecting you."

"I know that now." Lifting his gaze, he pinned me with a dark look. "But it doesn't change the fact that I want to be the one to stand by your side. I want to fight your battles. Me, honeybee. *Me.*"

The vulnerability in Levi's voice gutted me. Without thinking, I slid off the tub chair and threw my arms around his neck, holding him tight. He was such a contradiction. Cold yet warm. Hard but soft. Levi was like a man-child finding his own way in the world. Learning as he went.

Making mistake after mistake and not seeing where to put them right until someone intervened. He needed guidance. He needed love and affection and patience. But he also needed space and independence. He needed to feel secure without feeling stifled.

It was a delicate balance to find.

"What happens now?" he whispered shakily.

"I don't know, Levi. You tell me."

"Don't leave me, Bee." He pulled back to stare me dead in the eyes. "Promise me you won't leave me."

I COULDN'T STOP WATCHING her, wishing I knew Phoebe's deepest, darkest thoughts. Her desires. Her hopes and fucking dreams.

I wanted to remember last night, to remember what I said and what I did. The bruises and love bites all over her body were a pretty good indication, but it didn't dampen my need to know.

That was the thing about getting high; the buzz was incredible. For those few minutes or hours, the rush was everything. But the come down was usually pretty grim.

I felt okay, a little hungover, restless and thirsty. But I wasn't worried about me, I was worried about the quiet girl beside me.

After our conversation, after me getting on my knees and begging her not to leave me, Phoebe had kissed me on the cheek, and then gone for a shower. Now we were in the living room with Rafe and Eva, waiting for everyone else to join us for breakfast.

And she wouldn't look at me.

I reached for her hand, tangling our fingers together and pulling them into my lap. Phoebe finally flicked her eyes to mine, dropping them to our joined hands and back again. The faint smile tugging at her mouth wasn't nearly enough, but it was something.

Bedroom doors started opening, and Damon then Hudson padded into the living room.

"Morning," Hudson said around a huge yawn. "I see all's

well in loveville." His eyes went to where I was clutching Phoebe's hand.

"Hud," Damon warned. "Ali and Letty?" he asked.

"Will be here soon," Rafe replied.

"What's good?" Hudson eyed the counter full of pastries and fruit, pancakes and waffles. I'd barely eaten a thing, but I'd watched Phoebe devour a bowl of fruit salad with Greek yoghurt and an almond croissant.

"Since when did you get choosy about food?" Damon snickered, and Hud flipped him off.

They joined us and the six of us sat in thick silence, until Hudson said, "So are we going to take about the fucking shitshow that was last night, or what?"

Phoebe shifted uncomfortably beside me, but I wouldn't let her pull away from me. Not now. Not with my bandmates looking at me like I held all the answers.

"Where should we start?" Damon said calmly. He was the peacekeeper. The caretaker. The one we could always count on to be the voice of reason.

Rafe let out a heavy sigh, dragging a hand down his face. "At least the set was tight."

"Did you just make a joke?" I quipped.

The corner of his mouth lifted in an uncertain smirk, some of the cracks in our relationship smoothing out.

"Maybe we should wait for—"

Letty appeared, Alistair trailing behind. He looked a little worse for wear. At the sight of him, Phoebe snatched her hand free and tucked it into her side.

It fucking stung.

"Coffee, please tell me there's coffee." Alistair made a beeline for the coffee maker.

"Rough night, Ali boy? You and the brunette seemed pretty cozy on the ride back to the hotel."

"Hudson." Damon shook his head.

"Yes, well, I didn't come here to discuss my private life..." Heat crept into his cheeks.

"Are you... *blushing?*" I couldn't resist teasing him. Alistair generally had a stick the size of Tennessee up his ass. It wouldn't hurt him to let loose occasionally. Especially after Riley's betrayal.

"You're okay?" Letty asked me.

"I feel fine."

"Do you want to press charges?"

"No." I leaned back.

"Levi," Phoebe gasped. "She laced your drink with GHB. You could have—"

"Relax, Bee. It isn't the first time, and it won't be the last. I'm fine." Besides, I didn't want the headache of talking to the police and all that bullshit.

Her eyes drilled holes into the side of my face, but I didn't meet her lethal gaze. This wasn't a big deal. If I didn't care so fucking much about Phoebe, if I didn't want to be better for the band and the label... then last night would have gone a whole lot different. I would have accepted that drink, tongue fucked the blonde until she was dry-humping my leg, and then dragged her to the bathroom and given her what she wanted.

But I hadn't.

Because deep down, I didn't want to be that guy anymore.

What I wanted and what I needed didn't always marry up though.

"We got her details. She'll be blacklisted from all future events."

"Fine by me," I said. "I'm more interested in the fucker who put his hands on Phoebe."

Her breath caught, and Eva gasped.

Alistair frowned, rubbing his temples. "Yes, well, Dowager has assured me Mr. Milligan will be dealt with."

"Fired. I want him fired."

"Levi," someone scolded, but I was too far gone to recognize who.

"I realize Phoebe is a part of this team and that she and Hudson—"

Without thinking I snatched her hand and threaded our fingers together. "Not her and Hudson, Ali."

"Oh, shit..." That was Hudson. Rafe and Damon groaned, while Letty gave me a nod of approval.

She got it.

Maybe she always had.

"Wait a minute, what are you saying? Phoebe?" Alistair's confused stare moved to the frozen girl beside me.

"It's going to be okay, Bee," I whispered. "Just take a leap of faith with me."

Her eyes flickered to mine. She was pissed. Golden flecks burning deep in her honey eyes. But she didn't pull her hand away.

"I'm not hooking up with Hudson, Alistair," she said.

"You mean you and... *Levi?*" He leaped up. "Great. This is just great."

"Whoa, Ali, boy," Hudson stood too. "Relax."

"Let me guess. You all knew?"

Silence.

Deafening heavy silence.

"Fuck," he breathed. I don't think I'd ever seen him so angry.

Alistair didn't get angry, he got quiet and contemplative.

"It was gonna happen eventually." Everyone glanced at Hudson. "Maybe not Eva or Pheebs, but one day he would have found someone to put up with his bullshit."

"Cheers, man," I grunted.

"You're welcome."

"The label has rules for a reason," Alistair let out an exasperated breath. "Phoebe can't do her job effectively if she's—"

"I'll ask to be taken off the tour."

"What?" I tore my hand out of hers. "No way, no fucking way."

"Levi, relax," Rafe said. "No one is saying Phoebe has to leave. Are they, Ali?"

His jaw clenched and I could see his irritation at being backed into a corner. "We have less than a month until we leave for Europe. One month. I don't want even a sniff of this," he wagged his finger between the two of us, "going public. Understood?"

I nodded, risking a peek at Phoebe. Her face was pale, but she managed to choke out, "Understood."

"For now, if people get wind of anything, it'll be that you

and a Hudson are... well, whatever it is that Hudson does to women to get them into his bed."

"Oh, wouldn't you like to know." He smirked.

"That's bullshit," I said, feeling anger zip up my spine. "Phoebe's mine. I'm not going to let people think—"

"Yes, you fucking are, Levi. Because this band, believe it or not, is bigger than just you. People are counting on you, fans are counting on you. If this hits the press, it will create another storm we don't need."

"I—"

"Levi." Phoebe's voice demanded my attention. She shook her head gently, squeezing my hand.

"This stays between us," Alistair seethed. "I don't care what you two do behind closed doors, but the second you step outside, it stops, okay?"

"We understand", she whispered, cracking my heart clean in two.

I didn't fucking understand.

I wasn't a child. I was a grown man for fuck's sake. If I wanted to kiss my girl in public, I would kiss her in fucking public.

But somewhere in the back of my mind, buried underneath all the anger and resentment was a shred of rationality. Everything with Phoebe was still so new and uncertain. Sharing her with the world too soon could ruin everything before it even had chance to get started.

"Levi, I need to hear you say it," Alistair said.

"I understand," I mumbled.

The tension in the room seemed to lift. He marched out of the suite, taking some of the heavy mood with him.

"That went well." Hudson dropped down on the couch.

"He'll come around," Letty said. "It just caught him off guard."

"So what's the plan?"

"Plan?" Damon frowned at Hudson.

"Well yeah, you heard Ali. Everyone needs to believe she's hooking up with m—"

"Hudson!" Everyone yelled. Except me and Phoebe. She was watching me, her lips pressed together, keeping in whatever secrets she didn't want to tell me.

Maybe she was already regretting standing by my side.

Maybe she wanted to take it all back.

But it was too late now.

I wouldn't let her.

Phoebe was mine...

And I was never letting her go.

———

"THERE'S AN ARTICLE," Letty announced as the second bus began to roll out of Portland.

We'd all crammed on the Van Hool for the five-hour ride to Spokane.

"About me and Hudson?" Phoebe tensed beside me.

She'd been quiet since breakfast. We'd had an impromptu brunch with Dowager. He'd wanted to apologize, and personally reassure us that Milligan would be dealt with.

"It's only an online blogger connecting dots. Their *source* said they saw you and Hud looking pretty cozy last night."

My fist clenched... jealousy sweeping through me. But I

forced myself to breathe. This was the plan. Let people think Phoebe was his. Because Hudson didn't date. He didn't ever get caught with the same girl twice. Besides, as Letty had pointed out, Hudson had that way with women. He flirted, was touchy feely, a real charmer. He could have been jumping in to defend Phoebe because she was our assistant. Because he cared. Not because they were fucking.

"Let them talk. It's nothing that hasn't been spewed across the media a hundred times before. We don't mind being famous." He grabbed his junk, and the girls all muttered their disapproval.

"You know Molly will never want—"

"Don't," Hudson growled, his whole demeanor shifting. Molly was a sore subject. His Achilles heel, not that he'd ever admit it.

Damon stood up. "You need to man the hell up and admit you want her, before it's too late". He stomped off down the bus and disappeared into the bathroom.

"What the hell crawled up his ass and died?"

"It's his mom," Rafe said.

"Oh, fuck. Fuck." Hudson's expression softened.

"Yeah."

"I need to lie down." My head was pounding from all the talking and thinking. "Bee?"

"It's the middle of the day." Phoebe's brows knitted with concern.

"So? We're rock stars. If we want to sleep all day and party all night, that's our prerogative." It was supposed to be a joke, but she didn't laugh. In fact, she didn't smile at all.

"Please." I pouted, giving zero fucks that my brother and his girl, Hudson, and Letty were watching our interaction.

"Fine, fine." She gave me a small nod. "I'm just going to get a glass of water and I'll be there, okay?"

"Don't make me wait too long." I leaned in, brushing my lips over her cheek. I could feel myself crashing. Maybe it was the prolonged come down from the G, or maybe it was the fact I was bone-weary, but I needed to close my eyes for a second and just breathe.

"Go," she said, when I didn't move. "I'll be right there."

"Promise?" I whispered.

Phoebe smiled, the small action settling something inside me. "Promise."

I LET OUT a weary sigh as we watched Levi walk away and disappear into the bedroom at the end of the bus.

"You good?" Rafe asked me. My brows went up and he chuckled. "I think I owe you an apology."

"You don't—"

"Yeah, I do. I was a dick. But he's my brother and he's just so... so fucking complicated. This, the two of you... I won't lie, it scares me."

"You're not the only one." My gaze darted away from him, falling to my hands as I tried to regulate my racing heart.

This morning had really happened. Levi had outed us to Alistair with little thought to whether I was ready. I knew it was just something he needed to do, something he needed to believe in me, in us. But I was still trying to process what it meant.

"Maybe this is a good thing. It'll give him focus, something else to obsess over." Hudson leaned back against the curved bench that ran along one side of the bus and stretched his arms behind his head.

"That's what I'm worried about," Rafe said, eyeing me with concern.

"I should probably..." I flicked my head toward the closed bedroom door.

"You don't have to go after him, not if you need space."

"Yeah," I gave Letty a strained smile, "I do." Because I'd

made a promise to Levi, and I couldn't be another person to let him down.

Running myself a glass of water, I moved down the bus and slipped inside the bedroom. Levi was already sprawled out on his back, his eyes closed, and hands tucked behind his head.

"You're pissed with me." He didn't look at me.

"I'm not. I'm just confused."

"About me?"

"About everything," I admitted. "I didn't anticipate any of this, Levi. When I came here, I didn't expect to..." I hesitated.

"What, Bee?" Finally, he gave me his eyes.

"I didn't expect to fall for you."

"Come here." Levi crooked his finger at me, and I kicked off my pumps and joined him on the bed. He pulled me into his side, stroking his hand up and down my arm.

"I won't apologize for what happened earlier, with Alistair."

I peeked up at him.

"I'm not ashamed of you, Bee. You make me want to try to do better, to *be* better. I know you're scared. I know everyone is just waiting for me to screw up again. And maybe I will. Maybe I'll fuck this up before the tour is over. But I can't let you go."

"I don't want you to." My confession hung in the space between us.

"No?" Levi pinned me with an intense look.

I shook my head. "But next time you're hurting or

confused. I need for you to talk to me, not run off into the arms of the first girl you see."

"Technically, I didn't run—"

"*Not* the point." I gave him a pointed look.

Levi had made a huge step last night in removing himself from a volatile situation. I knew it meant something, and I knew he needed to see me putting my trust in him. But it didn't change the fact that when things didn't go his way, Levi lashed out like a petulant child who couldn't deal with his emotions.

"Can I ask you something?"

"Anything," he said, and part of me wanted to test his offer of candor. But there was one specific question I had on my mind.

"Why have you never had a girlfriend before?"

"Is that what you are, Bee? My girlfriend?" The corner of Levi's mouth curved with amusement. He was teasing me.

"I don't need a label. So long as you don't touch any other girls while we're... together." I watched his reaction to the word, but I found nothing but awe and honesty and acceptance.

This was really happening.

Levi Hunter was as good as my boyfriend.

"You're broken, Bee, like me. You think I don't see the shadows in your eyes, but I do. Your hair and ink and piercings; they're armor, aren't they?

"I—" He knew. Levi knew my secret and he'd never said a word.

"It's okay, if you don't want to talk about it."

"I watched Zephyr almost die," the words were like ash on my tongue. "And it was all my fault."

Levi tried to look at me, but I kept my body plastered to his. "I couldn't do it anymore. I couldn't watch him destroy his life, destroy us. So I tried to leave. I knew it was the coward's way out, to just sneak out and leave a note. But I couldn't..." Tears slid down my cheeks as I let myself remember.

It hadn't been one inciting incident; it had been years of being second string to the high. Zephyr loved me. I'd never for a second doubted that. But it wasn't enough.

I wasn't enough to make him want to stop.

"Bee, look at me," Levi shuffled onto his side, forcing me to give him my eyes. I squeezed them shut, wanting to keep my pain for myself. This was my burden to carry, my secret to bear. Yet, Levi—of all people—was here and he was asking me to let him in.

"There she is." He gently stroked my face, rubbing the tears away with his deft fingers. "I'm not him," he whispered, his voice cracked with emotion. "I'm not Zephyr."

No, Levi was worse.

I'd been with Zephyr in the early days, when drugs were fun, something to escape. I'd watched as his addiction spiraled out of control. I'd stood by as it took over his life. With Zephyr, I hadn't chosen to be with an addict. It just happened. One day, I was head over in heels with a guy, the next I was competing with drugs for his attention.

I'd chosen Levi *despite* his addiction.

I'd walked headfirst into the lion's den, knowing how this story would probably play out. And the truth was, I'd probably do it all again. Because I hadn't been able to save Zephyr. I'd walked away and it had almost killed him —and me.

When I'd gotten the call from one of our friends that he'd OD'd, I'd felt nothing but shame and guilt. He'd taken a lethal concoction of substances. Pumping his body full of drugs to ease the pain of me finally breaking free.

"No, you're not." I sniffled back more tears. Levi leaned in, touching his nose against mine until our breaths were mingled and our bodies were pressed impossibly close.

"I'm in control of this, I swear I'm—"

"For how long?" My smile was sad, mirroring the pain in my voice. "Part of it will always control you, Levi."

"I'll get help. I'll see a counselor, a shrink, whatever you want, Bee. I'm serious about us, about you... I don't want to lose you."

"I'm not going anywhere."

Relief settled in his eyes as he inhaled a sharp breath.

"I'm in love with you, Levi. It wasn't supposed to happen, but it did."

"Y- you... *love me?*"

I nodded, unsure whether it was the right time to say the words. But he deserved to know.

Levi deserved to know he was worthy of love.

"Fuck, Phoebe. No one's ever..."

"I know." I brushed my lips over his. "Your past doesn't define you. What happened with your mom, that was about her demons, her faults, not yours." I drew in a deep breath. "You were just a child. Children aren't born evil, Levi. They aren't born bad. And I'm so fucking sorry you had to grow up believing you weren't good enough. Because you are, you are Leviathan Hunter."

His breath was harsh, the sound reverberating between us.

"I think talking would help. To me, to a profession—" He tensed but I went on. "I'm not saying you have to do it today or tomorrow or anytime soon, but there's so much you haven't ever dealt with. You can't carry that forever, Levi. It's too much."

Silence descended over us. Levi watched me, absorbing everything I'd said. I didn't mean to unload all that, but I was glad it was out. It might have been too late to walk away from him, but I had no plans to stand by and watch Levi ruin everything he'd worked so hard for. I wouldn't be that girl again.

The girl who waited until it was too late.

"I'm here, Levi. I want to be here. But you have to keep trying."

"I am... I will... But facing the demons from my past, talking about her..." He expelled a strained breath. "It takes me to a dark place, Bee. Really fucking dark."

I leaned in and kissed him. Slow and tentative, my fingers sliding against his jaw.

"Then I guess I'll just have to be your light."

———

LEVI FELL to sleep like that, wrapped around me like a koala. I don't know if he was emotionally exhausted from our conversation, or whether he was so relieved, he managed to drift off. But after an hour, I finally slipped out of the bedroom and joined Rafe at the table.

"Where is everyone?" I asked.

"Eva's video-calling her parents and then wants to speak to Molly. Hudson is getting some beauty sleep, and Damon is... I'm not really sure."

"Is he okay?"

"Honestly, I'm not sure." Rafe rubbed his jaw. "How is he?" He flicked his eyes down the bus.

"He's sleeping."

A knowing smirk tugged at Rafe's mouth and I rolled my eyes. "Get your mind out of the gutter. We were talking."

"Talking? I heard that's what all the kids are calling it these days."

"I think we're okay," I said quietly, glancing toward the bedroom door.

"It won't be easy, you know, loving him."

"I know. But I can't walk away, Rafe. I won't."

"Good. He needs to know he's worth fighting for. It's all he's ever wanted."

"Doesn't mean I'm not scared though." My eyes flicked to his.

"We'll be here to pick up the pieces when things fall apart." His expression softened, and I frowned. "I don't mean like *that*." He smiled. "I just mean, you don't have carry this alone. We love Levi, so fucking much it hurts. But he's his own worst enemy sometimes. You've seen it, you know. He's different with you though, and we can all see he's trying. But it won't be an easy road."

"I've asked him to get help. I don't know if he will or if he's ready yet..."

"That's good. He needs to be challenged sometimes. We've stood by and watched him go off the deep end too many times." Rafe swallowed, his eyes glittering with regret.

"He's your brother, not your responsibility." I laid a hand on his arm.

"He's not yours either. But here we are."

His words were a heavy weight on my shoulders, but for the first time, I felt like maybe me and Rafe were on the same side—Levi's side.

A faint smile traced my lips. "Maybe we can carry him together."

The door to the bedroom opened and Levi stepped into the hall. He looked adorable, all heavy-lidded and sleepy. "Hey," he said reaching us. "What's going on?"

"We were just shooting the shit."

Levi dropped down on the end of the bench and hooked an arm around my shoulder, dragging my body back into his. "You left me."

"You were sleeping." I tilted my face up and Levi planted a big wet sloppy kiss on my lips.

Rafe chuckled, clearing his throat.

"What?" Levi asked.

"You're so fucking pussy-whipped. Never thought I'd see the day."

"I am, aren't I?" Levi puffed his chest, shooting me a blinding smile.

"You're such a goofball." I leaned my head on his shoulder, enjoying the feel of his arms around me.

"Don't worry, Bee," he whispered the words against the shell of my ear, "I'm still the hot shot rock star who will rock your world."

I glanced up at him and smiled.

You already do.

Things were good.

No, strike that.

Things were fucking great.

Phoebe had told me she loved me, and I felt like I was on cloud fucking nine. I hadn't realized how much I needed to hear the words until they formed on her pouty lips.

She loved me.

Me.

It blew my fucking mind. Especially after what she went through with her ex.

Fuck, listening to her confide in me about him, it was like a knife to my stomach. He'd loved her, he'd laid with her, kissed and touched her... but he'd squandered her love. Taken it for granted. And when she'd finally had the strength to walk away, he'd fallen into the clutches of darkness.

That last part I understood. If Phoebe ever left me, I would fall apart at the seams. I knew I was walking a tightrope of control. It's just how it was being an addict. You were only ever one drink or one hit away from a full relapse. But Phoebe filled some of the cracks inside me, and not just in a superficial, Band-Aid kind of way. No, she made me feel one step closer to being whole.

I knew I still had a long fucking way to go. I knew there would road bumps along the way. I knew I would have to continually fight the little voice in my head, trying to lure me to the dark side. But it didn't feel insurmountable anymore.

With Phoebe in my corner, I had something to fight for. Something to anchor me.

Someone to ground me.

And she loved me.

She fucking loved me.

I hadn't said it back because I'd been so stunned... and I didn't want to mess it up. I didn't want to ruin the first big milestone in our relationship.

I wanted it to be perfect.

But how did I put into words what she meant to me?

The thought hit me out of left field. I needed to tell her the same way I expressed all my thoughts and feelings, through music.

"You have that look," Rafe said as we sat around in the dressing room, waiting to go on.

We'd spent a grueling day in back-to-back interviews. After the shitshow in Portland, Alistair had given us the next few nights off. No extra shows or meet and greets. Part of me wondered if it was to contain the rumors slowly picking up pace about Hudson and Phoebe. There had been nothing in the mainstream press yet, but online sources had begun to run with it.

I was trying to not let it get to me.

Phoebe loved me.

Me.

It didn't matter what anyone else said.

"What look?" I answered my brother.

"The look that says you're up to something."

"No, I don't."

His brow quirked up. "Levi, I know you better than anyone."

"What's up?" Damon came out of the bathroom, still styling his hair.

"Levi has that look."

"Guys," Eva said. "Leave him alone."

"Always got my back, Angel." I flashed her a wolfish grin. "Always."

Hudson sauntered into the room.

"Where the fuck have you been?"

His cheeks were flushed, and his clothes were disheveled. "I... uh..."

"Let me guess, the cute brunette with the nose piercing?" I said.

"How'd you—" He gulped, his eyes flashing to Eva.

"Don't look at me." She shrugged. "I'm done being in between this weird contest you have going on with Molly."

"Contest?" That piqued my interest. "What contest?"

"There is no contest," he grumbled.

Eva scoffed at that. "Could have fooled me. So you're not making out with total strangers to get back at her for dating Carson?"

"Nope." Hud dropped on the couch with a shrug. "She can date whoever she wants."

"Hmm, Angel, I hate to break it to you, but I think they were doing a little more than making out."

He growled in my direction, flipping me off.

"Sometimes I wonder how this is my life." Eva groaned, and we all chuckled.

It was hard to imagine life without her now. She brought balance to the group. Perspective.

She filled a void we didn't even realize needed filling.

"I can't believe we only have five shows left until Europe."

We were doing shows in four smaller cities, before ending the domestic leg of the tour in Atlanta. There was a big after-party lined up. Then we had a month to recoup before setting off for the European leg.

"I heard European girls are—"

"Hudson!" Everyone yelled.

Letty slipped into the room with Phoebe in tow. I sat up, my eyes findings hers. She came toward me and I drank her in. Skinny jeans, baggy tank top layered over another tank. Smoky eyes and a slick ponytail. My girl looked hot.

As soon as she was close, I snagged her wrist and pulled her down on my lap. Her soft laughter was like music to my fucking ears as she wound her arm around my neck.

"Hi," I breathed against her lips, the rest of the room already forgotten.

"Hi." Phoebe smiled, lust and love glittering in her eyes, taunting me. Because I couldn't do anything about it, not yet. Not when we had a show to do imminently.

"I missed you." I stole a kiss, trying to resist the urge to plunge my tongue deep into her mouth.

"I was only gone an hour."

"An hour too long," I mumbled, unable to resist diving back in for another kiss. Phoebe curled a fist into my t-shirt, letting her mouth slide against mine.

Someone cleared their throat. "Okay, lovers." It was Hudson. Annoying fucker. "Let's not forgot where we are."

"Uh... sorry." Phoebe was flushed and I fucking loved that I was the one to put it there.

The door opened again, and Alistair stepped inside. Phoebe tensed, trying to wiggle off my lap but I locked my arms around her.

His eyes went straight to us, a deep frown crinkling his brows. I held his stare, daring him to say anything. It was a dick move. Alistair was our manager. He had our best interests at heart, I knew that. But Phoebe was non-negotiable as far as I was concerned.

I didn't just want her, I needed her. The sooner he realized that, the better this would go for everyone.

He cleared his throat, and finally glanced away. "All set?"

"We're good, Ali, boy. You don't gotta worry."

"We're on the homestretch now," he said, flicking his concerned gaze to mine again. "We only have to get through another five shows. Nine more days and then you can have some much-deserved downtime."

"Fuck yeah." Hudson fist pumped the air.

"Before you go out there, I have some news. I just got the official word *Drown* has hit number one on the Billboard Hot 100 Chart."

"W- what?" Eva gasped. "But... that can't be..." She clutched her throat, all the blood drained from her face.

"You're number one, Eva. Congratulations."

"Lap it up, Angel." I winked at her. "It's only a taste of things to come."

I hadn't wanted to record *Drown* for public consumption.

It was *my* song. But even I couldn't deny that Eva's lyrics and the female POV elevated it to something epic.

And now it was number one.

"We should celebrate tonight," I suggested, and everyone looked at me. "Relax, I'm not saying we do something stupid. Just the seven of us. Eight, if Alistair wants to come."

He rolled his eyes, muttering something about, 'only being our manager'.

"Sounds good," Letty said. "Are you thinking out or in?"

"In." I pulled Phoebe closer. I wanted to be able to hold her and touch her, I wanted to be able to fucking kiss her without fear of being caught by some mega-fan or wannabe journo.

"Can I bring a date?" Hudson asked and everyone yelled, "No."

"Joke." He groaned. "Geez, I was joking."

"Alistair, you in?"

"Actually, I'm not sure. My sister is in town."

"Ruby?" Rafe asked.

"Yeah. She's just passing through but wanted to see me."

"You should invite her," Eva said. "It'll be nice to see her again." We'd bumped into her at an industry thing a few weeks back.

"I'm sure Alistair already has plans," Damon said. It came out kind of strained, which was fucking weird because Damon was the most placid of us all.

"We were going to meet up for drinks," Ali said, "but maybe we can swing by the suite instead."

I watched Damon. His expression was hard, guarded. There was definitely something going on. Strange, because he hadn't whispered a word of it to me. I guess we all had our secrets though.

Damon wasn't like me or Hudson, or even Rafe in the early days. He hadn't hopped on the crazy train and lived and breathed the rock and roll lifestyle. Sure, he'd partied with us, hooked up with the occasional girl, and dabbled in some soft drugs here and there, but he didn't *live* it. He loved the band, he loved the music, but the life... he'd always acted like he could take or leave it.

"Where'd you go just now?" Phoebe raked her nails over my jaw, commanding my attention.

"Just thinking," I said, sucking her bottom lip into my mouth.

She smothered a whimper, wriggling on my lap.

"Do you think we have time to—"

Pressing a finger to my lips, she grinned. "Hold that thought, rock star, you have a show to do."

"I'll think of you, naked and waiting for me."

Conversations went on around us as we fell deeper into our own little world.

"Didn't you just suggest we celebrate tonight?" Her brow rose playfully.

"Yeah, but no one will notice if we disappear."

"Levi, everyone will notice." She chuckled.

"Are you two listening to a word I say?" Alistair's voice was like a bucket of ice water.

"Sorry, what was that?"

Hudson snickered, and I flipped him off.

"Forget it," Alistair grumbled. "Sometimes I don't know why I bother."

"I'm happy. Can't you just try to be pleased for me?" My brow lifted.

"Levi." There was a hint of warning in Phoebe's voice, but not even she was going to ruin my good mood.

"It's not going to work, Bee." I kissed her temple. "Nothing you say, or Ali says, or anyone says is going to dampen my mood. For the first time in my life, I feel... good. I feel really fucking good. So you can all worry about me or for me, or whatever... but I don't care."

Quiet snickers filled the room. Eva was smiling, pride glittering in her baby blues. Letty looked fit to burst, her smile so wide anyone would have thought she'd just been crowned number one on the Hot 100. Alistair looked as miserable as fuck still, his brows knitted together with concern. But I was done worrying. I had my band. I had my brother and Eva. I had music.

And most of all, I had my girl in my arms, and she loved me.

She fucking loved me.

"To family, good friends, and getting fucked-up." Hudson lifted his beer in the air and smirked. But when no one joined him, he added, "What?"

"You're an asshole, you know that, right?" Levi snorted, his fingers massaging my thigh as I sat perched in his lap.

The show had been a huge success. The crowd in Sioux City was electric, lapping up Levi's performance. He'd announced they had hit number one on the Hot 100 and pulled Eva out on stage to play three songs. The fans had loved it, echoes of 'more' and 'encore' rippling through the arena.

Watching them, you couldn't help but feel the Hunter-Walker magic that everyone so often talked about. Their bond was special, their music even more so. And everyone saw the change in Levi tonight. He was lighter somehow. More animated and excited. He'd strutted across the stage, high on endorphins. But I couldn't help the pang of worry I felt, that Levi was trading one addiction for another.

Me.

"Hey, what's wrong?" He tucked his chin onto my shoulder, his words a low grumble meant only for my ears.

"Nothing." I smiled back at him. His eyes held a new sparkle, but I still saw the shadows of pain. They would always be there. Until Levi took the giant step of talking to someone about his past, it would always haunt him. Nothing —not music, or his bandmates, liquor, drugs, or me—could fix that.

But he'd said nothing about seeking help, and he was so happy, I didn't want to push him too much too soon.

"Where the fuck are Alistair and Ruby?" Hudson grumbled. "I want to crack open the champagne."

"None of us even like champagne," Rafe said.

"Yeah, but it's a celebration. Can't have a celebration without champagne."

Just then, Damon's cell vibrated. "It's Ali." He scanned the text and his brow furrowed. "They're not going to make it. Something happened—"

"Are they okay?"

"Yeah, just says he's sorry but that something came up he needs to take care of." His expression darkened, only for a second, then his frown morphed into a smile as he pocketed his cell and gave the room his attention.

"Oh well, in that case." Hudson got up and went over to the counter, retrieving the champagne from the ice bucket. "I'll do the honors." He popped the cork and Letty leaped up to help fill the neat rows of crystal flutes. She handed us each a glass, and I watched the liquid fizz and pop.

"Does anyone want to say a few—"

"Hey, man, I've got this." Hudson shot Damon an irritated look. He puffed out his chest, running a hand through his damp hair. "Eva, Angel, Country... I won't sugarcoat it. I thought you joining the tour was the worst idea ever—"

"What the fuck, Hud?" Rafe balked.

"Relax, man. I've got this." He waved him off.

"As I was saying, I thought it was a terrible idea. We're rock stars, baby. We didn't need a girl tagging along, messing with our Feng shui. But I was wrong. You're the fifth piece to our puzzle, Eva. The light to our dark. The soft to our hard. I know Rafe loves you. I know that one day, he's going to put a ring on your finger and a baby in your stomach—"

"Oh, Jesus," Rafe murmured. "Somebody make him stop."

Hudson flipped him off. "You should be thanking me, bro. I seem to remember playing a vital role in operation 'make Rafe pull his head out of his ass'." He smirked. "Anyway, Eva, your heart might belong to Rafe, but you'll always be a part of this band. Congratulations on your first number one hit. I can't wait to see you soar to new heights. To the sweetheart of Country, Miss Evangeline Star Walker."

"Eva." Our cheers rang out through the suite, as she buried herself into Rafe's side, her cheeks a deep shade of pink.

"Speech, speech," Letty clapped.

"Oh no, I'm not sure—"

"Speech!" everyone yelled.

Eva rolled her eyes, shooting Letty an indignant look. But she was smiling, laughing right along with the rest of us.

"I'm not really sure how to follow that." She beamed at Hudson. "A year ago, my best friend pushed me so far out of my comfort zone, I wanted to hate her. For a hot second, I think I did. But performin' at the Jamesboro Talent Showdown changed my life... it changed it for the better. I got to know four guys who define the word family. Four guys who support each other through the highs and lows, and even when they're at odds with one another, they still have each other's back.

"It's been a dream come true tourin' with y'all over the last five months. I didn't ever imagine this life, bein' on the road, would be for me. But y'all make it so easy. I couldn't imagine bein' anywhere else." She swiped the tears from her eyes. "Wow, I didn't expect to cry. Damn you, Hudson."

"It's my specialty, making girls cry." He frowned. "No, wait, that doesn't—"

"Hudson!"

"Yeah, yeah, keep your hair on."

Eva chuckled, her laughter so warm and full of love, it was hard not to be affected. The girl from a small town in Tennessee really had found her place among this bunch of misfits. They loved her and she loved them.

"You complete us, Angel," Levi said from behind me, his words twisting something inside me. "And I'm so fucking happy my brother managed to get over himself and tell you how he felt. I love you guys."

The room went silent, the air thick with Levi's admission. This was a big deal. I could tell from everyone's shocked expressions that Levi had caught them off guard.

"What?" he let out a strained chuckle.

"Nothing, man," Rafe said, smiling. "We love you too. Always." Eva dropped down beside her boyfriend and the two of them nodded at Levi.

It was such an intimate moment between the three of them, I felt like an outsider.

Suddenly, I felt completely out of my depth.

"Excuse me," I said, standing. "I need a girl's minute."

They barely noticed as I hurried into Levi's bedroom and went into the adjoining bathroom. Closing the door, I braced the counter, unable to withhold the torrent of emotion rising inside me.

It was silly.

So what if Levi had told his brother and Eva he loved them. He was supposed to love them. They were family.

"Phoebe?"

His voice made me flinch. I didn't want him to see me like this, confused and upset. I didn't even really know why I felt this way.

All I knew was, hearing them all talk like that... it was so obvious their bonds went beyond being mere bandmates. They were a family. A unit. If one of them bled, they all bled. I'd known it before, but not like this.

No matter what, they had each other... while I had no one.

It had never felt more apparent than it did in this moment.

"Bee, open the door."

"Just a minute." My voice cracked.

I realized my mistake the second he tried the door handle and it opened.

"Levi," I said, turning away from him. "Please, just give a minute."

"You're crying?" He closed the door and stalked toward me. I felt the air shift around him, each step like a gunshot to my heart. "What is it, Bee? What's wrong?" His hands ran over my shoulders and down my arms.

"I'm okay," I sniffled, "I'm just being silly."

"Hey, don't do that. Not with me. Never with me." Levi turned me in his arms, but I couldn't meet his eyes.

I didn't do this—I didn't break down in front of my boyfriend and all his friends. I was the strong one, the fighter, the survivor.

"Honeybee, look at me." He gripped my chin and tilted my face up to meet his. "What happened?"

"I just got overwhelmed. It's silly." I dried my eyes. "I'm fine now, I promise." Forcing a weak smile, I tried to shirk out of his hold, but Levi backed me up against the counter.

"You're family too now. You know that, right?"

His sincere words were like a sucker punch to the chest and a fresh wave of tears spilled down my cheeks. "God, I hate this," I said. "I hate crying."

"Ssh, Bee." Levi pulled me into his chest, cradling me there. He didn't speak, he just held me, letting me purge my emotions.

When the tears finally subsided, I pulled away, and gazed up at him. "Sorry about that, I don't know what came over me."

"Don't do that. Don't act like you have to protect me from everything, Phoebe. I'm here aren't I? I'm right here, trying to be a better guy for you."

"Levi, I—"

"You're scared, I get it. You think I can't handle this—whatever *this*—is." His brows pinched as he released a heavy sigh. "I'm not a total asshole, Bee. Not all of the time."

"I know that, Levi." I brushed my thumb over his jaw. "It took me by surprise as much as you. I think... seeing you all like that tonight. Hearing Eva... You have this amazing, loyal family who will always be there. They'll always fight for you and stand by your side. I guess it reminded me that I don't have that."

There was me and there was my father, and he was as emotionally unavailable as he was physically. I didn't have a group of girlfriends to celebrate or commiserate with or talk about guys with. I had no extended family, no aunts or grandmas or cousins.

I was all alone in the world.

And until this moment, I'd thought I was okay with that.

But now I had Levi, and everyone was so set on reminding me to be careful with his feelings, to try my best to protect his fragile heart... that I hadn't spared much thought to what would happen if I lost him.

In some ways, since I arrived on tour with the band, I'd been trying to fix Levi, to keep him whole. I was a caretaker at heart. I had an innate need to want to look after people. But I'd been so wrapped up in my feelings for Levi, the intensity between us, I'd neglected to consider one vital thing.

Who would pick up the pieces of my broken battered heart if it all went wrong?

"I've got you, Bee. I've got you." Conviction coated Levi's words, and I wanted so desperately to believe him.

But Levi's feelings toward me weren't a permanent solution, it was a temporary fix.

A Band-Aid.

And when it finally came off, would there be enough left of him to love me?

Watching Phoebe cry shifted something inside me. My feelings about her were intense. I knew that. We all knew it. But it was how I experienced emotion, in powerful unrelenting waves. I was either low, my mood dark and desperate; or I was as high as a kite, thanks to the alcohol and drugs usually pumping through my system. I cared as deeply as I hated, the lines between the two often getting blurred.

But right now, watching my girl break apart at the seams, I wanted to take away her pain. For the first time in my life, I wanted to be someone's white knight.

The thought was so overpowering, fear snaked through my chest, taking hold of my lungs and squeezing the air right out of them. I couldn't breathe. So much self-doubt coursing through my veins, I was paralyzed.

What if I said the wrong thing?

What if I couldn't be who she needed me to be?

What if by loving her, I, in turn, ruined her?

A battle raged on inside my mind as I held her in my arms, wanting to absorb every ounce of her pain and take it as my own.

Phoebe hadn't talked much about her family, her life. I knew about her ex. I knew her mom had died and her father was some movie exec off doing his thing. But it occurred to me in this moment, that I didn't really *know* Phoebe. I didn't realize how lonely she was or how afraid.

She'd turned up on tour, so fucking strong, unwilling to

take any of our bullshit. My girl was a fighter. A survivor. But she was also human. She had fears and doubts and demons just like the rest of us.

And I didn't know because I was always so fucking self-absorbed. I'd been so desperate to lose myself in her, it had never occurred to me that she might also be losing herself in me.

Fuck.

I took a shuddering breath, trying to rein in the confusing tsunami of emotions racing through me.

"Levi?" Phoebe peeked up at me, her hands pressed firmly against my chest.

"I'm okay." I swallowed. I had to do this... I had to be the guy she deserved. Even if it was only in this moment.

"Come on," I said. "Let's go to bed."

"Bed?" She frowned. "But the celebrations—"

"Can wait." I gently tugged her into the bedroom and began peeling the clothes from her body.

My dick stirred to life, hunger gnawing deep in my stomach. I wanted her. I always wanted her. But this wasn't about sex. It was about her. About us. It was about me trying to show Phoebe that although I had a long fucking way to go, I could be the guy she needed.

When she was standing before me in nothing but her sexy as fuck zebra print bra and matching panties, I made quick work of stripping out of my own clothes. Then I scooped her up against my chest and carried her to the bed.

Pulling back the covers, I lay Phoebe down. Her eyes ran over my shoulders, my chest, the ink covering every inch of my skin. "You're so beautiful," she sighed.

I don't think I'd ever been called beautiful before in my life, but I loved how it sounded rolling off her tongue. As if I was the most precious thing she'd ever seen.

Phoebe moved over, making room for me, and I slipped in beside her. "This is nice." She sighed, and it was so deep, so fucking uncertain, that my gut twisted.

I hooked my arm around her waist and dragged her closer, until we were nose to nose, chest to chest, skin on heated skin.

"Levi," she breathed, her eyes fluttering closed.

"I don't want anything from you." *Lies. I want everything from you, Bee. Every-fucking-thing.* "I just want to be close, to feel your heart beating against mine."

"For a tortured rock star, you sure know exactly the right thing to say sometimes." She let the tip of her nose trail along my cheek. I inhaled deeply, breathing her in. Our lips moved together, seeking, searching. I didn't want this moment to become about sex or earthly desires, I wanted it to be about her. About me showing her, I could do this.

I could just *be* with her.

But we fell into the kiss fast and all at once. Phoebe whimpered the second my tongue slipped past her lips and found her own. But I kept it slow. Slow lazy licks. My hand trailed over her hip and slipped into the elastic of her panties, but I didn't go any further. I just wanted to hold her, to savor this rare moment of quiet with my girl.

My girl.

I wouldn't ever get used to saying that. To thinking or feeling it.

Could she really love me? Accept me, flaws and all?

"What are you thinking?" I asked her as she pulled away, inhaling a deep breath.

"About my mom. I don't let myself think about her a lot, but she'd have liked you."

My brow lifted at that, and Phoebe laughed softly. "She had a big heart with a soft spot for broken things. I guess that's where I got it from."

"She sounds nice."

"She was the best." A sad smile tugged at her lips. "I was a mess after she died. She wasn't just my mom, she was my best friend. I didn't have anyone... I mean, I had my dad, and later Zephyr, but it wasn't the same. So you're not the only one scared here, Levi. I know you think I have the power to ruin you, but you're not the only one with something to lose."

Fuck.

Her words were like shards of glass across my heart. She was giving me her heart, trusting me—of all fucking people —to keep it safe. I wanted to be that guy, I did. The need to protect her and love and cherish her burned through me like wildfire.

But I was so fucking scared of messing up.

I swallowed, my mouth dry.

"Levi?"

"I don't deserve you, honeybee." *I don't deserve any of this.*

"Let's not play this game. I'm here, aren't I?" She kissed me softly, letting her tongue slide over my lip piercings.

"Bee," I warned, smothering a groan as she wiggled her tight little body against mine. "We're supposed to be talking."

"What if I don't want to talk?" Lust glittered in her eyes. "What if I just want to feel?"

Without warning, I rolled her beneath me and settled between her thighs. The thin layers of our underwear weren't nearly enough to stop my dick searching for her wet heat.

"Levi," she gasped, staring up at me with stars in her eyes.

"How do you want me, Bee?" I licked a path up her neck to her ear, biting the soft flesh of her lobe. "Soft and slow or hard and fast?"

Molten lava flowed through my veins, my need for her so overpowering my skin vibrated. But I didn't want to rush this. I wanted to savor her, to take my time, and give her what she needed.

"You," she whispered, hitching her leg around my hip and grinding on me. "I just want you."

"Look at me, Bee." I eased away to meet her hooded gaze. "I want to hear you say the words."

She smiled at me shyly. "Make love to me, Levi."

Shit.

I'd wanted the words, but now they were out, lingering between us, I didn't know what to do.

I fucked. I used sex as a way to forget, to escape. I had a wicked tongue and a dirty mind... but making love?

What did I know about such things?

"Hey, it's okay." Phoebe smoothed her finger over my knitted brows, making some of tension in my expression ebb away. "We don't have to."

"I want to. Fuck, Bee, I really, *really* want to... I just..."

Darkness swarmed inside me, the urge to get up and run so fucking strong.

All I could hear was my mother's voice, taunting me. Mocking me. Reducing me to nothing but a series of cruel words.

Useless.

Worthless.

Evil.

Monster.

"Let me," she said, knocking me onto my back. Standing, Phoebe shimmied out of her underwear, and I was so fucking captivated by the way she wore her skin. So confident and sure of herself.

She was a goddess.

My little warrior.

I wasn't sure I would ever be able to put into words what she meant to me. What her faith in me to be better, meant.

She crawled onto the end of the bed, slowly pulling my boxers off, her eyes fixated on my dick as it stood proud, desperate for her touch.

"You okay?" Her voice was cracked with lust.

I nodded, unable to speak over the huge fucking lump in my throat.

Phoebe sat over me, grasping my shaft and slowly sinking down on me. We both groaned, the feel of her tight around me mind blowing.

"Fuck, Bee," I rasped, smoothing my hands along her thighs as she settled above me. "You're the light to my dark, the star in dark skies. You're the voice that I hear, when things don't go right. The angel on my shoulder, I can't let you go..."

"What was that?" Phoebe asked.

I frowned, not realizing I'd been murmuring the lyrics forming in my head. "Nothing. Are you going to sit up there all day or are you going to—"

She rolled her hips, circling them nice and slow.

"Fuuuuck," I hissed, grabbing her waist, wanting more. Needing it.

"No." She shook her head. "Let me..."

Hands pressed against my chest, Phoebe rode me slow and deep. I fisted the bedsheets, forcing myself not to take control, to simply revel in the feel of her owning my body. Taking what she needed.

"It's feels... fuck." My voice was rough against my throat, my body coiled tight with sensation, my veins swimming with liquid lust. She was so fucking beautiful.

She wasn't here because she wanted me for my fame and fortune or her five minutes in the spotlight.

I felt like the luckiest guy on the planet, brought to my knees by a girl with ink on her skin and scars on her heart.

"Fuck, Bee..." I rasped, barely able to get the words out. She felt divine, wrapped around my dick like velvet.

And I never wanted it to end.

"I'm so close," Phoebe panted, her eyelids heavy and lips parted.

"Use me, Bee. Take what you need," I gritted out, desperately fighting off my own release to make sure she came first.

"It's... God, Levi..."

"I know, honeybee, I know." I couldn't resist thrusting up inside her, making her cry out.

She was close, so fucking close.

But it was like something was holding her back. Sliding a hand between our bodies, I pressed my thumb against her clit and rubbed, and she shattered.

I curved my hand around her neck and pulled her down to me, capturing her lips and swallowing her cries of pleasure.

"I love you, Levi," she said.

Her words, the way she gripped me inside of her, her sweet as sin kisses; it was enough to tip me over the edge.

I held her close as we rode out the lingering waves. The words were right there, stronger than ever. But the second I opened my mouth, fear made me clam up and they died on the tip of my tongue.

"It's okay," Phoebe whispered, as if she could sense my inner turmoil. She pressed a kiss to my breastbone right over my heart, tracing the mark with her finger.

"I can wait."

PHOEBE

AFTER MY EMOTIONAL MELTDOWN, Levi spent every possible second trying to show me how much he cared. We'd become *that* couple, unable to keep our hands off one another. Finding as many ways as possible to be together.

We hung out with the band after shows or, if it was a night off, we escaped to Levi's hotel room and lost ourselves in one another.

After that night, the night where Levi had handed me control, he let me take the lead more often. Trusting me not only with his heart, but his body. But he still didn't say the words.

He still hadn't told me he loved me.

I felt it though. I felt it every time he looked at me, but something was holding him back.

I vowed to give him space, to arrive at things in his own time. But I couldn't deny that every time I said the words and he didn't say them back, another little piece of my heart withered and died.

There was only one show left until we made the journey back for the two final shows in Atlanta, home of Razorsharp Records HQ. Then we planned to fly straight out to Long Island after the wrap party the label had organized at The Riff Bar, one of the most exclusive clubs in downtown Atlanta.

I'd been caught off guard when the guys had all started talking about the trip as if it was a given I would be there. I mean, I wanted to go, but the way they just included me, as if I was part of their family now... it touched something deep inside me.

After the trip, everyone was taking two weeks to do their own thing. Eva and Rafe were heading back to Lyme, Tennessee, to spend some time with her parents. Damon was going to see his mom. Hudson was doing whatever Hudson did during his downtime. And Levi hadn't said anything yet about his plans. Part of me wanted to ask him to come back to Nashville with me. I had a cute little apartment we could hide away in, spending lazy days in bed, ordering takeout and enjoying life away from the spotlight. But I didn't want him to feel obliged.

There was also the small problem of my father. He still didn't know about the band, let alone Levi. And I wanted to keep it that way for as long as possible. But I knew I had to tell him eventually.

I just hadn't figured out how.

"Hey." Letty breezed into the suite. "Did you email HR back? They need to finalize the travel plans."

"Yep, I did it this morning."

"Awesome." She sank down on the couch.

"Are you sure the label still wants me—"

"We've been through this." She gave me a pointed look. "I want you on the tour. The band want you. I doubt we'll even get Levi onto a plane if you're not there, and Alistair will go along with whatever keeps him happy. When it eventually comes out that you and Levi are together, we'll deal with it then, okay?"

I nodded, swallowing the doubts I had.

"It'll be okay, Phoebe," Letty added. "You should be excited. Not many interns get this opportunity."

"I know, and I am. Excited, I mean. I just..."

"You're scared." I nodded, and Letty gave me a warm smile. "You wouldn't be human if you weren't. But I have a good feeling about everything."

"You do?"

"Yeah. The band is in a good place. I know a lot has happened, but with Eva on the tour, and now you, I don't know... it finally feels like things are slotting into place."

"Thank you, Letty, for everything." She had taken me under her wing, but more than that, she had become a friend. Something I didn't have all too much experience with.

"Now, now," she smirked, "don't go getting all emotional on me."

"I won't." I swallowed again. "I promise. How much longer do you think they'll be?"

The band was downstairs with Eva, having a photoshoot for *Rolling Stone* magazine. After *Drown* soared to the number one spot, everyone who was everyone in the industry wanted a piece of Eva and her Black Hearted boys, as the press was now dubbing them.

Letty checked her wristwatch. "Not much longer. Hudson and Damon are heading straight downtown to do the charity luncheon for kids in the care system, and I think Rafe mentioned he had plans for him and Eva. Which means, you and Levi have some time alone..." Her brows waggled suggestively.

"What are you going to do all day?" We had a rare

afternoon off. The next show wasn't until tomorrow but as the tour was winding down, the band's energy levels were starting to crash. They were exhausted.

We all were.

"Oh, I'm sure I'll find a way to keep myself out of trouble." My brows furrowed, and she chuckled. "I'll be fine, Phoebe. You and Levi make the most of it because once we hit European soil, something tells me life will get a whole lot crazier."

My stomach knotted. She was right, a world tour would be a whole other level.

"You know, if you wanted to go out, I could probably arrange something discreet for the two—"

"No." I shook my head. Sneaking around the on the buses and at shows was one thing, but being out in public was another thing entirely.

"Fine, but you have to prepare yourself for the fact this won't be a secret forever. One day, the world will know you're Levi Hunter's girlfriend."

Her words made my heart soar and my stomach sink all in the same breath. I loved being Levi's, his girl, his honeybee. But I didn't relish the day that I had to share him with the world.

Even though I knew that day would eventually come.

———

"LEVI, STOP, STOP." I tried to catch my breath as he was tickling my sides. We were supposed to be watching a movie, but Levi couldn't sit still, touching me and tickling me, anything to try to distract me.

I grabbed a pillow from beside me and swatted it at his face and the rest was history. He pulled me to the floor, pinning me with his hips, attacking me with his fingers.

"Do you surrender?" He grinned down at me.

"Surrender? We're supposed to be watching the movie." I tried to buck him off, but he was too damn strong.

"No, you wanted to watch a movie, honeybee, I wanted to do this." He leaned down, tracing his tongue up the slope of my neck, nipping the skin there, before kissing me hard.

A whimper spilled from my lips as his tongue plunged into my mouth and curled around my own. Heat pooled in my stomach, red hot flames licking my insides.

We had the suite to ourselves. Hudson and Damon would be gone hours, and Rafe had whisked Eva away on a date in an undisclosed located across the city. Letty and Alistair were meeting virtually with Dusty and his team to go over the final preparations for the world tour, and Johnson and Stalter were standing guard beyond the door.

We were alone.

Completely and utterly alone.

Levi was right, I didn't want to watch a movie. But I'd wanted us to do something normal, something couple-ish. I hadn't wanted to get too caught up in him, not when there were things we still needed to talk about.

"Levi, hold up." I managed to slip my hands free and press them against his chest. "We should talk."

"Talk?" He frowned. "You want to talk *now*?" He rolled off me with a frustrated groan. "You're killing me, Bee."

A soft chuckle vibrated in my chest. "I just figured we should probably talk about some stuff since the end of the tour is almost here."

"Okay." He found my hand, tangling our fingers together. "What's on your mind?"

"I just wondered what your plans are after the trip to Long Island?"

"I don't know." He shrugged. "I haven't really given it much thought. I just figured we'd either head back to my place or crash at yours or something."

Warmth flowed through me at how easy he made it sound. Levi was surprising like that. He spent so much time fighting his demons that when it came to making decisions, he often made his choice without realizing.

Like right now, he just assumed we would spend the rest of the break together, because to Levi, it was that simple.

"You're so freakin' cute." I ran my nose against his shoulder.

"Cute? I don't think I've ever been called cute, honeybee. Dirty-mouthed, reckless, rock star, maybe. But cute? Not so much." He flashed me a blinding smile that made my stomach clench. "Why do you ask?"

"Because we haven't talked about it and I didn't know if you had plans or anything."

His brows knitted. "We didn't? Huh." Confusion clouded his eyes. "I just figured we'd spend it together. I mean... if you want to?"

"I do." My lips curved. "I just didn't want you to think you had to spend it with me."

"Bee, when are you going to get it into your head that

I'm ass over elbow crazy about you? I hate it when we're apart."

Crazy about me... he was crazy about me.

I tried so hard not to feel a pang of disappointment, but I was only human, after all.

"We could have gone out, you know?" he said. "Between Letty and Johnson, they could have figured something out."

"It's probably not a good idea." His expression darkened so I explained. "There's only a few days left. Then we have some time before we leave for Europe."

"And when we're over there? Are we going to have to keep pretending then?" He didn't sound angry so much as defeated.

"Alistair seems to—"

"Fuck, Alistair, Bee," he hissed. "I only care about what *you* think. I know my life is a circus, but I don't want to hide this forever. I want people to know you're mine. I don't want to constantly have to worry that I'm too close to you."

"I'm scared," I whispered. The second the press knew, they would dig into my life and unearth all my secrets. My anonymity would be gone, forever. You didn't have a relationship with someone like Levi and maintain your privacy.

Was I ready for that?

Were *we* ready?

"Are you ashamed of me?" His question pierced the air... and my heart. I hated that it always went back to that. I wasn't ashamed, I was just worried about losing what we had to the inevitable media frenzy that would swarm us.

"Levi, you know that's not it."

"So, what's the big deal? You knew what you were getting into with me. I've always been honest about who I am, Bee. I thought you—"

"I do, so much." I cupped his face. "I love you, Levi. I love you so freakin' much. But going public will change everything, you have to know that."

"Yeah." He let out a resigned sigh. "I know. But we're going to be away for six months. Six fucking months, honeybee. Are you really okay sneaking around for that long? And after that? What happens then, huh?"

His intense eyes burned into me, searing my soul. Levi wanted more. He wanted to come clean. Maybe he needed the validation, or maybe he just wanted to finally be able to call me his without worrying who overheard.

But he still hasn't said the words.

"Maybe we can talk to—"

The blare of my cell phone cut through the tension swirling around us.

"Leave it," he said, clearly not ready to end this conversation.

"It must be Letty." She was the only person who ever called, and since she knew I was here with Levi, it was probably important.

I clambered to my hands and knees and crawled over to the coffee table. But the second I picked up my cell, dread slammed into me.

"Bee, what is it?" Levi was sitting up now, leaning back against the couch, watching me as I stared at my father's name flashing over the screen.

"I... uh, it's my dad." I barely got the words out over the lump in my throat.

"Well, don't just stare at the thing, answer it," he said as if it was that simple.

It wasn't.

This was the worst possible thing that could have happened today. Because my gut told me he wasn't calling to check in. He was calling because he knew.

My father finally knew the truth.

LEVI

Phoebe stared at her cell like it was the devil come to claim her soul.

"Bee," I said again, and she visibly flinched.

"I... uh, I'll just take it in the bedroom."

I watched her hurry into the bedroom and close the door.

What the fuck?

I knew from everything she'd told me that her relationship with her father was shaky. But this felt like more than just a little father-daughter rift.

I pulled myself up onto the couch and waited. It was killing me not to know what she was saying. I couldn't imagine he was all too thrilled with his daughter seeing a guy like me, especially after what went down with Zephyr, but she wasn't a child. Phoebe was a twenty-one-year-old woman. She could make her own choices, her own mistakes.

Not that I had any plans on becoming a mistake anytime soon.

Things were good. Great, even. I felt more stable than I had in years. I didn't wake each morning with a gnawing hole in my chest, and slowly, the constant hunger had begun to subside. I knew I wasn't healed; I wouldn't be for a long time. But it was a start.

And it was all thanks to my honeybee.

It was hard to believe that in just a few days I would be spending two weeks on a small island with my bandmates, my brother and his girl, and my girl.

My fucking girl.

I didn't think anyone could have predicted it. I was so fucking thankful though. Thankful to Letty for bringing Phoebe into my life, thankful to Phoebe for giving me a chance. I knew she was worried about the world tour, about revealing our relationship to the public, but the sooner we did it, the sooner we could get on with our lives. I had no plans to push her into the spotlight, but if they knew, then it wouldn't constantly feel like we were hiding and sneaking around. Besides, there were times when we were out and about, at interviews or meet and greets, that I just wanted to pull her close and kiss her. I drew strength from Phoebe. She was my light. My anchor.

My North Star in dark skies.

I pulled out my cell phone and made a note of some more lyrics. I'd been trying to put something together for her, but I was yet to share it with anyone. Humming the words, I typed and deleted, shuffled words around and added more, until I'd nailed two more verses. But Phoebe's raised voice caught my attention. I didn't want to eavesdrop; I didn't want to be that guy anymore. Paranoid and possessive. She sounded angry though, her voice rising above the silence. I got up and went to go to her, forcing myself to stay back. She'd obviously gone into the bedroom for some privacy, and I wanted to give her that.

I did.

But the second I heard her yell again, I stalked over to the door, pressing my ear against the wood.

"No, you can't... I won't let you," she shouted, her anger

palpable even from here. "Daddy, please, I'm begging you. I love him, I—"

I burst into the room and her head snapped up. "Levi..." she breathed, tears streaming down her face.

Anger welled inside of me.

"Hang up the phone, Bee," I gritted out, my jaw clenched impossibly tight. I didn't know what had gone down here, but whatever it was, it wasn't good if it had upset her.

"I... Dad?" she said, clutching the phone to her ear, her eyes never once leaving mine. "I have to go. We can talk about this later." Phoebe hung up, ignoring the shrill rants of her father on the end of the line.

"You weren't supposed to hear that," she gave me a sad smile.

"You were shouting."

"He's just so..." A heavy sigh escaped her lips. "He doesn't understand."

"He's not happy about us?"

"He was shocked to say the least."

"I- I don't understand..." We'd been seeing each other for weeks.

"He only just found out, Levi."

"What?" I reared back as if she'd slapped me.

"I didn't tell him." Guilt glittered in her eyes, taunting me. "I didn't want him to worry, and I knew he'd react badly."

"You didn't tell him?" I shook my head because it didn't make any sense. He was her dad, the only family she had left... and she hadn't told him about us?

About me?

"My father doesn't know I'm on tour with the band." She expelled a heavy sigh. "Well, he didn't. Dowager recognized me at the party, he just told him the news. That's why he was calling, to express his grave concerns about me working in such an 'unstable environment'." She mimicked the words.

"Hold up, you said Dowager told him... so he thinks you're seeing Hudson?"

Her expression darkened punching me straight in the stomach.

"I told him, about us. It was time."

"Time?" A bitter laugh bubbled up in my chest. "Fuck, Phoebe, here I am wanting to tell the whole world about us, and you haven't even told your dad. That's some messed-up shit right there." I rubbed the back of my neck, trying to get a handle on the anger swelling inside me.

She hadn't told him.

"I just didn't know how to tell him. After Zephyr—"

"I'm not your fucking ex," I snapped. "I thought we were past all this?"

"We are." She came closer but I jerked back. I didn't want her to try to comfort me, not when her betrayal was coursing through my veins like acid.

All this time, I'd been worried that I was Phoebe's dirty little secret... and I was right.

I was fucking right.

"You're ashamed of me," I spat, the words like a glacier between us.

"I am not ashamed of you. I just knew he'd do this. I knew he'd—"

"That he'd what? You're a grown woman for fuck's sake.

Does it really matter what your old man does or doesn't say?" I seethed. I couldn't stop. Suddenly, I felt like I couldn't trust anything coming out of her mouth. "I don't even know why we're having this conversation."

"Levi, please... just hear me out." Panic washed over her expression. But I couldn't think straight.

"I need to get out of here," I blurted out, grabbing the door handle.

"Wait," she cried. "He said he's going to have me pulled from the tour; that's what we were arguing about."

Her words echoed through me.

"It's not up to him." The words were a low growl.

"He says he has enough pull with the label to make it happen. Either way, he'll out us and they'll want me off your assignment. Alistair warned us this could happen."

I glanced back at her, hating the tears streaming down her cheeks. I wanted to go to her, to pull her into my arms and kiss them all away. But the little voice in my head had become a loud scream.

She'd kept me a secret.

Hidden me from her father, the one person she had left in the world.

Phoebe hadn't stood up and fought for us, for me... *because you're not worth it.*

"Maybe it's better this way." The words were out before I could stop them. I needed to get out of there before my anger exploded.

"Levi," she shook her head violently, tears running down her cheeks, "no—"

"We always knew this was only temporary, Intern." *I always knew fairy tales didn't come true.*

"But I- I love you. I'm yours." She sobbed harder, the sound splintering my chest wide open.

"No," I breathed, "you're not."

Maybe you never were.

———

"WHAT?" I barked at my bandmates as they all sat quietly, watching me.

An hour after I'd walked out on Phoebe, Alistair had summoned us to the suite. He wanted to deliver the news personally.

Phoebe was off the tour.

"That's some bullshit, right there," Hudson said.

"Who's her dad again?"

"It's doesn't matter who he is or isn't." Alistair let out a heavy sigh. "The point is she's off the staff. There's nothing we can do."

"Bullshit." My boot flew at the table, sending everyone's drinks flying.

"You need to relax."

"Don't fucking tell me to relax," I snarled at Rafe.

"So where is she now?"

"She already left." Letty's eyes drilled holes into the top of my head. But I couldn't meet her gaze.

Phoebe was gone.

Because her father demanded it.

Because the label demanded it.

Because you told her she wasn't yours.

I shut the voice down. This wasn't on me. It wasn't.

Was it?

Fuck, nothing made sense. My anger and pain were a wildfire inside me, making my blood boil and my skin itch.

She was gone.

My honeybee had left.

"I need to find her." I leaped up, and Rafe and Hudson shot up too.

"That's not a good idea, man," Hud held up his hands. "Let's just think about this. I'm sure Alistair can talk to the label. Right, Ali boy?"

But when I glanced at him, his expression said it all. The decision was made.

"Fuck." I jammed my fingers in my hair and raked them over my skull. "She's really gone?"

The fight began to seep out of me, and I dropped down in the chair.

I couldn't stand the six pity stares all trained on me. It was like hundreds of thousands of ants crawling under my skin.

"What?" I barked.

"Levi," Eva said softly. "We'll figure this out. There has to be a way to—"

"There isn't, okay?" I leaped up again, unable to stand it. Their sympathy. Their concerned fucking gazes. "She's gone. She fucking left me and nothing about this is okay." Before I knew it, I'd stormed across the room to the door.

"Levi, now is not the time to—"

"Hudson?" I snapped.

"Yeah, man?"

"Do everyone a favor and go fuck yourself." Damn near ripping the door of its hinges, I barged past Johnson and didn't look back.

I couldn't sit in there for a second longer. Not with them watching me, talking in circles like it was going to change anything.

Phoebe was gone.

And although I wanted to blame her, to pin this fucking shitshow all on her...

I knew I couldn't.

"THIS ISN'T A GOOD IDEA," Johnson said over my shoulder as I wandered down the street. I had no fucking idea where I was going but I needed the fresh air on my face, what little of it was visible from my poor attempt at a disguise—a ball cap and sunglasses. I looked like a fucking idiot, strolling the streets of downtown Des Moines. But I didn't care.

Finally spotting a bar, I slipped inside and took a seat at the counter.

"What can I get you?"

"Levi," Johnson moved behind me, but I ignored him, answering the bartender. "Double vodka on the rocks please."

Johnson cussed under his breath, but he didn't try to stop me. He'd been with me long enough to know there was no getting through to me when I was like this.

The bartender pushed the drink toward me, and I gave

him a tight nod, staring at the glass like it held all the answers to the universe.

Vodka had always been *her* poison of choice. I could still smell the foul scent on her breath as she leaned in close, whispering her words of hatred at me. I was just a kid, a boy. I didn't understand why she hated me, but I knew. I knew it right down to my soul.

Nursing the glass, I brought it to my nose, inhaling deeply. Just the smell turned my stomach. My hand trembled violently as I clutched the glass. If I could just drink it, if I could just separate her from this moment, maybe I could finally put my past to rest.

I could finally break free of that bitch's hold on me after all these years.

"Where are you?" Letty asked.

I clutched my cell phone in my hand, trying to smother the tears threatening to fall. I was surprised I had any left after the two-hour cry-a-thon I'd had since fleeing the band's hotel and checking into a motel just outside the city.

"I'm at The Lonestar Motel."

"Phoebe, what the fuck are you doing in a motel?"

"I panicked. After the lady from HR called and told me I was being relocated effective immediately, I just... I ran."

"This is a fucking mess," she breathed. "Are you okay? Do you need anything?"

"I- I don't know. Everything happened so quickly and I... crap, Letty, I really messed this up."

"You didn't. This is not your fault."

"I should have told him. I should have explained—"

"Nothing you could have said or done would have changed the outcome. Your father is an asshole by the way."

"You spoke to him?"

"Called him myself," she said with an air of pride. "I tried to reason with him, explain that you're a valuable member of the team. But he's adamant, you're off the band's assignment."

"I can't believe you did that."

"Believe it, girl. You're one of us now."

Her words settled something inside me. Levi might have walked away, shattering my heart in the process, but Letty was a good friend, and I was grateful to have her in my life.

"H- how is he?" I whispered.

"He stormed out about an hour ago. We haven't seen him since."

"He left?"

"Johnson's got eyes on him; he's been checking in with the others. So far, he's okay."

"God, what a mess." The guilt coiled around my heart, squeezing tighter. "I'm so sorry. I never meant—"

"What did I say a minute ago? This is *not* your fault. But we clearly underestimated your father's reach at the label."

"He's just trying to protect me." Despite his heavy-handed ways, I knew he only wanted to keep me out of the clutches of another toxic relationship. But he hadn't even given me a chance to explain... and then Levi had barged into the room and everything got super confusing and messed-up.

"He said I wasn't his." The words splintered something inside me.

"He's confused and he's hurting," Letty said, and I could hear the sadness in her voice.

"Do you think he'll do something stupid?" I couldn't live with myself if Levi tried to hurt himself because of me.

"We won't let him, I promise. Besides, it's not Levi I'm worried about right now, it's you. You shouldn't be there all alone."

"I'm okay."

"It's not right." She let out an indignant huff. "You should be here."

"The label said—"

"I don't give a flying fuck what the label said. They don't

understand what it's like on the ground, managing these guys, keeping things running smoothly. We need you, Phoebe." She hesitated. "He needs you."

"They were pretty clear that if I didn't return to Nashville by tomorrow, then I wasn't to bother."

"That's just fucking wrong. Have you tried calling him?"

"My father?" I scoffed. "He's fielding my calls via his assistant."

"Coward."

"He doesn't enjoy confrontation." He preferred to handle his business in a more direct and to the point approach. But I still couldn't believe how unyielding he'd been about this. As if I wasn't old or wise enough to make my own mistakes and shoulder the consequences.

"This couldn't have happened at a worse time," she muttered. "Shit, sorry, I didn't mean..."

"It's okay." She was right. The end of the tour was imminent. The band had three shows left to get through. The one tomorrow in Milwaukee, and then the two shows in Atlanta.

The last thing they needed was for Levi to go MIA. All because of me. Because he thought I'd betrayed him.

If only I'd have gotten to my father first.

But Letty was right. It wouldn't have changed anything. After Zephyr, he would never have accepted Levi—he never would.

Not that there was even a me and Levi to accept anymore.

"But I- I love you. I'm yours."

"No," he breathed, "you're not."

The words repeated in my head, over and over, taunting me, shredding my heart in two.

I wanted to believe Levi was just lashing out because I'd hurt him, but I knew Levi well enough to know he didn't hand out second chances.

You got one shot to prove yourself, to earn his trust... and in his eyes, I'd broken it.

Pain rolled through me as I sat in the small, dingy motel room. It was a far cry from the hotels I'd stayed in with the band. But I was no longer *with* the band. I was an intern at the label; the girl who got coffee and filed paperwork.

I wasn't sure I could go back to that, not now I knew what it was like to be right there in the thick of it. But I needed this job, I needed the steady income. I was a twenty-one-year-old college dropout with a very lacking resume. For as much as I hated to admit it, I needed my father's connections if didn't want to end up working a dead-end job.

"Phoebe, are you still there?" Letty's voice pulled me from my depressing thoughts.

"Yeah, I'm here."

"Is there anything I can do? Anything at all?"

"No, I don't think so."

Even if Levi would hear me out, it wouldn't change the fact the band was due to leave for their world tour in a little over a month. And I'd be stuck in Nashville.

It couldn't work.

Levi there and me here. He'd grow frustrated, angry... he'd get drunk or high to try and fill the void and eventually he'd lose control... he'd find some pretty French girl or British girl to chase away the pain.

It was always going to be hard being on tour with Levi...
but being thousands of miles apart for six months at a time?

Our fragile relationship couldn't withstand that.

If there was anything left.

Tears pricked the corner of my eyes as I swallowed over
the ball of emotion lodged in my throat.

"When are you leaving?" she asked, because like me, she
knew I didn't have a choice.

"My flight is tomorrow."

"I'll find him. I'll talk to him."

"Okay," I said.

Even though we both knew it wouldn't matter.

———

THE NEXT MORNING, Letty sent me a car to take me to the
airport to catch my flight from Des Moines to Nashville.

For a second, when I'd spotted the familiar black SUV,
I'd half-expected to find Levi sitting inside waiting for me.

Of course, he wasn't.

I'd cried the entire journey. But when I touched down in
Nashville, I'd dried my tears, pulled up my big girl panties,
and told myself that I would be okay.

I'd survived Zephyr.

I would survive this.

As I exited the airport and joined the line for a taxicab,
my cell started vibrating. Hope filled my chest, but quickly
turned to dread when I saw my father's number flashing on
the screen.

"Hello," I said with little emotion.

"I just wanted to check your flight was okay?"

"You mean you wanted to make sure I was on the flight?"

"Phoebe, don't take that tone with me, young lady."

"Dad," I sighed, "I'm really not in the mood to argue."

"I got you that internship because I wanted more for you than a life shackled to some junkie. A rock star, Phoebe, really?" he sneered. "Levi Hunter is nothing more than—"

"*Don't*. Don't you dare talk about him like that."

"Don't tell me you actually fell for the guy?" He scoffed as if the idea was preposterous. "I thought you were smarter than that."

"Yeah, well, I guess I never was very smart when it came to trusting the men in my life." I hung up and shoved my phone in my pocket.

The women in front of me glanced back and gave me a sad smile. I didn't return it, glancing down at my feet. All I wanted was to get to my apartment and shut the world out.

"I'm heading downtown if you want to share the fare?" The woman asked as a cab pulled forward.

"Uh, no thank you." This time, I did smile.

She went on her way and I waited for the next cab. When it rolled to a stop, I climbed in and barked off my address. The guy had his music turned up, so it was hard to miss Drown blasting through the speakers. "Eyes so deep I fall and fall, can't crawl out, and I can't breathe. These feelings crash over me..."

Levi's voice was like a punch to the stomach, and I smothered the sob racking through me.

I wouldn't cry, not here, in the back of a stranger's taxicab.

"That was *Drown* by the formidable Black Hearts Still Beat featuring Eva Walker, the hottest track in the country right now," the radio host said. "And now we welcome Levi, Rafe, Hudson, and Damon onto the show. Welcome guys."

"Thanks for having us."

I was frozen, paralyzed on the cool leather seat. "Can you turn it up please?" I blurted out, needing to hear it word for word.

Less than twenty-four hours from when he walked away from me, Levi was live on national radio. I grabbed my cell phone to text Letty, when I realized I already had a message off her. I must have missed it in my haste to get off the phone to my dad.

LETTY: **He's back and he's okay... I just thought you should know.**

RELIEF FLOODED ME. Levi was okay. He was okay...

This was a good thing. The best news I could have hoped for given everything. But as the radio host interviewed them, their voices began to turn to white noise over the roar of blood in my ears.

Levi was okay.

And yet, I'd heard nothing from him.

Not a damn thing.

———

LEVI DIDN'T CALL. He didn't text or send a message through Letty. It was as if he'd disappeared from my life as quickly as he'd barreled into it.

It hurt.

It hurt so fucking much.

He'd cast me aside as if I was disposable. Insignificant. But maybe it was better this way. Our relationship had been intense, a whirlwind that had swept us up and devastated me in its wake.

He'd never been able to tell me he loved me... and I realized now, maybe there was a good reason for that.

Maybe, in the end, I hadn't been enough for him.

I didn't doubt he cared for me, that in his own way, Levi had fallen for me—or at least, the illusion of me—but perhaps, I'd been wrong.

Perhaps it had never been love for him.

It was no easy task, returning to the office. Everyone was excited about the weekend. The label was flying out everyone and anyone connected to the band for the tour wrap party. It was a big deal.

Of course, I'd been left off the guest list. But it didn't matter.

I wouldn't have gone anyway.

LEVI

"You good?" Rafe eyed me carefully. I'd gotten used to his heavy stares over the last few days. Ever since Phoebe left.

I was... present.

That's all I could offer them right now. I'd gotten through the last show. I hadn't gone off the rails, despite how much I wanted to. And I'd made every one of our scheduled interviews.

By all accounts, I was excelling at not fucking up, but it didn't mean on the inside I wasn't slowly drowning in a pit of self-hatred and loathing.

I hadn't drunken the vodka that first night without Phoebe. In the end, I'd traded it for my usual Jack and Coke. For whatever reason, I couldn't lay my past to rest.

And it bothered me.

A lot of things bothered me.

Like how I couldn't sleep at night without Phoebe beside me. Or the gaping hole I felt every time I watched Rafe and Eva together, kissing and laughing, lost in their own little world.

Everyone gave me space, but not too much space. It was Riley all over again, them waiting for me to snap, me resenting them for it.

"Levi," Rafe's voice cut through my thoughts.

"Huh, what?" I asked, blinking over at him.

"I asked you if you were good?"

"I'm fine."

Fine.

I fucking hated that word

Not good, not bad... *fine*.

It was a nothing word, steeped in fake reassurance and forced platitudes.

But *fine* got people off your back, *fine* let them tell themselves everything was okay.

"Last show of the tour," he added, as if I cared. As if those words were supposed to mean something to me.

Nothing meant anything without her here.

Phoebe.

My honeybee.

I hadn't spoken to her in five days.

It felt like five fucking years. But I hadn't known what to say. This was all new territory for me, and I wasn't sure how to navigate these uncharted waters. All I knew was, every day that went by that I didn't talk to her or see her, the gaping hole in my chest cracked that little bit wider.

Letty said she was working at the Nashville branch of Razorsharp. I knew they kept in touch, I was relieved. Phoebe didn't have many people in her life she could turn to.

"This is probably for the best, you know," Rafe said, as we watched Eva wrap up her set.

"How can you say that to me?" I shook my head, anger skating down my spine. "You got your girl. You got everything you ever wanted."

"Levi, that's not—"

"I love her," I heaved the words, feeling their weight press down on my chest. "I'm ass over elbow in love with her and I couldn't say the words when it mattered most. So don't stand there and tell me that it's for the best. I lost her, Rafe.

I lost the one person who saw past all this bullshit." My eyes flicked to the stage. "Phoebe saw me, and now she's gone."

"I'm sorry," he murmured. "It was a dumb thing to say. I just hate seeing you so numb."

"I've spent the last ten years of my life numb, it's nothing new."

"You really love her?" He regarded me with a strange look.

"I do." It had just taken losing her to make me finally be able to say the words. Talk about bittersweet irony.

"You should tell her."

"What?" My brows knitted. "In case you didn't notice, she left."

"So? You're Levi fucking Hunter. Figure out a way to get her back."

His words echoed through me.

Get her back...

"Are we interrupting something?" Hudson and Damon joined us. Eva was on her final song, the crowd electric as she serenaded them with tales of friendship and first love.

"Levi's in love," Rafe said as if it was the simplest thing on earth.

"Well, duh, of course he is." Hudson grinned at me. "The question is, what are you going to do about it?"

"Don't look at me," I grumbled, feel irritation zip through me. "I was hoping you'd have the answer."

Phoebe was in Nashville. It was a four-hour ride. We had the after-party tomorrow night at The Riff Bar...

"What?" Damon asked as my eyes lit up.

"I have an idea," I said, feeling a lick of anticipation, a

tingle of Hunter magic I hadn't felt in a really long time. "But I'm going to need your help."

———

"ANY SIGN OF HER?" I drummed my hand against my thigh as I kept my eyes trained on the door.

The club was already crammed, the who's who of the label all here to celebrate the end of the tour and the beginning of another.

Letty had wrangled the four of us into matching black dress shirts and jeans, insisting that we put on a good show for the bigwigs. Alistair was already working the room, shaking hands and rubbing shoulders with the guys who signed off the checks.

There was a buzz in the air, the world tour the hot gossip on everyone's lips.

"She'll be here," Eva said with more confidence than I felt.

Stalter had called ahead to say they were running on time, but she was already ten minutes late.

Fuck.

I needed a drink or something to take off the edge, but since I'd made some pretty hefty promises to stay clean, I chugged on my bottle of Perrier, hoping the ice-cold liquid would douse the nerves zipping through me.

"Guys, I want you to meet Franny Mineston."

Alistair appeared with a beautiful woman in tow. She was older, her hair pulled off her face in a sleek bun, a dusting of makeup accentuating her natural beauty. Fuck me. If I wasn't a reformed man, I wouldn't have thought twice about offering to rock her world.

As it was though, I only had eyes for one woman tonight.

And she was late.

"Levi Hunter," she drawled with a slight southern twang. "I've heard so much about you." She leaned in, sliding her lips over my cheek.

Something snaked up my spine, a tingle of awareness. Slowly, I turned to find Phoebe standing there, watching me. Watching Franny linger too close, her hand still on my arm.

Hurt flashed in her big honey eyes and her step faltered. I yanked my arm away without apology and strode across the room. "You're here," I breathed.

"We need to talk," she hissed, yanking me into the corner of the room. "You sent Stalter to kidnap me, that is unaccept—"

I pressed a finger to her lips, silencing her. "I missed you too, Bee."

Her expression softened, but only for a second. Then fiery indignation blazed in her eyes.

"I know you have questions," I said before she could get in another word. "I know you probably want to chew me out for the next twenty minutes. But I'm asking you... no, I'm begging you... to give me five minutes to show you why this is a good idea."

"W- what? You're not making any sense. You want me to ... *what?*" She gazed up at me with cloudy eyes.

"Five minutes." I leaned in to kiss her on the cheek, catching myself at the last second.

Phoebe's breath hitched and I smiled to myself. It was

good to know that she was still affected by me, even if she did want to kick my ass.

"Okay then," she mumbled, uncertainty thick in her voice.

I hated that I was the one who'd put it there. But I couldn't take back what was done. I could only look forward.

Phoebe had taught me that.

"I think there are a couple of people who want to see you." I pointed to Letty and Eva and they waved at Phoebe.

"Levi, what is happening right now? Why am I here?"

"Don't you trust me, Bee?"

She narrowed her eyes at me. "I thought I did."

Ouch.

That stung. But it was nothing I didn't deserve. Before I could stop myself, I leaned in again and pressed my lips against her cheeks. I needed something, anything, to tide me over for the next few minutes.

This was my big moment.

Fuck, I wanted a drink. Instead, I settled for another sip of my water.

Phoebe eyed the bottle in my hand, and her brow quirked up.

I chuckled. "Sobriety never tasted better." I winked and stalked away, heading for the stage. My palms were slick, and my heart was crashing wildly against my chest. I'd performed to crowds of fans, tens of thousands of fangirls all wanting a piece of me. I'd sung at small intimate events, caressing the audience with my voice, my lyrics. I'd done television and radio interviews, taken part in industry awards, but I'd never been more nervous than I was right now.

My bandmates met me at the side of the stage. Rafe pulled me in for a hug. "You've got this," he whispered, holding on a little tighter. When he eased back to meet my eyes, what I saw there almost wrecked me. "Give us a second," he said to Hudson and Damon.

"Show time, Hunter." Hudson grinned.

"Come on, we'll see you out there." Damon gave me a small smile before climbing the stage.

"I just wanted you to know I love you, man," Rafe said thickly. "Sometimes I think I should have done more. I should have set her straight—"

"No, Rafe. *No.*" I curved my hand around the back of my brother's head and pressed my forehead to his. "What happened, it isn't on you. Never think that."

"I fucking hate her for what she did to you." His chest heaved with the weight of his words. "I don't think I've ever said that before. But it's true. I only ever cared about what one person thought of me growing up, and that was you, bro."

"It's you and me," I said over the lump in my throat. "Always."

He swallowed thickly as I felt the tension between us melt away. "Always. Ready to go get your girl?"

"Hell yeah." I smirked, and we walked out on stage together. Exactly the way it was supposed to be.

The heat of the lights blazed down on me, my skin sizzling with anticipation. But the second my eyes landed on her in the crowd, everything slowed down until I could breathe again.

Phoebe was here.

My honeybee.

My girl.

She stood wedged in between Letty and Eva, tears already glossing her eyes.

A bolt of nervous laughter shot through me as I perched on the stool and waited for Hudson's opening beat. We hadn't had much time to practice, but as the music washed over me, a deep sense of peace settled in my soul.

Oh, pretty angel, give me your eyes
Come back to me, I need you right here

Oh, pretty angel, show me your smile
Come to back me because I can't be without you

You're the light to my dark, the star in dark skies
You're the voice that I hear, when things don't go right

The angel on my shoulder, I can't let you go…

Skin like silk, eyes like honey, this girl will rip out your heart before
you can blink
But she can have it, take it all from me
She's my hope and strength, the one that I want
My fire and my fight, the one that I love
She's my savior, my life… she's my honeybee

Oh, pretty angel, give me your smile
Stay with me always, I need you right here

Oh, pretty angel, show me those eyes
Don't ever leave me, I can't be without you

You're the light to my dark, the star in dark skies
You're the voice that I hear, when things don't go right

The angel on my shoulder, I can't let you go...
No, I won't let you go

I FINALLY OPENED MY EYES...
And all I saw was her.
My honeybee.
The girl who'd saved me.

I couldn't breathe.

Letty clutched my hand, squeezing gently every now and again to make sure I was still alive.

Levi Hunter had written me another song.

But not any song.

A love song.

My body shook gently as I tried to fight off the swell of emotions rising inside me. I'd been waiting for him to say the words, and he'd chosen here... surrounded by all these people.

"Phoebe?" Letty said, as I began to back away. I needed air. It was too hot in here, too dark and claustrophobic. The walls closed in around me as Levi watched me from the stage.

"I- I just need..." To go. I needed to go.

But I was rooted to the spot, held captive in Levi's dark gaze as he strode across the room to me.

"Bee," he whispered, reaching for me.

That one little word broke me. Tears spilled freely down my cheeks.

"Shit," he rasped, pulling me into his arms.

"We'll just be..." Letty pulled Eva away, leaving us alone.

Levi's grip on me tightened, as if he never planned to let go. "I'm so fucking sorry," he said. "I should never have said that. You're mine, Bee. Of course you're fucking mine."

I finally lifted my head to his, drying my eyes with the back of my hand. "You wrote me a love song."

He nodded shyly, rubbing his jaw. "I've been writing it for a while."

"You have?" I balked.

Levi ran his thumb through my tears, swiping them away. "I've wanted to tell you so many times. But every time I tried it was like this fear would take hold and I couldn't do it. I'm messed-up, Bee. Really fucking messed-up."

A couple of people brushed past us and Levi growled, pulling me further into the shadows. I noticed Johnson and Stalter move with us. Always there in the background, guarding Levi.

"After you left, I went to some bar. I sat there for an hour trying to drink a glass of vodka. An hour. But I couldn't do it. No matter how much I tried to break her hold on me, I couldn't do it."

"Oh, Levi…"

"I'm going to see somebody," he said. "Fiona. She's nice. I think she'll be able to help me."

"A therapist?"

He nodded. "She comes highly recommended. It'll be hard with being on tour, but she thinks we can make it work."

"That's huge, Levi. I'm so proud of you."

He glanced down, rubbing the back of his neck. When he looked up again, I saw a flash of vulnerability in his eyes. "I don't want to be like this anymore, Bee. I want to be better… for you."

"Levi, I—"

"Just hear me out, please."

I nodded, feeling a tight ball of emotions lying heavy in my stomach.

"I spoke to the label."

"W- what?"

"I had a conference call with management this morning. I told them that having you on the tour was non-negotiable. If I couldn't have you there, then I wasn't going."

"Levi, you can't—"

"Already did." A faint smirk traced his lips. "You're too important to leave behind, Bee." He inched closer, taking the air with him. Levi's hand glided down to my neck, holding me gently. My breath caught in my throat as my body hummed with anticipation.

"I love you, Phoebe Halstead. I don't know when or how it happened, but I fell, Bee. I fell so hard that I must have hit my head or something because I know I've been an asshole. I know I should have called or texted; but the truth was, I was scared. I was fucking terrified I'd ruined the one good thing in my life."

He leaned in, touching his head to mine, breathing deeply. "I love you, Bee. So fucking much. And I know I'm hard work, I know I'm not gonna change overnight, but I'm here and I'm trying. So, what do you say, honeybee? Want to see the world with me?"

My heart raced in my chest as Levi's confession flowed through me.

He loved me.

Levi Hunter loved *me*.

I didn't know which part to focus on. The fact he'd

finally declared his love for me, or that he'd given the label an ultimatum about me.

It was a lot to process.

But then, being around Levi had never been a walk in the park. He felt differently to most people. His emotions were often exaggerated and larger than life.

But he loved me.

He'd chosen me.

I wasn't foolish enough to think there wouldn't be relapses, or bumps along the way, because addiction was a long, painful road to recovery. But there was no mistaking the steely determination in Levi's eyes.

He wanted this.

He wanted me.

"Yes," I breathed. "Yes, I'll go on tour with you."

"And the other part?" he asked in a soft whisper, as if he was almost scared to say the words.

"What other part?" I teased.

"Yeah, Bee, the part where you're mine forever?" His mouth moved dangerously close to mine.

"Oh, that part... well, I guess we could give it a shot. But I don't want you to get your hopes—"

Levi smashed his lips to mine, swallowing my words. I moaned at the taste of him, the feel of his hands on my body, his tongue curling around my own. A couple of people cheered, and I was sure I felt the flash of camera, but it didn't matter.

It didn't matter that we were in a roomful of staff from the label, because I was the girl who owned Levi Hunter's heart.

He'd given it to me.

Handed it over willingly, and this, right here, our lips sliding together, was my promise to keep it safe.

"I love you Leviathan Hunter," I breathed against his mouth, finally coming up for air.

His eyes sparkled with relief, but then smile tugged at the corner of his mouth. "I love you too, Bee. And I can't wait to rock your fucking world later."

———

"TONIGHT WAS A GOOD NIGHT," Letty said as we all stood near the bar, watching the party rage on around us.

"The fucking best," Hudson declared. "I'm so happy for you guys."

"Is he okay?" I whispered to Levi, who had his arm wrapped around my waist as I stood with my back to his chest.

After very publicly claiming me as his, Levi had refused to let me go. We'd spent the entire night chatting to people and working the room together, some part of us always touching. I saw the stares of curiosity, heard the whispers, but I didn't care. Nothing was going to ruin this night; not a damn thing.

"Okay?" Hudson overheard me. "I'm better than okay, Pheebs, I'm fan-fucking-great."

"I'm sad she couldn't come too," Eva said, laying a hand on his arm.

"I'm not sad... why the fuck would I be sad?"

Hudson drained the rest of his beer. "Molly isn't my girl,

we're not together... fuck, I need another beer. Hey, Bryan, get me another." He waved his empty at someone.

"I think you've had enough," Damon said.

"Relax, *Dad*. It's a party. We're celebrating. Levi finally grew some balls and got his girl. Rafe and Eva are having a kid—"

"What the fuck?" Levi tensed.

"Uh, Hudson, no we're not." Eva frowned, looking to Rafe who just shrugged. "Why would you say that?"

"Not now, but you will. You'll get hitched and have babies and ride off into the sunset with your little blonde-hair, gray-eyed, guitar playing kids and all live happily ever—"

"Okay, that's it," Damon grumbled. "I'm cutting you off." He intercepted the beer from the bartender and refused to give it to Hudson.

"You're no fun."

"And you're embarrassing yourself."

"Lighten up, man. At least I'm a happy drunk." Hudson slung his arm around Damon's neck. "Did I ever tell you how much I love you, D? I've been thinking now that these fuckers are all wifed up, maybe you and I should... you know?" He waggled his brows, and the rest of us tried to smother our amusement.

"I'm glad you're all finding this funny," Damon rolled his eyes.

"Oh, look, it's Ali boy. Ali, we love you, man."

"Uh, thanks." Alistair's brows bunched together. "Everything good here?" He ignored Hudson.

"Yeah, we're good." Levi tightened his hold on my waist.

"Phoebe, I just wanted to apologize—"

"No apology needed."

"Yes, well," he grimaced, "I still feel like I let you down. Both of you."

"Relax, Ali, it all worked out in the end."

"You know, Dominic loved *Honeybee*, he wants to talk to you about—"

"No," Levi said without hesitation. "*Honeybee* is Phoebe's song. Only she gets to say what happens to it."

Oh my.

Warmth washed over me.

"I see," Alistair said. "Well, maybe that is a conversation for another day."

But I already knew the answer. Levi had already given the public *Drown*. But *Honeybee*, that was ours. It was one part of him I wasn't prepared to share with the world.

Ever.

"When do you head out?"

"Tomorrow afternoon," Rafe replied.

"Hell yeah. Two weeks of sun, sand, sea, and s—"

"Hudson!"

"What? I was going to say salad. I need to lose a few pounds before we head to Europe." He patted his rock-hard abs. I knew, I'd seen them enough during my time on tour with the band.

"Hmm." Levi brushed my ear. "Two weeks of nothing but sun, sand, sea, and you. Sounds like my idea of heaven."

My stomach clenched. This morning, I'd been resigning myself to another day fetching coffee and filing paperwork.

But now, I was standing with the world's hottest rock band on the cusp of their first world tour.

"Hey, you okay?" Levi asked.

"Yeah." I tipped my face to his. "Just thinking how quickly life can change."

"No regrets?" His eyes darkened.

"Only one." His brow quirked, and I added, "Letting you walk away."

"Sometimes you have to lose everything to realize what you had. I'll never walk away again, Bee. And if I try, promise me you'll make me stay."

"I promise, Levi. I'll be your anchor."

Always.

WE FINALLY LEFT THE PARTY. Security flanked the seven of us as we made our way outside to the *click click click* of cameras. But we never made it into the car. A commotion behind us drew our attention and we all turned to find Hudson on his knees, staring up at... Molly?

"Mol?" Eva barged through the crush to reach her best friend. "What happened? What are you doin' here?"

Mascara-stained tears slid down her cheeks as she hiccoughed. "I- I... I got here and then security wouldn't let me in. I- I... I waited."

Hudson leaped and flew at the doorman, knocking his big body into the wall. "You wouldn't let her in? Are you a fucking idiot? That's Molly... it's—"

"Hud." Rafe and Damon yanked him back, directing him

to one of the cars. Letty jumped into action, checking the man over

"Should we do anything?" I asked Levi.

"They can handle it."

Eva wrapped her arm around Molly and led her to the car the guys had just shoved Hudson inside.

"Levi," Johnson said, directing us to the first car. We slid inside and I glanced back, trying to make sure everyone was okay.

"They'll be fine," Levi said.

"But Molly—"

"Not our problem, Bee. Not tonight." His eyes sparkled with wicked intent as he traced the lines of my face. "You're really here," he whispered, reaching out to ghost his fingers over my face. Relief washed over him, as if the events of the night were finally hitting him.

"I'm here, Levi."

I was vaguely aware of the privacy screen rolling up, separating us from security. Part of me wondered if Levi had planned it this way.

"Alone at last." He leaned in, brushing his lips over mine.

"Here?" I whispered.

"I need to be inside you, Phoebe," his voice cracked, "more than I have ever needed anything else."

"So what are you waiting for?" My lips curved.

A deep growl reverberated in his chest and then he was on me. Kissing the air from my lungs and clawing the clothes from my body.

"Levi, slow down." Pushing him off me, I hitched my dress around my hips and straddled his legs.

"Fuck, Bee, you are fucking perfection. But if you don't speed things up, I'm going to—"

"Patience, rock star." I cut him off with a bruising kiss. Levi slipped his tongue into my mouth as he grabbed my hand and pressed it against his dick. "Let me take care of you," I said, knocking his hand away. He let out an indignant huff but finally relaxed against the leather seat.

I slowly unzipped his pants, pulling him free. He was so hard and heavy in my hand. I smothered a whimper. Pumping him a couple of times, I rose up on my knees slightly and worked him inside me.

Our muted groans filled the car as I sank down on him.

"Fuck." Levi buried a hand in my hair and kissed me deeply. "I can feel you everywhere, Bee."

"M- move," I choked out, overwhelmed at the feel of him.

We rocked together, slow torturous circles that hit the deepest parts of me. Levi didn't try to take control or fuck me harder... he just went with it.

"God, it's..." The words got stuck in my throat as he thrust inside me, short shallow strokes that had me whimpering above him.

He curved a hand around the nape of my neck, anchoring us together. "I'm never going to let you go, Bee. You're mine now. Mine."

"Good," I said. "Because you're mine too."

My broken, black hearted bad boy of rock.

And I didn't ever plan on letting him go.

LEVI

"WHERE DO you think you're going?" I snagged Phoebe around the waist and dragged her down on top of me. Her soft laughter wrapped around me like a blanket. I wanted to bask in it. Drown in it. I wanted to bottle it and keep it with me always.

It was official.

Levi Hunter had lost his balls.

No, I hadn't lost them—I'd handed them willingly to a girl with ink on her skin and scars on her heart.

Phoebe.

My honeybee.

My every-fucking-thing.

It had been a week since the wrap party. One week since I'd gotten up on stage and sung a love song to the girl who owned me, heart, body, and black fucking soul.

It had been the best damn week of my life. No fangirls, no paparazzi, no media. It was just me, my girl, and our closest friends and family. Letty had organized the entire thing.

Two weeks at her family's beach house on a secluded beach situated on Long Island.

It was perfect.

Well, it would have been if it wasn't for Molly's unexpected arrival.

We were still in the dark about her sudden appearance that night. All Eva had told us was that something had happened back home, and Molly needed to lay low for a while. Of course, we weren't going to send her away.

Not that Hudson would ever have allowed it.

He'd gone into full alpha protector mode since we found her that night, standing outside the club with tears rolling down her cheeks.

It was their business though. I was just relieved to be spending two weeks with my girl. We had the best fucking bedroom, with a balcony overlooking the ocean. I'd fucked her on it more times than I could count. Sometimes hard, fast sex, reveling in the way her cries filled the salty air; other times it was slow and deep with her riding me back to front as we both stared out at the horizon.

Sex was our language of love. We didn't need words or lyrics to tell the other how we felt. It was all in the way she kissed me, or the way I touched her.

I couldn't get enough.

"Yo, lovebirds, breakfast is here," Hudson yelled.

"No," Phoebe murmured, tucking herself back into the crook of my arm. "I'm not ready to get up."

"So we stay in bed," I said, dropping a kiss to her hair.

"No, we should join them. I feel like I've been stealing all your time."

"Seriously?" I nudged her out of my side and stared down at her.

"I don't mean it like that. I just... they're your bandmates, Levi. This is your vacation."

"And you're my girl."

That made her smile. "I am, aren't I?"

"You so are." I brushed my lips over hers. "And now the whole world knows it."

"Ugh. Don't remind me." Phoebe grumbled, and I chuckled.

The story had run two days after the event, and it hadn't taken long before a journo reached out to the label for comment on the rumors that Levi Hunter was officially off the market.

I'd told Alistair to confirm it. Phoebe had refused to talk to me for an entire day. Until I'd pinned her to the bed and done wicked things to her body as way of an apology.

She'd gotten me back the next day though, when she'd called her dad and made me clear the air with him.

That had been a fun conversation.

One I didn't ever plan on reliving.

But Mr. Halstead hadn't hung up on me, which is more than I could have hoped for. He made me promise never to break his daughter's heart, and I made him promise never to take her away from me again.

We ended up agreeing to disagree.

My therapist called it progress. I called it my girl owning me by the balls.

Phoebe pressed a lingering kiss to my lips before climbing out of bed. My eyes feasted on her curves as she pulled on some bootie shorts and a band t-shirt.

"Thank God for bootie shorts," I mused, and she smirked over her shoulder. "Keep looking at me like that, Bee, and we'll never make it to breakfast.

Her eyes lit up with mischief as she darted for the door. "You'll have to catch me first, rock star."

PHOEBE

By the time Levi arrived in the kitchen, I was already tucking into a stack of pancakes.

"Morning," he said to everyone.

"Rough night?" Rafe asked, and my eyes immediately went to Levi's very bare, very marred chest.

Heat flooded me.

"What can I say? My honeybee likes to bite."

"Too much information for breakfast," Damon grumbled. "Go put a shirt on, Jesus."

"Relax, Donnelley. You just need to get laid, remove that stick from—"

"Levi." Rafe shook his head.

I held out my hand, beckoning Levi to me. He came willingly, wearing a wolfish grin.

"You ran, Bee."

"You should have chased me."

He laughed. A real honest-to-God laugh. It made everyone stop what they were doing, all eyes trained on Levi.

"What?" He frowned, rubbing a hand down his face to hide the slight stain to his cheeks.

"You are so freakin' adorable," I whispered.

"It's good to see you like this, bro," Rafe said. "It's been a long time coming."

Something passed between the two Hunter brothers. But then Molly stepped into the kitchen, taking all the air with her.

"Uh, hey, sorry... I didn't mean to interrupt." Her arms were wrapped around her waist like armor.

"You're not interrupting." Eva rushed to her side.

Two seconds later, Hudson appeared. His hair disheveled, wearing nothing but some black shorts.

Eva bristled at the sight of him, and he let out a heavy breath. "It's not what you think, Angel."

But it was *something*.

Molly was broken. Quiet and skittish, nothing like the voracious outgoing girl I'd met before.

But no one was telling us anything. Just that she needed some space.

Eva tended to Molly while Hudson went straight for the liquor cabinet.

"Seriously?" Levi balked. He hadn't touched a drop of alcohol since we'd arrived. Every other day, he disappeared for ninety minutes for his session with Fiona, and every day, he searched me out afterward.

He was changing.

Healing right in front of my eyes.

Levi still had a long way to go, but he was trying, and that was all any of us could ask for.

After Zephyr, I'd truly believed love couldn't fix a person. That I wasn't enough.

But love was a reason to fight.

It was a reason to try to change and lay your demons to rest.

Love was strength.

And I was enough.

Every day... every touch... every kiss... every time Levi sank inside me, I felt it.

My love hadn't been enough to save Zephyr, but it was enough to make Levi want to fight.

In the end, love was enough to save him.

PLAYLIST

Zombie – Bad Wolves

Mad at You – Noah Cyrus, Gallant

Ruin My Life – Zara Larsson

Outnumbered – Dermot Kennedy

7 Minutes – Dean Lewis

Gone – Red

Break In – Halestorm

All I Need – Within Temptation

Ashes of Eden – Breaking Benjamin

Last Stand – Adelitas Way

Rue – Girl in Red

Broken – Seether, Amy Lee

Better Than Today – Rhys Lewis

Lay By Me – Reuben

Nothing Breaks Like a Heart – Mark Ronson ft. Miley Cyrus

I Wanna Be Okay – Blindlove

Maybe It's Time – Sixx:A.M.

Let Me Love You Like A Woman – Lana Del Rey
Where's My Love – SYML
You Are The Reason – Callum Scott

AUTHOR'S NOTE

Oh Levi, my beautiful black hearted soul.

What a ride these two characters took me on. I hope you enjoyed reading their story as much as I enjoyed writing it. I can't wait to bring you Hudson's and Damon's stories next year.

As always, a huge thank you to my team:

Andie, Nina, Anna, and Tracy... you all keep me sane. Ginelle, thank you continuing to pick up my proofreads at the drop of a hat. To Sarah Puckett and Michael Johnson for bringing the series to life in audio (and Doug Johnson and Jon Ryno for the amazing songs) – it's been wonderful to hear my lyrics come to life. To my promo team, you ladies rock, and my readers / spoiler groups – your enthusiasm and support for my characters and stories makes it all worthwhile. To Give Me Books for always organizing all of my series promotion.

And finally, to the bloggers, reviewers, and

bookstagrammers who continue to support me, without you I wouldn't get to do this, so thank you. THANK YOU!

Until next time,
L A xo

ABOUT THE AUTHOR

Angsty. Edgy. Addictive Romance

USA Today and *Wall Street Journal* bestselling author of over forty mature young adult and new adult novels, L A is happiest writing the kind of books she loves to read: addictive stories full of teenage angst, tension, twists and turns.

Home is a small town in the middle of England where she currently juggles being a full-time writer with being a mother/referee to two little people. In her spare time (and when she's not camped out in front of the laptop) you'll most likely find L A immersed in a book, escaping the chaos that is life.

L A loves connecting with readers.

The best places to find her are:
www.lacotton.com